DIGITAL
FIRST

DIGITAL FIRST

THE SIX REALIZATIONS TO TRANSFORM
YOUR BUSINESS

A LEADERSHIP FABLE

VAMSHI GUNTHA

SHAHRUL LADUE

Henderson Delridge

DIGITAL FIRST

THE SIX REALIZATIONS TO TRANSFORM YOUR BUSINESS

A LEADERSHIP FABLE

Vamshi Guntha and Shahrul Ladue

Published by Henderson Delridge
Seattle, Washington, USA

ISBN: 978-1-958839-01-0

Edition: 2022

To all tenacious digital leaders who inspire us and give us hope.

To our parents.

EARLY PRAISE FOR THE BOOK

99% of the books on digital don't address the part of the process where 99% of the value is created: Execution. Vamshi addresses this complex issue head on. If you want to become digital-first, read this book first.

— Anand Laxshmivarahan,
Group Chief Digital Officer & Innovation, Vedanta Limited

Loved the case study style of narration of Fitness First's journey to become digital-first. I felt the story is very well constructed and explained in layman terms. Especially, the narration with mentor is very good. The simple explanation of purpose and how it ties to the digital journey is something I loved.

— Jayaprakash Bhaskarabatla,
Engineering Leader, Google

The book is holistic in terms of the current challenges we see during digital transformation. It's an effortless and refreshing read as a fable. I particularly liked Charan's character, his timely wisdom and his Nostradamus characteristics of predicting.

— Varun Manian,
Managing Director, Radiance Realty & Radiance Media Group

The book resonates very well. It's a creative and engaging way to talk about a business topic.

— Tim Bowman,
Head of Compete, Asana

Vamshi has delivered an incredibly concise, relatable, and practical fable that can serve as a playbook for any executive driving a digital transformation. The book is the distillation of his decades of experience advising senior leaders on winning strategies and solutions. A must-read!

— Praveen Vukkalam,
Managing Director, one of the global banks based in India

A gripping fable for executives and leaders hungry for driving transformation through digitization and leading with purpose!

— Suresh Namala,
Executive Director, IT, Seattle Genetics

A well-written book outlining the nuances of digital transformation in the form of a fable. The book would be valuable for folks interested in transforming with digital.

— Samik Raychaudhuri,
Director, Product (Cloud & AI), Oracle

Fantastic read! The book introduces what are normally complex ideas in a subtle and easy-to-understand manner. The 'fable' in the book is thoroughly enjoyable. Keeps the reader hooked without losing focus on the central idea of what it takes to transform an organization.

— Sandeep Maram,
Vice President, Swiss Re

Digital transformation is business transformation first. Vamshi portrayed the transformation journey well and dealt with the business challenges in a very lucid manner. A compelling read for organizations looking to adopt digital in their strategy.

— Kalyan Guntha,
Founder & CEO, Tectalik, Pathfinder award winner from Times Group

AUTHORS' NOTE

In the digital era where the bold eat the complacent, it is inevitable that every business will become a digital business. Companies that fail to transform will flame out or fade away. Leaders in all industries have realized that adopting digital is no longer an option.

Over the past decade, we have been advising senior executives and driving digital transformations at multi-billion-dollar traditional companies. We have seen and experienced the challenges of digital transformations first-hand, learning from multiple failures and several successes. As we guided executives through the challenges of transformation, we saw six broad themes emerge, which we called *The Six Digital First Realizations.*

This book has two main purposes: to share the six digital-first realizations and to provide a playbook that will enable leaders to unlock value from the transformation journey. We also chose to write this book in a business fable format for two reasons.

First, we wanted the book to be highly practical and close to real-world experiences so everyone could absorb the nuances of transformation. We tell the story of Neo Ray, a Chief Digital Officer who takes on the challenge of putting Fitness First Inc. on a digital-first trajectory in one year. The simple narrative helps readers understand the six digital-first realizations and demonstrates how organizations can create order out of chaos.

Second, we wanted to illustrate how purpose-driven organizations with aligned teams can push boundaries and deliver game-changing results. We've added examples of real-world companies and summaries of the realizations at the end of each section. Most of the examples show how companies applied the realizations successfully—we've also included a few cautionary tales.

The book is divided into six parts. Part 1 covers the two foundational elements of any successful digital transformation: a transformative customer-centric purpose that goes beyond profits and the need to digitize the core business while also exploring new digital business models. Both are necessary for any transformation to succeed.

Parts 2 and 3 cover the practicalities of how to get started with digital transformation. These include the minimum requirements to make any transformation successful, including a business plan, leadership, team, delivery model, and funding. It also covers some big changes that are needed, particularly departures from how traditional companies approach value measurement, team structure, and innovation.

Parts 4 and 5 show how to scale a digital transformation, and how to prioritize and govern multiple initiatives simultaneously. It also covers how to shift the company culture and imbibe a digital mindset amongst the leaders.

Part 6 provides a sneak-peak into how Fitness First operates like a digital-first organization after accelerating on the trajectory set by Neo during his first year.

This book is targeted toward executives who need to make their businesses resilient with digital. You will relate to Neo's journey and will learn a multitude of ways to solve your challenges. For leaders that have yet to begin a digital transformation (or have tried and failed in the past), we hope to inspire you toward a renewed commitment and give you the confidence that you can win. For those who have already made significant progress with digital transformation, you will find ideas and frameworks that will help deliver consistent, long-term success. Regardless of the stage your company is in, we know that leaders must constantly demonstrate conviction, grit, and decisiveness to fully realize the opportunities with digital.

It has been our mission to guide leaders in creating new, multi-billion-dollar growth opportunities. This book is our humble attempt to help you unlock massive value through digital transformation.

CONTENTS

THE SIX DIGITAL-FIRST REALIZATIONS

1. Purpose:
   Organizations must create a transformative customer-centric purpose that goes beyond profits.

2. Dichotomy of Digital:
   Organizations must focus on digitizing the core business while also exploring new digital business models across the value chains they serve. Both are necessary for the transformation to succeed.

3. The Real Measures:
   Measurement and metrics must focus on what you are transforming with digital – core business vs. new business – and how quickly are you transforming with digital. Not just ROI.

4. Innovation Pods:
   Deploy small, autonomous teams composed of customer-obsessed intrapreneurs to deliver digital initiatives.

5. Digital Innovation Approach:
   Solve customer problems rapidly with the five-step Digital Innovation approach: (1) Frame the challenge, (2) Know the customer, (3) Ideate to solve the right problems, (4) Envision a cover story, (5) Create a service blueprint

6. Digital Governance Model:
   Accelerate the digital-first journey through a clear set of Guiding Principles and a multi-faceted Digital Governance model that guides the Innovation Pods and removes blockers.

PART 1
THE WORLD
UPSIDE DOWN

DISGRACEFUL EXIT

I am *Neo*, and yes, I share the same name as Keanu Reeves from the Matrix Trilogy. Unlike Neo from the Matrix, I don't have superpowers to manipulate a simulated reality. But my clients used to call me a "Digital Alchemist" — someone who transforms things for the better with digital.

I moved to the US for my Master's at Wharton, where I met the love of my life, Tina. After graduation, we spent most of our time in Seattle, where our daughter, Riya, was born. I traveled cross country helping clients on their digital transformation journeys, while Tina worked at Microsoft in Seattle, so she could balance our demanding jobs and parenting. It was all going well until my dad was diagnosed with cancer.

I convinced Tina to relocate to Bengaluru for a year to help me take care of my parents. Quitting our dream jobs and leaving the country that shaped me into a Digital Alchemist was not easy. It was an even tougher decision for Tina, who had never spent more than a few months in India.

After battling cancer for a year, Dad lost his fight and left us all. Mom spiraled into depression; she needed us more than ever. I convinced Tina that we continue in Bengaluru for a little longer to take care of Mom. Little did I know that one year would become three years.

I have fond memories of Bengaluru; I was born here. The canopies of trees that lined its roads, the delicious street food, and the abundance of greenery made it a city that was easy to love. But everything was different now. I saw problems all around: road rage, over-crowded places, pollution, and poor infrastructure. It took me weeks to get over all the changes. Then I started seeing these problems as opportunities. India was at the cusp of a digital revolution, powered by smartphone adoption and inexpensive data plans. And Bengaluru was the Silicon Valley of India. It was the perfect platform to launch the startup idea I envisioned while at Wharton.

I co-founded Digi Gate with Ayaan, a former colleague and good friend, and his friend Arjun. Together we built a technology platform to simplify security and property management for large apartment communities, with a simple mobile app interface for the residents. We grew fast, and after two years we had more than 2 million apartment residents using our app daily in 15 cities. Then online shopping demand spiked. I saw the early indicators that online buying behaviors were changing, likely to the benefit of a few e-commerce giants. Many local businesses would be negatively impacted. I saw a way to help. Inspired by the Indian Government's Aatmanirbhar Bharat mission to make India self-reliant, I saw a unique opportunity to empower neighborhood stores (Kiranas) with a new feature on Digi Gate—a marketplace for essentials. It'd bring neighborhood stores online, benefiting not only the millions of Digi Gate's existing residential customers with faster and more convenient service, but also helping local businesses survive.

I formed a small autonomous team called an Innovation Pod and moved with full force to create the marketplace. The pod had a Product Manager, who played the role of a Lead; Business Designers to uncover customer needs and conceptualize the solution; Visual Designers to bring the concepts to life on a digital canvas; and Full-stack Developers to get the marketplace up and running. [*Innovation Pods and how they power digital transformations are discussed in detail in Part Three*]

My move created friction with the founding team. I worried that not everyone understood my vision, so I decided to meet my co-founders and two of our investors—collectively acting as a board—to get formal approval for the marketplace opportunity.

As I rode the elevator, I thought I had probably overdramatized the magnitude of today's meeting and the situation in general. I told myself that the board would understand the long-term customer opportunity, and that they'd unanimously approve my new digital business model that would empower local businesses.

I was the first to arrive in the conference room, followed by my Pod Lead. We had prepared a detailed presentation, explaining the opportunity, the new Innovation Pod model, progress made so far, early test results, and the launch plan.

As we were arranging the presentations, Mike Curt walked in. Mike was from Ant Capital, one of our first investors and a staunch advocate of my ideas. With Mike and Ekta Reddy from Soft Ventures, we had a strong board powering Digi Gate to become a unicorn soon.

After some small talk, Mike flipped through the presentation. He was intrigued by the rapid progress we'd made. "I like the new thinking regarding autonomous teams. You guys have made decent progress, and in such a short time." He saw the launch plan and asked, "How many neighborhoods are you planning for the soft launch?"

I checked my watch anxiously as the rest of the board was nowhere to be seen.

"Neo?" said my Pod Lead.

"Hmm?" I muttered, distracted.

My Pod Lead clarified for Mike, "Five neighborhoods, three in Bengaluru and two in Chennai."

Mike focused on me. "Are you alright, Neo?"

I pointed to the empty chairs. "I'm wondering where everyone is. I know Arjun, Ayaan and Ekta are here, I saw them entering the elevator. But I'm not sure where they are now."

Just when I was about to call Ayaan, all three entered the room.

I smiled at my co-founders. "Glad you all are here. I thought you guys didn't know where the meeting was." I pointed to the presentations on the table and was about to start the discussion.

Arjun interrupted. "Neo...I have something to share with you. It's important that we discuss it now." He looked hostile.

"More important than the new digital business model?" I asked.

He nodded and said in a harsh tone, "The board has just taken a vote."

"Excuse me? What did you say?" I was perplexed. I looked at Ayaan and Ekta and got a muted response.

Mike interjected, "What are you talking about, Arjun?"

Arjun looked at me and said, "We need to talk. Please sit down."

I realized that something was wrong, terribly wrong. I sat down heavily. "What was the voting about? How come I was not there?"

"Neo, we had to meet because of you." He stressed the end. "For the past couple of quarters you've been missing all critical meetings. You've been distracted with your pet projects that have got nothing to do with our core business. Ayaan and I have been running the show."

A cold hand reached inside me and grabbed the bottom of my stomach. I looked at Arjun and Ayaan. "I thought we were co-founders and partners in crime."

Arjun went on. "Yeah…except that we had our best quarter ever, and it was when you were least involved." He paused for a moment, and then pushed ahead. "We voted on whether you should continue as the CEO. I'm sorry, Neo—you are out!"

My face was hot. How? Why? We always had an understanding—Arjun & Ayaan would take care of the core business and I would focus on adding new revenue streams. I couldn't believe they used it against me.

I glanced sharply at Mike. "Did you know about this?"

Arjun intervened. "Sorry Mike, we all know how close you are with Neo. We needed to act in the best interest of the company. Rest assured; we want you to continue as a board member."

I started to realize that this was a game cleverly played by Arjun, maybe for months. Arjun always had a cutthroat streak running through him. It was Ayaan who had brought us together, who had played the peacemaker between us. But now, somehow, Arjun had gotten Ayaan entirely on his side. They were united. "You can't do this. I started this company, for God's sake."

"I'm sorry, Neo, but the company has moved past you," said Arjun. "We are not a tiny startup anymore, exploring random things. The board felt we need a CEO with a track record of quick results, someone who will shorten the cash cycle so we can survive. All you were doing was," he paused for a dramatic effect, "*burning cash*."

He handed me a piece of paper. "We had a quorum, and the vote was unanimous. Except for you and Mike."

I slumped deeper into the chair. This couldn't really be happening. I built the team. I created the digital product and business model. I put in my blood, sweat, and tears to get us to the "soonicorn" status Digi Gate was at now.

I heard myself say, "Who is going to be the new CEO?"

Arjun cleared his throat. "I had to accept that responsibility. Believe me, I didn't want it to be this way, but you have given us no choice." Arjun blinked at me, all false humility. But he must have been laughing inside.

What followed next was surreal. Arjun asked his executive assistant (EA) to open the door and two security guards stepped in.

"Neo, these men will escort you out. Your personal items will be brought to your house tomorrow. You can leave your computer here."

As the security guards escorted me out of the room, I saw Arjun asking his EA to dump my presentations in the shredder. He then took my seat at the end of the table and continued the meeting. Ayaan didn't look me in the eye, not once.

The security guards, who saluted me every day, now marched grimly by my side as they walked me to my car. I got into the car and felt the only thing I was still in control of was the wheel.

———

After fifteen minutes of staring at the windshield, my haze of disbelief had turned into rage. For the next few hours, I sat in my car calling lawyers and talking lawsuits. I was desperate to get my startup back. The lawyers were eager, but they warned me that the fight could take months, possibly years. Then I just sat doing nothing, staring at the building, unable to drive home even as all my old staff got in their cars and left for the day.

My phone dinged. *Hey honey, home soon?* read a text from Tina.

I couldn't bear to tell Tina the truth over text, so I replied, *Dealing with a work emergency, I'll be back soon.*

Around 6:30 pm I heard a buzz on my phone. I quickly picked it up to see if it was an update from the lawyer's office.

It was a text from Mike.

Let's meet at 7 pm. Our usual!

I was glad to hear from Mike, the only person I felt was still on my side. I sped my car to Toit in Indira Nagar, where we usually met for drinks.

I found Mike sitting at a booth in the back corner. Our drinks were already served. I took a sip and then chugged the whole thing. It felt awful. I ordered a refill. As the server made my drink, there was an awkward silence. I was chugging my second drink when Mike said, "Slow down, buddy. I want to help, but before I do that, I need to get the details right."

I finished draining the second drink and said, "What's left for me, Mike? I lost everything."

"No, you did not," he challenged. "Have you even read the terms sheet Arjun gave you?"

I ground my teeth in anger hearing Arjun's name. "Mike, please don't say that traitor's name."

"Okay, but did you read the terms sheet?"

"Of course I read it. Honestly, I could care less."

"You should care for it—it's a good deal. You keep your stock, and you'll collect a payout if the company gets acquired or goes public. If you sit tight, you could be a rich man in a few years." He paused and thought for a moment. Perhaps to find the right words. "Neo…I met with Ekta and Ant Capital leadership. Sorry to say, but no one wants to rock the boat. Digi Gate is on its way to paying us back ten times over. Investors are happy with that kind of return."

"But Mike, we could do so much more with some additional time and investment."

"I believe you, Neo. I kept the copy of your presentation; there are some incredible ideas there. I tried to talk to Ayaan, but…Arjun has locked him down."

"I've been talking to some lawyers. I'm going to fight—I've got a good case," I added furiously.

"That's your right, but what do you expect to achieve? You'll be litigating this for months, maybe years. And say you get control back; the company won't be the same one you left. Sorry to say, but Arjun is putting out a press release tomorrow announcing your departure and his promotion. They've already announced the change to all the employees. If you litigate, you'll probably destroy both yourself and the company. Just sit tight and cash out at the right time."

"I don't care about the money. That's not why I started. I wanted to make a difference. Change people's lives."

"You can still do that, just not at Digi Gate. In fact, I just thought of an idea. There is another company we are invested in: Fitness First Inc. They could really use someone like you there."

"As CEO?" I asked curiously.

"No, they already have one, and she's not going anywhere. They need a Chief Digital Officer (CDO). In the United States."

My eyes lit up when I heard *United States.*

He went on. "Fitness First is looking for a CDO who can put them on the right trajectory to become a digital-first organization and get the digital transformation right—this time around."

I crossed my arms. "What do you mean by *this time around?*"

Mike took a deep breath and said, "Well, let me lay it out for you. They've tried before to digitally transform. But the failed attempts over the past two years cost the previous CDO his job. We now have one year left to get things on the right course. I feel if there's anyone who could do it, it would be you. You would be a great fit for the role."

"Hmm," I said with hesitation. "I'll need to think about this. I'm not sure if I'm ready to give up on Digi Gate just yet. And I would need to talk this over with Tina."

Mike nodded. "I understand. Go home. Do some research. Talk to Tina. But Fitness First needs a CDO soon, so I can't give you much time. Can we connect again tomorrow?" he asked.

"Yeah…sure."

I drank a glass of water and headed out. As I drove back from Indira Nagar, one of the plush neighborhoods in Bengaluru, every bit of the journey annoyed me—the potholes, the white cabs, the yellow-topped autorickshaws, and the swarm of bikes that squeezed in between every possible space in the traffic. The restless drivers and mind-numbing honking made me feel that everyone was in a mad rush to get home. But I drove much slower than normal.

I was not ready to face Tina. I did not have the courage to tell her about the eventful day. Would she feel like all her sacrifices had lost their meaning? She quit her job for me. She never wanted to relocate to India. She struggled to settle down in a new country. She was taking care of Mom and continued to stay in India because of my startup. Now I would have to tell her that I was just fired from my own company, and that the past three years had been for nothing.

BRASS TACKS

As I entered the living room, Tina looked up from her smartphone. "Hi, you're late." She stood up. "Like my dress?"

She wore a blue pleated gown with rich golden embroidery. I quickly glanced at it and replied automatically. "Yeah, looks great."

"Do you remember these?" she asked, pointing to the earrings that I could barely see in her mass of curly ringlets.

"Nice," I said.

"Gee, you're not enthusiastic at all. You gave me these on our first anniversary. Remember?"

My whole body stiffened, and my eyes widened. I was a deer in the headlights. It was our anniversary that day. I did not buy a gift. And to top it off, I totally forgot about it.

I hugged her and wished her a happy anniversary.

"Finally, you remembered," she said.

"Sorry, I had a rough day."

"Ah, poor baby," she said. "I've got a great idea. Let's go out for dinner, and you can forget all about it."

I shook my head. "I can't." I took a deep breath. "I got fired from Digi Gate today."

She laughed, a short bark of surprise. "What?" She peered at me. "Are you serious?"

I explained what happened and how the situation went out of control.

"Neo, I'm so sorry," she said. "If you just want to relax and get this out of your mind, that's okay. We can have a quiet evening at home."

"Thanks, Tina. Actually, I want to eat something fast and then get started researching an opportunity in the US." Aargh. Why did I mention the US?

Her face changed. Did it brighten? "The US…really?" she asked.

"Yeah. Mike told me about an opportunity for a Chief Digital Officer in Bellevue."

That piqued her interest even more. "Bellevue? We could move back home?" We had lived in Bellevue before relocating to Bengaluru and we had both loved the Northwest region of the US. "How soon before you can join?" she asked.

I was in disbelief. I felt myself glaring at her. I thought she cared more about Digi Gate, but she seemed ready to move on right away. "You really want to get out of Bengaluru as fast as you can, don't you?"

Tina softened. "Neo, this isn't my hometown. I don't have the same sentimental feelings for it that you do. You know how much I've struggled," she said.

"What did you want me to do?" I said furiously. "Everything just happened, one thing after the other since Dad was diagnosed with cancer. Everything was out of my hands."

"Out of your hands? Really?" she said with sarcasm.

"Tina, I do not have time to get into a fight." I frowned at her. "I can't believe you are in such a rush to leave. I still think I should fight for Digi Gate."

Her lips thinned, and I could see she was keeping control of her temper. "Neo, I left my career behind to move to a new country. I have been compromising and adjusting all along. You said that fighting for Digi Gate probably wouldn't work. Is it any surprise that I would be excited about moving back?" She turned partly away from me, her eyes wet. "I miss my family too, you know."

I swallowed, a pit of shame building in my chest. Tina had been holding the family together—taking care of Riya, helping Mom through her depression, and running the family. I took her in my arms and hugged her. "I'm sorry."

She stepped back and looked at me. "Will you at least seriously consider the opportunity that Mike suggested?"

I shrugged.

"I'm not saying you have to take it. Just look at it objectively. Maybe it could be a good thing," she said. And then she emphasized. "Neo, you've been so wrapped up in your work that you barely think about your family anymore. We moved to India because of family. I tried to accommodate as much as I can, but now it's getting tough for me."

I knew that Tina missed her life in the US. She had told me many times that even when I was a consultant and traveling a lot, she felt closer to me. I am home every night now, but my mind has been at work.

I promised her that I would seriously consider the opportunity and went to the dining room to eat something fast. I could smell that Mom was cooking her legendary Chicken Biryani.

Mom could tell right away that something was wrong and asked me if everything was alright. I shook my head. A few minutes later, Mom quietly handed me a plate of food. She sat next to me and watched me eat.

After a few minutes she said, "When your dad was fighting cancer, he would still try to do things to take care of me. Little things, but it was how I knew he loved me." She paused, then continued, "No matter what, you must put Tina and Riya first, because they will be with you for your whole life. Work comes and goes, and even parents do. You need to think about what will make Tina and Riya happy, because every moment is precious. Even now, I wish I had just one more day with your dad."

I was at a loss for what to say and sat eating in silence. Then I promised Mom that I would take care of the family and get things back on track. I went to my bedroom and checked my email. Nothing from the lawyers. I pulled up the Fitness First website.

Tina came to the room, looking tired. She must have been putting Riya to bed. I followed her into the dressing room and watched as she removed her jewelry and makeup. I was hoping that she would start a conversation because I needed her guidance. Although I hated myself for turning our anniversary night into a personal counseling session, I didn't want to gamble.

"Tell me again which company Mike was referring to?" she asked.

Thank God. She initiated a dialogue. "Fitness First Inc. It sounds exciting, but I don't know whether I'm ready. I don't know whether they have the right team."

"What, specifically, doesn't feel right?"

"I don't know. The fitness market is new to me, and I just don't know…"

She interrupted, "You've said *I don't know* a few times already. Maybe let's start with what you *do* know?"

I nodded. "Yeah, I'm struggling to organize my thoughts. I know that the previous CDO was fired. I know that they didn't see any promising results even after two years of work. I know that the CEO is there to stay, at least for a while. It's why they're failing that I don't know, and I'm worried that I'll fail, too." [*Reasons why digital transformations fail are discussed in detail in Part Two*]

Tina rolled her eyes. "Can you at least approach the opportunity with an open mind?"

"I'm feeling a bit skeptical and close-minded right now," I added sheepishly. "Very pessimistic, even."

We walked back to the bedroom and sat on the bed.

Tina took a breath to gather her thoughts. "Do you agree that Mike knows you pretty well, and that he wouldn't say you're the right fit for the role unless he really believed that?" She smiled in a warm and motherly way. "I think you need to leave your apprehensions behind, both about yourself and Fitness First."

I listened intently.

She continued, "Didn't you say you're not sure if you're ready?"

I nodded.

She threw a pillow at me. "When opportunity comes and knocks at your door, always be willing to take a chance. And this time around, you can make a sacrifice for me—going back to the US."

She was right. I must have an open mind. I agreed and dove back into my iPad. I immediately uncovered some interesting things about Samantha Martinez, the CEO of Fitness First.

A Harvard MBA with management consulting experience at Big 3s and now a newly promoted CEO in her thirties.

Samantha was not any of that.

Rather, she was an Economics graduate from University of Rochester. She grew up in a small town in Ohio. She joined Active Health Inc. as a management trainee and worked her way up, starting in marketing and public relations, then did rotations in Business Development and IT, where she led a handful of digital initiatives that added new revenue streams and catapulted Active Health to a new level. Active Health was then acquired by Fitness First a few years back, where she became Senior Vice President of Sales. When the previous CEO and founder retired three years ago, she impressed upon the board that she was the one to lead Fitness First Inc.

Quite an accomplishment.

Fitness First's Annual Reports revealed more about the company, board, executive team, and financial performance. They were a 19-year-old organization and had four business verticals: health clubs, workout equipment, supplements and expert consultations.

Health clubs business: *The largest vertical with $1.2 BN revenue and 450+ health clubs spanning across the US. 100+ health clubs were from the Active Health acquisition. Health clubs had been growing at a CAGR of 13%, but that growth had recently slowed dramatically. Revenue guidance for the year was not rosy with revenue falling below $1 BN.*

What could be the digital play here? What would have cost the previous CDO his job?

Workout equipment business: *Second largest vertical with $345 MN revenue. A steady growth at a CAGR of 16%, with significant growth recently. Growth could have been even greater, and there was manufacturing capacity available, except that they were experiencing supply chain and on-time delivery issues.*

The recent growth was great, but they wouldn't be able to sustain that growth if they couldn't streamline their supply chain.

Supplement and expert consultation business: *Experts ranged from personal trainers to nutritionists and mental health professionals. Supplements* *ranged from vitamins to protein powders. While the expert consultation business had been growing at CAGR 13%, the supplement business had grown at 24%. Combined revenue from both the businesses was $320M.*

I turned off my tablet. Tina was already asleep next to me, breathing quietly. Fitness First seemed like a solid company. They had most of the ingredients required to elevate customers' lives by providing high-quality fitness and health experiences.

Why did Mike think I would be a great fit? Granted, I had some success in finding innovative solutions when I was consulting with large companies, and Digi Gate taught me a great deal about how to lead an organization. But I didn't know how to transform a 19-year-old fitness behemoth. Should I put my career at risk by accepting an unimaginable task—putting a traditional business on the right trajectory to become digital-first? And in *one year?*

If I failed, my career would go into oblivion—both in the US and in India. Forever.

But if I got it right, I would be a Chief Digital Officer of a large traditional organization, in the United States, where Tina's heart was. I owed that to Tina. The job could go a long way toward fixing my family life.

I sent a text to Mike that I was keen to move forward. I got a reply immediately.

Great! Let's meet in London for the Digital Unplugged conference later this month. Plan your travels.

MEET THE MENTOR

The next two weeks were good, except for avoiding calls from news-hungry journalists and well-meaning friends and colleagues who heard about my sorry exit from Digi Gate. I spent quality time with Tina, Riya and Mom. I was more than resolved to try my best and land the job at Fitness First.

I headed to London to meet Mike at the Digital Unplugged conference. On the first day, I went to the breakfast buffet at the conference hotel. It was packed with business types like me. As I was looking for a place to sit, my eyes paused on an old man who looked familiar. He was wearing an immaculate striped suit, sitting alone with his book in one hand and a coffee in the other. I felt like I knew this guy. He looked like Charan, the Business Management professor from Wharton, with whom I had endless debates during my masters. He was considered a management guru. At first, I was not really sure if it was him. As I stared at him, he glanced at me and raised one bushy eyebrow in an unspoken question: do I know you?

"Charan?" I asked him.

"Yes?"

"I'm Neo Ray. Remember me?"

He didn't say anything.

"I knew you some time ago. I was a management student at Wharton. We had endless debates on digital business models and two-sided networked platforms. In fact, I won a business model innovation competition and got an award from you. It was for security management."

A small flash of recognition finally hit him. "Of course! I do remember. *Neo*, was it?"

"That's right."

He looked at my full plate, then at the crowded dining area, and gestured to the seat across from him.

I sat down. "So, how are you these days?"

"Busy," he said. "Very busy. And you?" He closed his book, giving me his full attention.

"Well, not so much. I'm here for a job interview," I added. "What about you?"

"I am here to give some guidance," said Charan.

He seemed bored with this line of chat. A second of awkward silence passed between us. He tapped his forefinger on his book and watched me chew.

I rallied. "Remember the business model innovation award I got? On security management? I built a startup in India based on the idea. It's going to be a unicorn soon."

Charan nodded. He seemed more interested.

"Funny, I got fired from my own company because the board didn't want to invest in a new line of business. I guess I will be busy with my new assignment—making Fitness First Inc. into a digital-first organization."

"I see," said Charan. "What's the role you are interviewing for?"

"Chief Digital Officer. The previous CDO was fired for his failed attempts. Now it's my turn to put them on the right trajectory. That too in one year," I said.

"That's interesting. How big is the company?"

I gave a short summary of the details I'd gathered.

Charan leaned forward. "Interesting. What's your plan for how you'll transform them into a digital-first organization?"

I felt myself freeze. I had my doubts in the first place whether I was a good fit for the role. Now he asked if I had a plan. I really didn't want to reveal my ignorance. "I've got some ideas." I nodded enthusiastically, hoping to avoid any further questioning.

"Great," he said. "Since you've done some background research and have started on a plan, help me clarify one thing. What's the purpose of Fitness First?"

"I'm not sure I understand," I said.

"What is there to understand? It's a simple question. What is the purpose of Fitness First?"

I couldn't hold back my smile.

"Well, it's obvious isn't it? To make money?"

"No," he said. "That's old-school thinking. Let me rephrase it for you. *Why does Fitness First exist?*"

My smile froze. I leaned back, looking at him. What the hell did he mean by that?

"You mean their reason for being?" I asked.

"Exactly. Every organization exists for a reason." He paused. "Different question. Do you know why the previous CDO was fired?"

"No," I admitted.

"You said the transformation had been going on for more than two years with no significant results? Is that correct?"

"Hey, Charan, what is this?" I asked him.

"Just tell me," he said. "Did the transformation lead to mixed results or no results?"

"Offhand, I have to say I don't think it delivered any significant results. I mean, why'd they fire the previous CDO if the results were great? But I'd really have to check the details."

"Check with the team if you'd like," he said. "But I'm going to do you a favor, since you're one of my old students. If there's no clarity as to their purpose...and the last CDO was fired...and transformation is taking years and years—then you will be fired, too."

How did he know? How could he predict? In the pit of my stomach, I was getting the same feeling I'd have if I was in a cable car high in the mountains and the cable broke.

"Wait a minute. How do you know about this? Do you have some insider information about Fitness First?" I asked him.

He smiled. "You have more insider information than I do. But I see these symptoms in a lot of traditional organizations that embrace digital. Fitness First is not alone."

"But aren't you a management guru?"

"Well, I'm more like a doctor. Maybe sometimes a trauma surgeon. I fix poorly managed organizations," he said. "And right now, you could say that I'm working in the highly traumatic field of fixing organizations trying to drive business transformation with digital."

"Whatever it is you're into, you definitely put your finger on a couple of my biggest problems, I have to give you that," I told him. "How come—"

Charan jumped in his seat. He reached into the pocket of his striped pants to take out his smartphone, which was buzzing furiously. "Sorry, Neo! I'm going to be late."

He stood up and reached for his bag.

"That's too bad," I said. "I'm kind of intrigued by what you said. And a bit apprehensive."

He paused. "Yes, well, if you start to think about what we've been discussing, you could probably get yourself out of trouble."

"Hey, maybe I gave you the wrong impression," I told him. "I know there will be problems, but I don't think I'm in deep trouble."

He looked me straight in the eye. It felt like he knew what was going on, precisely.

"Listen," I said, "I've got some time to kill. Why don't I walk you down to wherever you're going? Would you mind?"

"No, not at all," he said. "But we have to hurry."

I got up and grabbed my coat and laptop bag. Charan was already edging his way towards the hallway. He waited for me to catch up with him. Then the two of us stepped out into the corridor where people were rushing everywhere. Digital Unplugged was one of the busiest conferences and people came in from across the globe. Charan set off at a fast pace. It took effort to keep up with him.

"I'm curious," I told Charan. "What made you suspect something might be wrong in Fitness First's transformation journey?"

"You told me yourself," he said.

"No, I didn't."

"Neo," he said. "It was clear from what you said that Fitness First is not running the digital transformation efficiently. In fact, they are doing the opposite. They are running the digital transformation very inefficiently."

"But how did you guess that?" I wanted to know.

"If their purpose was clear, you would have discovered it in your research. Since their purpose is not clear, how in the world can the company determine where to focus with digital? It is critical to get the purpose right during a digital transformation journey. For that matter, any transformation journey."

Purpose again, I thought.

He continued. "Every organization has a soul and a purpose for why it exists. An organization that defines their purpose with absolute clarity inspires employees to something greater, the kind of mindset that makes them believe a cultural shift is possible. These organizations can harness the power of purpose to drive performance and profitability and enjoy a distinct competitive advantage. There are countless studies to prove that."

We rushed around a corner. In front of us were metal detectors and security guards. It looked like there was a high-profile event in the ballroom. I had intended to stop and say bye to him there, but Charan didn't slow down.

"Just tell me, what is the purpose of your digital startup?" he asked as he walked through the metal detector. "To you, personally, what does it mean?"

I put my laptop case on the conveyor and followed him through. I was wondering what he wanted to hear.

"Well...let me think. We're into security management. We want to make security management simple and easy. That's our purpose?"

"Wrong," he exclaimed.

I felt insulted.

"Think again. What would happen if your product or service didn't exist?" he asked.

"I guess…residents would lack a sense of safety and security?"

"That's correct!" said Charan.

"I understand now. Our purpose is to provide safety and security to residents."

"Exactly! And perhaps that might be the reason why your marketplace idea was abandoned," he said.

That hurt again. But I wondered—how would organizations evolve if their purpose remains the same?

"Will a company's purpose ever change?" I wanted to know.

"It will. Progressive organizations define purpose with a long horizon. For example, take Amazon. Their purpose is to become *Earth's most customer-centric company*. I think they may replace *Earth* with *Universe* when Mr. Bezos' dream to conquer space is realized. Organizations may rethink their purpose based on changing market dynamics," clarified Charan.

I thought for a moment. I never defined a purpose at Digi Gate, but we prioritized initiatives with an unstated and unspoken purpose in mind.

He continued. "There are two types of purpose statements. A *Transformative Purpose* is defined to help customers achieve a more balanced life. It's one in which different human needs are integrated more cohesively and harmoniously. A *Linear Purpose* will push the organization to develop strong technical assets which, in turn, will help the business achieve linear growth."

We were rushing down the hallway. I was trying to match Charan's pace.

"So, you mean each digital initiative will need to align with the purpose of why Fitness First exists? If not, it'll lead to an ill-coordinated effort and will likely be directionless?" I asked.

He nodded and said, "Neo, I have come to the conclusion that aligning initiatives to a company's purpose is necessary to bring that company closer to realizing its purpose. Every initiative that brings a company closer to its purpose is *aligned*. Every initiative that does not bring a company closer to its purpose is *misaligned*. Do you follow me?"

"Yeah, but…really? That's just common sense. Isn't it?" I asked.

"It's simple logic, is what it is. But purpose-driven organizations are more likely to win—they attract the best talent, unify efforts, inspire richer innovation, make faster decisions, are more trusted, have greater loyalty, and attract larger investments," he said. *[Refer to real-world case studies at the end of Part One]*

We stopped. I saw a cardboard cutout in front of the ballroom of someone who looked like Charan. I looked again. It *was* indeed Charan. I was stunned to see that he was the keynote speaker of the Digital Unplugged conference.

Suddenly, Charan started to look like a guru in digital transformation. He was joined by a conference coordinator who escorted him backstage. I trailed along, and surprisingly no one said anything.

"Okay," I said. "I get it—I need to know the purpose. And then I bring in the right tech: Artificial Intelligence, Machine Learning, sensors etc."

He smiled ruefully. "Sorry to say, but purpose is not your only problem. I just realized that you have a bigger problem. You don't even know what digital really means. And, by the way, there is only one definition of digital, no matter what company it is."

That stumped me. The conference coordinator was whispering something into her headset and motioning Charan to stand behind the curtains on stage. I could hear someone introducing Charan to the audience behind those giant curtains.

"Wait a minute! What do you mean I don't know what digital is? I know what digital is," I told him.

The conference coordinator was glaring at me now. I was sure she'd figured out that I wasn't supposed to be there. Charan didn't seem rushed. "Really? Tell me what digital means to you."

"Digital is cloud, analytics, scalable technology." I clarified.

He shook his head. "Wrong. That's not it."

I stared at him blankly.

The conference coordinator had caught Charan's elbow and was trying to steer him. "We will be ready in 30 seconds!" she said anxiously.

Charan told her, "Okay." Then he turned to me. "Come on, Neo! Quickly! Tell me what digital means to you. If you know what it is."

"Using technology to achieve the purpose?" I suggested.

He looked surprised.

"Not bad, Neo. You've gotten closer than most people."

The conference coordinator looked tense. "Sir, 10 seconds," she said coldly.

Charan acknowledged her. "Neo, you've gotten one thing right. You cannot understand the true meaning of digital unless you know what the purpose is. Until then, you're just playing a lot of games with tech. Stay for the talk—I'm sure they'll find you a seat."

He waved goodbye to me and the conference coordinator, who sighed in relief. Charan stepped onto the stage to roaring applause from the audience.

UNLEARN TO RELEARN

As I followed the conference coordinator, I heard Charan sharing the conversation we just had with the audience. The coordinator put me in the front row, in an empty seat usually reserved for VIPs. As embarrassing as it was, I was really hoping that Charan would clarify the true meaning of digital to the larger audience.

He said, "I promise to demystify what digital really means. But before that, let's look at *why* digital is important now, more than ever."

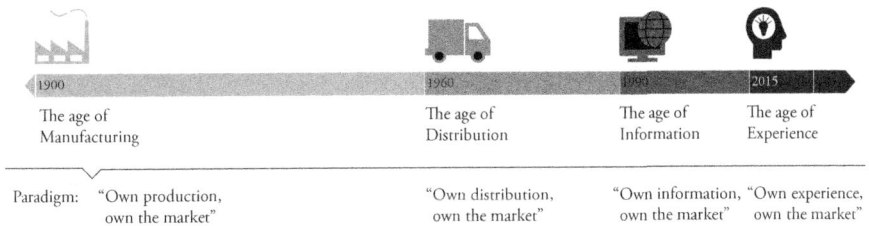

1900		1960	1993	2015
The age of Manufacturing		The age of Distribution	The age of Information	The age of Experience

Paradigm:	"Own production, own the market"		"Own distribution, own the market"	"Own information, own the market"	"Own experience, own the market"

Source: Forrester Research

"From the Age of Manufacturing in the 1900s through to the Age of Experience we are in now, our expectations have evolved right along with advances in industry, technology and information. Nowadays, the traditional thinking of faster, cheaper, and better is no longer enough to create differentiation. That path results in commoditization and a race to the bottom, driven by endless price wars." He paused to let that message sink in.

"In the Age of Experience, digital has become a critical differentiator for delivering compelling products and services. That effect has been accelerated recently. Organizations have realized that adopting digital is not just critical to be relevant but also to be resilient to future disruptions."

A few heads nodded in agreement.

"But digital means different things to different people. If you ask ten executives what digital means to them, I can guarantee that you will hear ten different answers." And then he asked the same question he had posed to me minutes before. "So, what does digital really mean to you all?"

A hand shot up. "Digital is anything that has to do with technology. Artificial intelligence, sensors that power the Internet of Things, drones, cloud. All these things are digital to me."

"Hmm…okay."

Another hand went up. "Social media platforms like Instagram that power our digital marketing?"

Someone called out from the back, without raising their hand. "What about smartphones, tablets, wearables?"

"Okay…anyone else?"

"My team uses Hyperion and Power BI to crunch numbers and provide analytics. That's digital to me."

The audience kept calling out technologies. As they did, Charan quietly wrote them on the whiteboard:

Social, Mobile, AI & Analytics, Cloud, Drones, IoT

There was a murmur of laughter in the audience. "Are you saying we're all getting smacked by digital?" asked a gentleman wearing a blue suit with suspenders and round glasses. "I'm definitely getting smacked by the cost of my IT budget," said someone from the back.

More laughter.

"Precisely." Charan didn't smile. In fact, he looked like he was delivering a eulogy at a funeral. His response was a bit unsettling to the audience. And me.

"I have asked the same question to some of the smartest C-level executives, including their boards. The answers I heard from them were no different from what I heard from all of you. And all the technology is fine at one level. However, when you start to look at how companies are investing in digital, you discover a lot of misalignment. People pulling in different directions."

He spread his hands wide. "Digital has two aspects. One is economic and the other is operational. Most of us interpret digital from an operational perspective—how do I leverage digital to go faster, cheaper, or better?"

I decided to take advantage of my front row, VIP seat. "Can you explain?" I asked. I knew this time he wouldn't punt my question with another question.

Charan smiled. "Sure. When a new digital technology arrives in the market, there is a frenzy for adoption. Today it's artificial intelligence. Tomorrow it's blockchain or brain computer interface. The question mostly, though not necessarily all the time, centers around how digital can improve operational aspects." He looked at the audience and said, "There is nothing wrong in focusing on operational aspects; they are important. And by operations, I mean anything you want to make faster, cheaper, and better in your day-to-day activities. But focusing only on operational aspects is not enough to extract the true value of what digital can offer."

There was absolute silence among the audience as they waited to hear what Charan would say next.

"Now let's talk about the most interesting part—the economic aspect of digital. It is important for organizations to understand how their overall value proposition is changing or will be changing, and where it is going with the emergence of *every* new digital technology. Remember, digital has the potential to shake up every element of the value chain."

What he said was enlightening yet confusing. I raised my hand again and asked, "Can you give an example? Maybe from the fitness industry?" It didn't hurt to try.

He gave a short bark of laughter. "Sure, the fitness industry…let's take ClassPass. It's a digital platform that provides access to fitness classes at different health clubs via their mobile app. All you have to do is pay a flat fee every month to get access to any health club and fitness classes in their network. With ClassPass, a new business model was created that never existed before. It was possible because of a digital platform and a two-sided network."

A hand went up. "What's a two-sided network?"

"Good question. In this example, on the one side, ClassPass has consolidated a fragmented set of health clubs—call them service providers—through their asset-light digital platform and connected them to the customers on the other side—call them service receivers."

He then stressed a point. "An interesting thing to note is that the source of disruption isn't from an existing fitness player, but someone from outside the industry."

Charan had the attention of the audience. He added details of how digital helps redefine the value proposition. "Digital platforms enabled ClassPass to *bundle* the value proposition based on variables that would deliver the most value—say service-based, i.e., pricing based on classes and nutrition experts; or region-based pricing, i.e., pricing differently for New York and New Jersey. Not only did the profit pools shrink for the fragmented players, and the value transferred primarily to customers, but the pie was redistributed to ClassPass."

He paused for a moment and said, "Digital has a potential to bundle, like you saw in ClassPass, and unbundle as well. Let me explain unbundling."

Charan thought for a moment and created a hypothetical example. "Say a health club not part of ClassPass provides a combo package which includes access to the health club and also 10 expert consultations. With ClassPass, the combo package can be unbundled, and customers may be given an option to just buy access to the health club and let them pick expert consultations from wherever they want—either from ClassPass or from outside."

A few audience members were furiously taking notes. Charan pushed on.

"As new digital technologies enable new distribution models, businesses swing back and forth like a pendulum, implementing bundling or unbundling options to adapt to the changing customer demands and needs. Usually, bundles start out great, until they tip over on their own weight. Then customers start demanding only parts of the bundle. That's when we see the pendulum effect swing back to meet the customer, shifting the distribution model."

A light went on in my head. I raised my hand. "So, the economic aspect of digital will center around new business models, value creation and new possibilities anywhere in the business or in the industry. And we need to pay attention to it…all the time." It was sort of a question.

Charan nodded. "Exactly right! With new digitally inspired business models, profit pools will shift. A few players end up taking most of the profits, and surprisingly, they often come from beyond the industry. Digital can shakeup traditional business models overnight. It can blur the barriers to entry. Digitally savvy entrepreneurs can compete with well-established incumbents. If traditional organizations play it safe and focus only on the operational aspects and drive incremental changes and innovation around the edges, it's an end game."

"How can we keep an open mind to the economic aspect of digital?" someone asked.

"There is no magic formula. However, if you have a digital mindset, if you appreciate the true meaning of digital and if you constantly look for the "Art of the Possible," you will likely discover possibilities. Sometimes ahead of the competition."

He flashed up a slide that stated,

Digital enables a company to achieve its purpose by creating new business models, reimagining customer experiences and increasing employee productivity

He continued. "Every organization must balance the outcomes of the economic and operational aspects of digital. Digital technology can be anything."

"Is there a difference between how Digital Giants like Amazon or Google approach this, compared to traditional organizations?" asked a gentleman.

"Digital Giants are born digital. They balance it well, sometimes with near perfection. However, traditional organizations must also master the art of balancing the *dichotomy of digital*. On one hand, digital must enable them to add new digital business models. And on the other, the core business must be digitized—that business still needs to be maintained. Remember, digital doesn't always mean disruption. Traditional organizations must perform the balancing act cautiously if they want to be a digital-first organization."

Since Fitness First was a traditional organization, I wondered how the previous CDO balanced the dichotomy of digital. I raised my hand and asked, "Is there a recommendation on the right balance?"

"Well, there is no one-size-fits-all to define the perfect balance. Usually, traditional organizations start with 80% of their resource investments dedicated to digitizing their core business. They focus on the remaining for business building with digital. However, industry shifts, emerging trends, and new entrants can all influence the mix."

The rest of the session was a blur. In just a few conversations, Charan made me realize that there is so much more to becoming a digital-first organization than I initially thought. Truth is, I didn't know how to be a good CDO of a traditional organization. The gap between my actual skills and the skills I needed was dauntingly wide. Could I bridge that gap with the right coaching? And in time to put Fitness First on the right trajectory before the year ran out? It seemed impossible.

SHEDDING FEARS

Any confidence I had in the morning had been torn away by the discussion with Charan. After Charan's keynote ended, I trudged back to my room. I thought about calling Mike and telling him that I couldn't take the meeting. But I knew that I didn't have a lot of options, and the idea of looking for a different opportunity filled me with despair.

My phone buzzed. It was a video call from Tina. A few positive words could turn despair into hope.

I grabbed a seat and took the call.

"Daddy, look what I made!" Riya's little face beamed with excitement. She showed off her artwork on the card she made for me. The card had four astronauts taking off on a rocket from India and the rocket had the words "*To the US*."

"Do you like my card, Daddy?"

"I love it, sweetheart," I said.

"Look, Daddy. You are an astronaut going to the US."

I smiled and said, "It's brilliant." Riya was fascinated by space and loved hearing about the billionaires and their companies putting their hearts and souls into making humans interplanetary. She wanted to go to Mars one day.

"Who are the others, sweetie?" I wanted to know.

"It's Mommy. Me. And granny," she said. "We are coming to the US with you. Mommy said you will take us with you soon."

I froze. I swallowed and blinked back tears. I tried to clear my throat to speak.

Tina noticed and said, "Okay, say bye to Daddy."

"Bye Daddy!" Riya gave me a virtual kiss.

My heart was breaking. Tina took the phone and asked, "Everything alright?"

"Nope. I'm realizing that the opportunity at Fitness First will be much more complex than I initially thought."

"How so?" she asked.

"Remember Charan from Wharton? I bumped into him here in London. We had a short debate…again."

Tina was shaking her head as if to say *not again.*

"Charan is an expert in fixing organizations that are *trying* but *failing* to embrace digital. It looks like I need to unlearn and relearn the basics of a digital-first organization—it's very critical to set the foundation of the journey," I added.

"What are you worried about?" she asked.

"Well, the process of unlearning and relearning and the time left."

"Neo, you were near the top of our class. And you've always been curious. If anyone can figure it out, it's you."

Tina was right. I decided to make this work.

"Listen, I gotta run. I'm meeting Mike for lunch and I need to do some prep. I must pull together some thoughts from what I've learned!"

I hung up and went down to the hotel bar. I ordered a drink and pulled out my iPad to write:

Transformative Customer-centric Purpose	→	**Balance the Dichotomy of Digital**	→	**Align Digital Initiatives**

First, I needed to define the purpose of Fitness First—why do they even exist? I flipped through the folder where I'd gathered the annual reports of Fitness First. I read through the filings and my notes and refreshed my memories from the meetings with Mike.

Vision   *— **Undisputed market leadership**.*
('The What' we want to accomplish)

Mission	*— **Deliver innovative fitness***
('The How' we want to accomplish)	***options to our members**.*

While the vision and mission of Fitness First was clearly articulated, the purpose of *why Fitness First exists* wasn't. Since Fitness First was into health and wellness, the purpose statement must be grounded with the health and wellbeing of its customers. It must be transformative, like Charan mentioned. After all, what's the point of having a linear purpose when the Digital Giants were already hungry to get into health and wellness?

A transformative purpose by its very nature had to be centered on addressing the core needs of the customer. The needs must not be addressed just at the surface level, lest it become a linear purpose. Customer needs had to be integrated more cohesively and harmoniously, and it needed to be action-oriented for the customer. The purpose statement had to be something we could deliver with our current capabilities or with capabilities we could realistically build in the future.

Make our customers fit?

Nah, that's too linear.

What was the *why* behind what Fitness First's customers did? Were they okay if they were just *fit*? Or would they be focusing on health and happiness? Focusing on fitness could limit the scope to physical health and nutrition. What if we expanded it to overall health? What if Fitness First helped its customers on their path to overall health—physical and mental health?

That was it. I took my iPad and wrote:

> **Be the best in the world at helping individuals**
> **and families on their path to better health**

I looked at it carefully.

The statement went beyond *what the customer does* by integrating more cohesively and harmoniously with the core needs of the customer. *Check.*

It delivered personalization that creates differentiated experiences for our customers. *Great.*

It was action oriented. *Perfect.*

It was transformative in that Fitness First could focus on a broad range of products and services in health and wellbeing for the greater good of the customer. *Terrific.*

And Fitness First's four business verticals had capabilities to deliver on the purpose, right off the bat. I felt I was off to a great start.

Now I had to worry about balancing the dichotomy of digital. *How do I do that?*

Fitness First was a 19-year-old incumbent. Guaranteed that the company would be fraught with legacy systems, operations, procedures. Therefore the majority of the digital transformation efforts had to be focused on re-inventing the core. But the threat of Digital Giants and start-ups was also high, so we would need to carve out time and resources to introduce new digital business models. In fact, in order for Fitness First to win in the long term, it would need to double down on building new digitally innovative value streams before it was too late.

As my iPad screen filled with notes, I started to look forward to the meeting with Mike. Charan had given me the key to unlocking digital transformation success. Clarify the purpose, then align all efforts against that purpose. Master the balance between the operational and economic aspects to extract the true value of digital. Once the balancing act was managed, all I needed was to bring the plan to life. I could create Innovation Pods similar to the one that had delivered rapid results at Digi Gate. With multiple Innovation Pods in place, Fitness First would soon be on a good trajectory.

I felt good about how I was reinventing myself. I pulled some facts and figures to convince Mike why *purpose* is critical. In the next thirty minutes, Dr. Google gave me everything I needed on the benefits of becoming a purpose-driven organization. I made a list of key points:

Business oriented:
- 79% of business leaders surveyed by PwC believe that an organization's purpose is central to business success[1]
- Purposeful companies outperform the stock market by 42%[2]

- Companies without a sense of purpose within their vision/mission underperform the market by 40%[3]
- Purposeful companies report 30% higher levels of innovation and 40% higher levels of workforce retention than their competitors[4]

Customer oriented:
- Millennials who have a strong connection with the purpose of their organization are 5.3 times more likely to stay[1]
- 79% of customers are more loyal to purpose-driven brands, and 73% said they would defend them. Another 67% said they are more willing to forgive a purpose-driven company for any mistake[5]
- Customers view purpose-driven brands as being more caring and, as a result, are more loyal to them[5]

I looked around and felt as if I had just come out of a long trance. Everything looked familiar but seemed new. I took a couple of deep, easy breaths. I stretched and the muscles in my shoulders relaxed. Time to meet Mike and blow his mind.

1. PwC Study on 'Putting Purpose to Work'
2. DDI World's Study on Global Leadership Study
3. Conference Board/EY Global Leadership Study
4. Deloitte Study on Purpose with an Impact
5. Cone/Porter Novelli Purpose Study

THE BIG MEETING

As I walked to the lunch meeting, I thought about how useful Charan's discussion had been. If I could convince Charan to be my mentor, I was sure I could ace the transformation. But before I asked for his help, I needed to secure the job.

I went to the banquet hall where Mike had made a reservation for a table. As I walked towards Mike, I saw someone sitting next to him. She looked a lot like Samantha Martinez, the CEO. Yes, it was her. Odd—Mike had never said she was joining.

She was casually elegant, wearing a plain grey V-neck cardigan and a perfectly fitted black dress. Her jewelry was limited to a watch and earrings. Dark hair in an "up" style, nothing to distract from her face, which was commanding, with high cheekbones and sharp angles, softened just enough by her youth to look appealing, if not exactly pretty. Lively dark eyes fixed on me as I approached. My new boss if this went well.

"Good afternoon. I'm Neo." I stretched out my hand to shake.

She had a firm grip, confident. "I'm Sam. So, you're the guy?"

I shook hands with Mike and looked her straight in the eye with a smile. "If you mean your potential CDO, then yes!"

Sam smiled thinly and continued her curt questioning. She appeared curious and anxious at the same time. "Your background is in startups. What makes you feel that you can get us out of this abyss in one year?"

Sam wasn't wasting any time, getting right to the point. I glanced at Mike, who gave a slight shrug.

I thought for a moment and gathered my thoughts. "Well…taking Fitness First out of the abyss in one year isn't impossible. It's just that we need to follow certain ground rules that are unique for transforming a traditional organization. It's totally doable, but only with a well-coordinated effort. Let me explain in three steps."

I had Sam's attention. "First, every organization, more so traditional organizations, must have an absolute clarity of purpose, the lack of which leads to siloed and misaligned digital efforts."

"What do you mean by purpose?" asked Sam.

"The reason for being. Why Fitness First exists. In fact, I looked at the annual reports to get clarity on its purpose."

"And?"

"Well, we need to create one. One that is transformative, motivating, and inspiring."

"I don't understand. Can you give an example?" Sam asked.

I dove in. "Imagine a company that makes watches. This business could envision its purpose as helping people be on time—and that's linear, leading to linear growth opportunities. A linear purpose will push the organization to develop technical assets which, in turn, will help the business achieve linear growth."

"In a transformative purpose, the watch company might frame their purpose as helping people achieve a more balanced life, one in which different needs are integrated more cohesively and harmoniously. Not only will the purpose deepen the meaning of what the company does, but it will also expand the make-up and scope of products and services it can deliver, and the very impact it can have on the lives of its customers." I felt very lucky I'd met Charan that morning.

"Interesting," said Mike.

As Sam was internalizing, I quoted Charan, "Purpose-driven organizations are more ambitious, they attract the best talent, unify their efforts easily, inspire richer innovation, make faster decisions, and attract more investments."

I quickly summarized the research studies outlining the benefits of a purpose-driven organization, driving home the message of what Fitness First was lacking.

"Second, we must define digital initiatives with a good balance of digitizing the core businesses and at the same time launching new digital business models. The choice of initiatives and how these initiatives unify our efforts sets the stage for the type of digital future we want to create. It's equal parts art and science."

"What if we just focus on digitizing the core business?" she asked.

"Digitizing the core business will help, definitely, but ultimately it just delays the inevitable. It's like rearranging the deck chairs on the Titanic. Disruption of the business model is going to occur. If we don't disrupt ourselves, one of the Digital Giants or a new start-up will disrupt us. Our direction and trajectory must be changed with new digital business models before it's too late."

Having led digital initiatives at Active Health Inc., Sam appeared to appreciate what I said. She asked, "What's the last step?"

I went on. "The digital initiatives must be driven by Innovation Pods—"

Mike interrupted. "Are those the small autonomous teams you launched at your startup?"

"Yep."

Mike continued. "Sam, I saw these pods in action. They are like workhorses, delivering game changing value in a short time."

Sam's interest grew.

"Yep, Innovation Pods are like speed boats. The more speed boats you have, the easier it is to change the direction of the Titanic before the inevitable."

Sam seemed impressed. She asked curiously, "Can everything be done in the next twelve months?"

"We can make a lot of progress. But it requires a well-coordinated effort across the company."

"Okay. Can you define the purpose of Fitness First and get started?"

I smiled and nodded, not quite believing what I was hearing. Was that a job offer? Am I in? I wanted to ask.

Sam stood up abruptly. "Okay, I need to rush. It was nice meeting you, Neo. We are looking forward to working with you more closely." She shook my hand again and requested that Mike join her for a minute. As she started to walk out, Mike motioned for me to stay seated. He accompanied her to the exit, where they spoke briefly in low voices.

HUMILITY

Mike came back to the table, beaming. "Good show, Neo," said Mike. "Congratulations! You are in."

"Really? I guess I expected…more of a process? But this is great!" I was thrilled. I thought about Tina first. She would be excited to hear the news.

He went on. "Sam's EA will reach out to you to take care of the next steps. We could set the Monday after Thanksgiving as your start date. But just to be clear, you've got one year," he stressed.

"I know. I know," I said. We both smiled. At least he did, I wasn't sure if I was smiling or not.

Digi Gate was still on my mind. As we walked out, Mike suggested that I move past my startup and not even think about any legal battles. He insisted that I focus on what I had on hand—get the trajectory right at Fitness First in one year.

The thought of one year reminded me of Charan. I rushed to the conference and saw that he was still there. Hesitantly, I went near him and waited for him to finish shaking hands with some of the conference attendees.

"That was eye-opening, Charan," I intervened.

"Hey, Neo! You are back. Good to hear that you found it eye-opening. Will you remember the points while you are exploring your new opportunity?" he asked.

"Actually, I wanted to talk to you about that. I just met with the CEO, and I got the job."

"Congratulations! I hope you avoid failure. Success is possible, just not easy."

"It's an odd situation I'm in," I admitted. "I have a strong feeling that there will be many nuances to this digital transformation at a large organization that I don't yet understand. And I know I will be doomed at Fitness First if I don't get it right the first time. You predicted that."

"Yes, I did."

"So, I'd like your time. Help me find answers that will keep the digital transformation journey alive and kicking at Fitness First."

Charan looked away for a moment. He genuinely seemed to consider it.

"I'll tell you my problem," he said. "I have a crazy schedule through March. With the commitments I already have, there is no way I can spend time helping you in the way you are expecting from me."

I sighed, very disappointed. I said, "Okay, if you're too busy—"

"Wait, I'm not finished," he said. "That doesn't mean you can't get started by yourself. I don't have time to solve all your problems for you. And that wouldn't be the best thing for you anyway—"

"What do you mean?" I interrupted.

He held up his hands. "Let me finish! I think you can solve some of your own problems during the initial months. What I will do is give you some basic rules to apply. If you and your people follow them diligently, I think you will be off to a great start. Fair enough?"

"But, Charan, I've only got twelve months."

He nodded impatiently. "I know, I know. It's more than enough time to show progress. If you are diligent, that is. And if you aren't, then nothing I say could save you anyway."

"Oh, you can count on my diligence, for sure," I clarified.

"Shall we try it then?" he asked.

"Frankly, I don't know what else to do. Well, I guess I'd better ask what this is going to cost me. Do you charge by the hour or something?"

"No, I don't charge by the hour," he shared. "But I'll make a deal with you. Just pay me the value of what you learn from me."

"How will I know what that is?" I asked.

"That's easy. You should have a reasonable idea after we've finished. If your transformation journey ends up doomed, then obviously the value of what you learned won't have been much; you won't pay me anything. If, on the other hand, you learn enough from me to make millions, then you should pay me accordingly."

I laughed and said, "Deal!"

Handing me his business card, Charan said, "Until next time, Neo. Call me once you settle in."

Then he rushed away. I followed him out to the lobby. As I turned, I saw Charan talking to a gentleman in a vintage suit. The man led Charan to a limousine waiting at the curb. I heard the man say, "After the investor meeting, we will meet the chairman and…" As they approached the limo, a chauffeur hopped out to open the rear door for them.

Waiting inside for them was a man who sported a salt and pepper beard. He smiled and shook Charan's hand. The chauffeur closed the door and the limo quietly merged into traffic.

THE BITTER PILL

I was excited about the future possibilities and how Charan's mentorship could elevate the game for me. With my future mostly sorted, I decided to make it up to Tina.

I took her to the same restaurant we couldn't go to for our anniversary. I walked with her into the restaurant and the maître d' led us to a table with a white linen cloth and flowers elegantly arranged for the occasion. We were given a welcome drink, and the menu for the night was set to the side.

"Tina, I have a surprise for you." I gave her the offer letter I got from Fitness First.

Tina saw *Fitness First Inc.* on the letterhead. She screamed with excitement.

"You made it? Wow, congrats! I knew you would!"

She was relieved and already thinking of the United States. She started talking about the Bellevue neighborhood, the school district, and the fact that Riya hadn't really adjusted to living in India.

But her excitement was short lived as she scanned through the paper—a term sheet stating that I accepted the position of an *Interim* Chief Digital Officer and that I had twelve months to deliver outcomes. She was alarmed.

A waiter interrupted us to ask if we were ready to order. Neither of us had opened the menu—the conditional offer had sucked the oxygen out of the room for Tina. I asked the waiter to just bring whatever was best.

Tina went on. "Why does it say you have twelve months? It looks like a conditional offer. What happens if you can't deliver?"

"Don't worry, Tina. I got this! With Charan by my side, I'm confident I'll knock it out of the park. In fact, we're both confident that we'll get it right in twelve months."

"And you want Riya, me and Mom to come with you on the strength of that belief?" she asked.

I nodded hesitantly, knowing that I might not have given this enough thought. Again.

She looked upset. "You have no idea what's happening in the family, Neo. I'm concerned about the fact that your mom has been depressed since Dad died. And I'm really worried about what will happen to her if we move to the US now. The newness, the adjustment, and the uncertainty of your job will create more stress than comfort," she explained.

I felt ashamed that I hadn't realized how lonely and depressed my mom had been. I started to say, "I will find some other—"

She interrupted me. "I am not quite finished. Finding a new opportunity is out of the question." She took a deep breath. "We will have to make Fitness First work. You need to make it work with Charan. I need to make it work with the family here."

"What are you trying to say?"

Between us, the waiter set down two elegant silver plates, starters, and a basket of bread. He put out butter and silverware. Neither of us were in the mood to savor the delicacies.

"I will stay in India with Riya and Mom," said Tina in a reassuring tone. "But you need to find a way to bring the whole family to the US."

I was speechless. I felt guilty that my career was again taking priority and adding to the already stressful situation Tina was in.

"Just like the Fitness First contract, you have one year to bring everyone together," she added.

Tina's willingness to sacrifice and her resolve to find a way amazed me. I held her hand and assured her that everything would fall into place—and quietly wished that the stars would align for me to make everything work at Fitness First.

FIRST DIGITAL-FIRST REALIZATION

Purpose

Organizations must create a Transformative Customer-centric Purpose that goes beyond profits.

Every organization has a soul—a purpose for why it exists. Organizations that can harness the power of purpose will drive better performance and profitability and enjoy a distinct competitive advantage. There are two types of purpose statements:

A Transformative Purpose will help customers achieve a more balanced life. It's the one in which different human needs are integrated more cohesively and harmoniously.

A Linear Purpose will push the organization to develop strong technical assets which, in turn, will help the business achieve linear growth.

If an organization's purpose is transformative and is defined with absolute clarity, it inspires employees to aspire to something greater—the kind of mindset that makes them believe a cultural shift is possible and that any transformational change can be managed effectively.

Let's take a look at Microsoft. In a company defined by intense rivalries, empire-building and cutthroat competition, Satya Nadella, the CEO of Microsoft, did something spectacular. He took the entire company back to its roots, looking to a period before Windows when its software tools were used by other companies to build their own technology. He reinforced the purpose and communicated across the organization during town halls, emails, etc.

> *We empower every person and every organization on the planet to achieve more.*
>
> – Microsoft.com

"That fundamental notion that we build tools, build platforms so that others can build more technology, I think is more relevant, more needed in 2019 than it was in 1975," said Nadella. Combined with a growth mindset and customer obsession, Nadella reinvented Microsoft to achieve a transformative purpose. It became more ambitious, attracted the best talent, inspired richer innovation, and was more trusted.

Like it did at Microsoft, a well-written purpose statement will guide everyone from the board to frontline staff during hard decisions.

CVS Health is a US-based healthcare company and the owner of the CVS Pharmacy retail chain. CVS was originally founded as Consumer Value Stores, but over time their leadership began to guide the company based on the core values of Convenience, Value and Service. CVS evolved and reimagined its purpose:

> *Bringing our heart to every moment of your health.*
> – CVS Health

CVS leadership saw that the company had a purpose beyond just making money; they wanted to achieve something bigger. So much so that CVS announced it would stop selling any tobacco-related products in their thousands of stores. It was a decision that would cost the company $2 billion per year in revenue. There was no campaign nor pressure from competition to do so. It was a hard decision, but it was guided by their transformative purpose.

The news was met with overwhelming support from the general public. Research stated that customers who purchased their cigarettes exclusively from CVS were about 38% more likely to stop buying cigarettes altogether. CVS heard from their customers, "When you quit, I quit."

Customers who used the drugstore for other items—whether it was their over the counter or personal care items or even pharmacy items—continued to remain loyal CVS customers. In fact, CVS attracted new customers.

CVS is the epitome of a purpose-driven organization. It had the courage to make bold decisions and a willingness to take risks for the greater good of the customer. It was guided by their transformative purpose.

While writing a transformative purpose, be sure to address the core elements:

- Go beyond what the customer does by integrating more cohesively and harmoniously with the core needs of the customer,
- Aspire to deliver personalization that creates differentiated experiences for customers,
- Be action-oriented on behalf of the customer,
- Provide an opportunity to add a broad range of products and services for the greater good of the customer, and
- Ensure that the organization has most of the core capabilities needed to deliver the purpose, right off the bat.

SECOND DIGITAL-FIRST REALIZATION

Dichotomy of Digital

Organizations must focus on digitizing the core business while also exploring new digital business models across the value chains they serve. Both are necessary for the transformation to succeed.

Digital can shake up traditional business models overnight. It can blur the barriers to entry. Well-established incumbents can suddenly be disrupted by the entry of a Digital Giant or a savvy start-up. With new digitally inspired business models, profit pools shift. Winners take the majority of market share and profit, and they often come from beyond the industry. To extract the real value of digital, traditional organizations must understand and balance the dichotomy of digital.

There are two aspects to digital—economic and operational. Most traditional organizations interpret digital from an operational perspective—how do I leverage digital to make my core business faster, cheaper, or better? Focusing only on the operational aspects can yield benefits, but only delays the inevitable disruption. To be clear, traditional companies must invest in transforming their core businesses, unlocking the maximum amount of value from digital at scale. But they must also invest in new digital business models.

It's this balancing act that must be performed cautiously by traditional organizations. For that, it's important for traditional organizations to first understand the economic aspect of digital. Specifically, they must consider how their overall value proposition might change as a result of the transformative purpose. By aligning digital technology to the transformative purpose, traditional companies can find ways to shake up every element of the value chain.

Let's take a look at Kohl's, an American retail chain selling everything from clothing to toys to home and kitchen products. In 2017, Kohl's piloted a returns program at ten of its stores in partnership with Amazon, a direct competitor. The partnership enabled Kohl's to accept "eligible" Amazon items—without a box or label—in stores, where associates then packaged the items and sent them back to one of Amazon's return centers at no additional cost to the customer. The pilot was a success—in 2019, Amazon returns digital kiosks were rolled out to all of Kohl's 1,100 stores.

"The nationwide rollout of the Amazon Returns program is our single biggest initiative of the year," said Michelle Gass, Kohl's CEO. "Our top strategic priority is driving traffic, and this transformational program does just that. It drives customers into our stores, and we are expecting millions to benefit from this service."

By leveraging their physical store footprint to solve a real problem facing digital customers (returns are a hassle), Kohl's created a totally new value proposition and turned a disrupting competitor (Amazon) into a strategic partner. At least 2 million new customers visited Kohl's stores in 2020 as a result of the Amazon Returns program. According to Kohl's, a third of these new visitors were millennials—a coveted growth demographic.

When it comes to products and services, digital has the potential to bundle and unbundle offerings. Industries swing back and forth like a pendulum, implementing bundling and unbundling options to adapt to changing customer demands and needs. Usually, bundles start out great, until they tip over on their own weight and customers start demanding only parts of the bundle. That's when we see the pendulum swing back to meet customer demand and shifts in distribution models.

Reliance Industries Limited (RIL) went from being a conglomerate largely focused on traditional sectors like petrochemicals, textiles, etc. to a new-age tech and digital giant. RIL has played a major role in bridging the urban-rural digital divide in India with its flagship product—Jio Platforms. Launched in 2016, Jio onboarded a huge user base by offering free voice calling and 4G data to its users. Jio also introduced cheap smartphones to the market, allowing them to capture an even wider base of customers in India. With its recent partnership with Google, Jio Platforms unveiled the Jio Phone Next, an ultra-affordable Android 4G-smartphone, to unlock the price-sensitive customer base.

"As technology becomes a driving force in all businesses and facets of life, the future belongs to organizations that can lead and leverage the digital revolution," said Mukesh Ambani, Chairman of RIL.

With its family of start-ups, partnerships and acquisitions, Jio Platforms is in a position to offer novel technology services in a wide range of critical fields, such as education, healthcare, media and entertainment, logistics, toys, online search, financial services, and marketplace. Its partnerships and collaborations will enable Jio Platforms to bundle and unbundle products and services to cater to the unmet and unarticulated needs of customers during the entire life cycle of a customer. RIL's digital innovations are helping to power RIL's aspiration to become one of the top 20 companies in the world.

Traditional organizations must move outside their comfort zone. Focusing on operational improvements, incremental changes and innovating around the edges might feel like the safe path, but it leads to disruption and destruction. C-level executives and business leaders must embrace a transformative purpose and have a digital mindset. They must constantly look for the "Art of the Possible" to discover new value creation opportunities. They must balance the dichotomy of digital, keeping in mind their transformative purpose and thoughtfully selecting digital initiatives that pave the way toward becoming a digital-first organization.

Transformative Customer-centric Purpose → **Balance the Dichotomy of Digital** → **Align Digital Initiatives**

Ideas to remember

- Vision answers "*The What*" you want to accomplish. Mission answers "*The How*" you want to accomplish. Purpose answers "*The Why*" you want to accomplish.
- In this day and age, if a company creates a purpose that is purely centered on making money, they might be perceived as self-centered. In fact, Environment, Sustainability and Governance (ESG) investments have been gaining momentum. The US and Europe alone represent 80% of global sustainability and responsible investments during 2018 to 2020. Enterprises from traditional organizations to Digital Giants are promising to become carbon neutral. A *transformative customer-centric purpose* will enable organizations to go beyond money making and help them to be relevant to the customer and the community at large.

- Purpose is not just critical for digital transformation but also paramount for any business transformation. Initiatives must be aligned to achieve this purpose.
- To balance the dichotomy of digital, traditional organizations usually start with 80% of their resource investments dedicated to digitizing their core business, with the balance allocated toward business building with digital. However, industry shifts, emerging trends, and new entrants can influence this mix.

PART 2
BRACING FOR IMPACT

THE NEW BEGINNING

I reached Trinity Towers, one of the tallest buildings in Bellevue by 7:40 am and headed straight to the 24th floor, where I was greeted by HR. I finished the formalities in fifteen minutes. Sam's assistant arrived and escorted me to Sam's office on the 25th floor.

"Welcome aboard, Neo. I've been looking forward to today." Sam smiled but appeared impatient. She remarked, "I really need you to get the team moving with the purpose you mentioned in London, and I need the Pods aligned. I want results quickly."

I was taken aback by Sam's expectations and the rush for results. Pods didn't exist yet at Fitness First and establishing a Pod takes time. We needed the right team composition to make it autonomous. Further, I was sure that implementing the dichotomy of digital would be complex, especially during the first few quarters—it's like building a plane while flying it. I needed to get it right the first time. But she was not in the mood to listen.

I nodded hesitantly but the little voice in me screamed: *don't try to rush things that need time.*

She steered me to a packed conference room and said on our way, "Let's not waste any time getting you in front of the team."

The setting was glamorous, yet ominous, like something right out of a movie. We were in the most formal conference room in the building. It provided a breathtaking view of Mount Rainier. Members of the Senior Leadership Team were gathered around a large table, with their lieutenants sitting in chairs along the walls. Apparently, this was a breakfast meeting to discuss supply chain issues. I was hoping I wouldn't be asked to solve it with digital. It was my first hour at Fitness First, for God's sake.

The Senior Leadership Team (SLT) in the room thanked Sam for her impromptu visit, as they wanted to get her perspective on a couple of issues. I observed the SLT as they interacted—Sam's visit turned into a thirty-minute discussion. What I witnessed was nothing less than corporate theater. The focus was not on real issues—each person had their own agenda and efforts were not unified. The few solutions presented were incomplete, and no one took the lead in trying to get to a decision. Overall, it was chaotic.

As the discussion bounced back and forth, I analyzed the team and their personalities. When considered individually, the SLT seemed well-intentioned and reasonable, though there were a few exceptions. It wasn't unusual from the set of people that one might typically see at the top of any corporation. The team members sitting along the wall only spoke when called upon.

Not knowing what to do, I went to the breakfast island to grab a bite. Just when I bit a mouthful of croissant, I heard Sam announcing my name.

"Okay, guys. We have Neo Ray, our new CDO. You all know what's been happening with our digital transformation during the past two years, and I've brought Neo to kick things back into top gear. This boat has a giant hole in it. And Neo is here to fix it and get everyone rowing in the same direction. I'm not interested in any more excuses or explanations. I want results. Neo is the right person to make us digital-first."

I quickly gulped the croissant, wiping my mouth with a tissue with one hand while waving my other hand to the room. Talk about a first impression.

I mustered all my energy and spoke with enthusiasm. "Hello, everyone. I am Neo and I'm looking forward to working with you to make Fitness First a digital-first organization."

"What does digital-first even mean?" The voice was filled with sarcasm. It was Stan, a tall gentleman, who I later learned was the least popular among the SLT.

I clarified, "Digital-first is the new way of doing business. It means reconsidering every aspect of our business to use digital and elevate our game."

Before I could add more details, Sam interrupted, "Look guys, today is *Day One*. It's a fresh start for everyone. I expect to see big results, fast. Neo is here. We are sorted. So, let's get out there and attack this digital transformation. Alright?" Sam abruptly exited the conference room, and I followed her, shocked at her abrupt leadership style.

As we were walking in the hallway, Sam told me she was a big believer in empowering her executives, and that she wouldn't be standing over my shoulder as I drove the digital transformation. She suggested that I connect with Lisa Naro from the central digital team to get started.

I thanked Sam for trusting me. I asked if I should come to her for approvals to enter into partnerships and collaborations while building an ecosystem for Fitness First. Sam insisted that I need not bother her with these things and that I move forward as I felt right.

I was somewhat perturbed by Sam's leadership style. Digital transformation requires a leader who is inclusive, inspirational, and purpose driven. Furthermore, it couldn't be driven by a single person or two. It takes a village. And the SLT at Fitness First was an interesting mix.

The Senior Leadership Team of Fitness First

Samantha Martinez aka HiPPO – CEO

Sam was the Highest Paid Person in the Office (HiPPO). The more I saw Sam in action the more I felt she was a true personification of "command and control" and believed in a hierarchical style. She just wanted people to follow her orders. An ambitious and impatient Type A executive.

Stan Watson aka ZEBRA – Chief Operations Officer

A true New Yorker, Stan had moved to Seattle for work. He was tall and tanned, generally curt and a bit rude. Before he joined Fitness First he was the VP of Operations at a large computer manufacturing organization. Stan was the least popular amongst the SLT and personified someone with Zero Evidence But Really Arrogant (ZEBRA). He was known to roll his eyes in disgust when someone talked about operations issues or when someone came up with a new business idea—mainly because he would instantly get into the nuances of execution and downplay the ideas.

Of all the SLT, Stan was the most impacted by Fitness First's recent manufacturing challenges and would likely welcome digital solutions with the potential to streamline operations and simplify his team's work.

Tim Anderson aka The Fence Sitter – Chief of Sales

Tim was the most tenured member of the SLT. He had been with Fitness First for more than a decade and was the frontrunner to be the CEO. He lacked a digital mindset—where one believes that business problems could be solved efficiently with digital, and he adopted a wait-and-see attitude for anything outside his domain. That said, Tim was well respected by the SLT and the board because of his track record of not missing sales targets. Tim was under a lot of pressure to up his game and was very concerned about his and his team's sales quotas and incentives.

Anna Chang aka The Evangelist – Chief Marketing Officer

Marketing was a critical function at Fitness First. The board had been ecstatic to get someone like Anna Chang. Anna was Asian American and one of the women executives on the SLT, bringing diversity to the team. She had graduated from Chicago Booth.

Anna strongly believed in the experience economy and the power of digital to deliver game-changing customer experiences. She was considered a brand-building genius among her peer group.

Neel Mehta aka WOLF – Chief Technology Officer

With advanced degrees from Cambridge and Berkley, Neel was a prized possession of the board. He had a track record of success as a Chief Architect at a technology company in the Bay Area. Neel was a key member of the SLT and personified someone who is Working on the Latest Fire (WOLF). He had an excellent intellect but wasn't great at management and execution. He was known to constantly check emails or work on something during meetings. He spoke little but whenever he did, he had something important and constructive to say.

He was a big believer in digital and was trustworthy and low maintenance. The SLT was awed by Neel's ability to find solutions but frustrated by the way things were managed in IT.

Susan Smith aka Dr. No – Chief Financial Officer

The final and most important member of the SLT was Susan. She had played a key role during Fitness First's IPO and during the acquisition of Active Health Inc. and the supplements business. A stickler for detail, Susan was a seasoned finance executive with experience in the fitness industry. Prior to Fitness First, she worked at 24/6 Fitness as Finance Director. Susan treated the company's money as her own and commanded respect from the SLT. While the board had so far given the SLT free rein when it came to budgets and investments, they did so only because they knew Susan would not let things get out of hand.

THROUGH THE LOOKING GLASS

I went to the 20th floor to find Lisa. As I walked to her cubicle, she noticed me and became uneasy.

"Are you Lisa Naro?" I asked.

She nodded and said, "You must be my new boss." She stood up and we shook hands. "The third one in three years."

I was appalled to hear *the third one* but I tried to stay calm. "What do you mean by the third one?" I asked.

"Well, there were two CDOs before you."

Two? Was the first one fired too? My curiosity grew. I knew any further discussion would open a can of worms, so I changed the topic.

"By the way, did I see you in the meeting this morning? You stepped out early," I said.

"Well, the digital solution to solving our supply chain issues didn't make sense. It's a tech-first approach."

"What do you mean by a tech-first approach?" I asked.

"Simple. They start with the tech and then try to make it work."

I frowned. "Care to explain?"

"Sure. In the supply chain meeting, there was a discussion about how artificial intelligence and machine learning could be used to solve our supply chain and on-time delivery issues. Apparently, a few tech partners came in last week to share some solutions with these technologies. As exciting as that may sound, many of our issues are foundational and don't require a complicated technology solution. If you start with tech, you end up chasing tech and force fitting tech. Like someone with a hammer treating every-thing like a nail."

She had a point. While it's not totally wrong to collaborate with tech partners to get inspiration and an understanding of the "Art of the Possible," it would be wrong to force a fit. A tech-first approach leads to adding new technology to old school thinking, and then expecting transformation to happen. Like Charan said, it'd be like playing a lot of games with tech.

I wanted to know if she knew the right approach, since she didn't like the tech-first strategy. So I asked, "What should they be doing instead?"

Her response was instant. "A customer-first approach—you start with the customer and work backwards. And customers can be internal employees or external customers."

I brightened up and nodded in agreement. I was glad that Lisa was on the team, but I wondered why she didn't voice her concerns in the meeting. "Did you think the SLT wouldn't care for a customer-first approach?"

She thought for a moment and said quietly, "They want things quick and easy. Some members of the SLT get wrapped up in the coolness of tech. In many cases, tech partners present use cases and our SLT immediately directs the team to add new digital initiatives. My worry is that we end up becoming tech obsessed. But every single one of us must be customer obsessed."

She was absolutely correct but I was baffled that she didn't speak her mind like she was doing with me. "Every single point you shared makes perfect sense. But why didn't you voice your thoughts in the meeting?" I asked.

"Why would I?" she said without any hesitation.

I was taken aback that she didn't care or didn't have the courage to be a changemaker. I tried to inspire her. "We must speak our mind to do what is right—right for the customer and right for Fitness First. Each of us must be empowered to do what is right."

She looked unconvinced. "Look, Neo…it's a dead horse. I really don't want to lose my job like the others."

It took more than a few seconds for her words to sink in. I was startled and wanted to know more. I was immediately thinking of my predecessors and the culture they created.

"Why would you lose your job? Is that the precedent set by the previous CDO?" I tried to not show any frustration.

She shook her head. "Joe didn't. In fact, he himself was fired. It's such a disgrace that we let that happen." Joe was the most recent CDO.

"Wait, you're sympathetic towards Joe? Why?" I wanted specifics. The gorier, the better.

Suddenly, I realized we were talking in the open at Lisa's desk. I hinted to her that we should go to a quiet place. She grabbed the pack of cigarettes lying on her desk and walked me to the smoking zone near the entrance of Trinity Towers. I hate smoking but at that time I didn't care. I wanted to know what was going on.

Lisa took out a cigarette and a shiny looking lighter. She lit the cigarette and asked, "You don't know why Joe had to leave?"

I shook my head.

She took a puff and said, "You're not going to like it. And you're not telling anyone that I told you, especially Sam."

I assured her that it would be confidential. I couldn't believe that I was having this conversation on the first day of the job…and with my direct report.

She took a puff. "Where do I start?" It was clear that there was a long list of issues. She decided to start with Vitamin M—money. "Let's talk about finances." She thought for a moment and said, "We monitor the wrong measures. It's Return on Investment (ROI) all…the…time. Customer metrics like Net Promoter Score, churn, etc. are never even considered. Furthermore, ROI is measured way too early and the funds are cut off if the ROI isn't met."

"Okay, that doesn't seem right," I said.

"There's more! Budgets are allocated to each business separately. With decentralized budgets, each business drives digital initiatives on their own—mostly in silos. We have duplicate digital initiatives and a lack of unified design language. In fact, digital assets like a website or app created by each business look completely different than those created by other businesses.

Just imagine the customer experience. All of this makes it look like customers are interacting with different companies," she added.

"Yikes."

"You have to hear Bert's story. He was our first Chief Digital Officer, the one before Joe. Bert was a technologist who came from a successful retail startup. Sam wanted to bring on a new line of products and sell it through a mini-store concept at our 400+ health clubs and an online store. It took eighteen months for Bert to launch the retail channel, which should have taken about three months."

And then she shared a shocker. "Fitness First is siloed and fraught with layers of bureaucracy and processes. Our organizational structure is not conducive to delivering digital interventions at speed."

I asked, "Did Bert get buy-in from the SLT?"

"Of course he did."

"And the delays occurred despite the support from leaders?"

She continued. "He secured executive sponsorship and funding for IT engineers and he attempted to implement agile to speed up delivery. But he quickly realized that he just couldn't go at the speed of a startup."

"Where did he face issues?" I wanted to know the specifics.

She appeared tense as she shared Bert's experiences. "Every step until launched. He was strangled because of bureaucracy and endless processes."

"Can you be a little more specific?"

She took a second cigarette and lit it. "Yeah, the online-category leader was reluctant to provide access to online sales data—data-access constraints. The store head was wary about Bert conducting customer surveys—customer-research constraints. Bert was told not to meddle with terms and conditions and waivers—legal department constraints. He was expected to run risk and compliance checks, even for customers who already had a relationship with Fitness First—risk-department constraints. Onboarding new vendors took three to six months due to our complicated vendor selection processes—commercial department constraints."

I was rattled. But I tried to convince myself that Bert must not have had the right team composition, like the one in an Innovation Pod.

She took one puff after another as she shared Bert's chronicle. "While Bert was going through these hoops, he was shocked to see IT resources unilaterally pulled off the work whenever there was a crisis. Each time engineers were reassigned, most of the momentum was lost. After eighteen months of running from pillar to post, the retail stores were finally launched—both a mini-store at health clubs and an online store—but it wasn't smooth sailing."

"Insane."

"Yeah and to top it off, Sam came in at the middle of the project and threw more bodies at the problem. She asked Bert to double down and speed up the launch. Adding more people halfway through slowed us down. And the real problems were never solved. Layers of bureaucracy, too many processes, siloed digital teams and initiatives—like we were operating on islands. None of these were solved," she added.

"What happened to Bert?" I was intrigued.

"He resigned after the launch. That's when we got Joe as our CDO." She put the cigarette out in the sand pit and took another from her pack. "Sam was frustrated that it took 18 months to launch the mini-stores. She wanted to deliver outcomes with speed. She suggested that Joe create an agile organization. After a couple of weeks, Joe created an agile transformation strategy and recommended that we start small with one team and two digital initiatives. Sam did not agree. She wanted to show quick results. She wanted to convert the whole company to an agile organization right away. Everyone was reorganized into squads at the behest of Sam—it led to a 10% reduction in staff. The new structure rubbed the existing employees the wrong way. Another 5% of the staff left because of the abrupt change."

"Do we have an agile organization in some form now?" I asked.

She chuckled and shook her head. "After six months, Sam declared that it was a disaster and put the blame on Joe. She demonstrated an absolute lack of transformational leadership and patience."

Lisa's insights started painting a picture of how Sam acted as a CEO. I wanted to get more clarity. "What about Sam? How is she?"

"Lately, Sam has been short-term focused. She wants to prove herself to the board…and to the street. In the name of speed, technology is brought in like a toy and it's making us a tech-obsessed company. She lacks a long-term digital vision required for a large organization. Although she was successful at Active Health, she is struggling to run Fitness First. The two CDOs were fired not because of their lack of competency but because of Sam's inability to drive large-scale transformation successfully. Since she is so autocratic and she wants to show results quickly, the rest of the team is losing their identity."

Hearing about Sam, I felt my whole sense of gravity shift.

Lisa saw my restlessness and said, "I know I have been sharing only negative stuff. I must say, I like the people and culture sans Sam. People want to make this digital transformation work but we need to protect the resources to make change happen. Fear of failure must be addressed, and it must be perfectly okay to fail. That's when innovation thrives."

I took a deep breath and nodded, acknowledging everything Lisa shared. I thanked her for trusting me and sharing her thoughts candidly. As we walked back, I felt a strange mix of distress and hope. Distress about the situation and the thought of *What the hell did I get myself into?* Hope because I found an ally in Lisa, who I thought would be a great lieutenant.

That night I hardly slept. I thought about everything that Lisa shared. I felt I was losing the game even before I started. On one hand, I wondered why Mike never shared any of this. On the other hand, I felt it was quite likely that Lisa might be overthinking and overreacting. I felt my strategy—purpose, aligning digital initiatives and Innovation Pods—would stream-line *everything*.

The next day, I walked to Lisa's desk. With a sense of urgency, I said, "Lisa, pack your stuff and—"

She interrupted. "Darn! I knew this would happen."

"Wait, what would happen?"

"Me getting fired!"

I laughed and shook my head. "No! You are not getting fired. In fact, you're moving next to my office on the 28th floor with the big guys. We are going to do amazing things together."

She had a strange look on her face.

"Facilities will move the heavy stuff. In the meantime, get your laptop and let's go to my office. We need to talk about something important."

As we walked to my office, I explained my strategy to her, i.e., purpose, digital initiatives, and Innovation Pods. But I felt there was a need to do something bigger. I looked at her and said, "For every digital transformation to be successful, there are certain basic things that must be true."

"You mean that if you remove any one of those basic things, the transformation would be guaranteed to fail?" she asked.

"Yes, exactly right. Since you've been in the thick and thin of past digital transformation efforts here, what comes to your mind?"

I was interrupted by a buzz on my phone. It was a reminder of an upcoming meeting. I glanced at my calendar and saw that it was packed for the week. How did that happen? There wasn't a spare hour. Most of the meetings were like the supply chain meeting—weekly recurring meetings with 20 or more people and no clear agenda or purpose. As we entered my office, I asked my EA to clear my morning. I picked up a marker and wrote *Retrospect* on the whiteboard.

"Sorry, please go-ahead Lisa."

"I'd say clarity of the digital team's role. We've had several issues in the past with role clarity. It's important that everyone knows what we do. Moreover, how we integrate with business."

"Isn't it obvious that we enable the organization to achieve our purpose and business goals and that our role is to create digital solutions rapidly?"

She chuckled with sarcasm.

I added, "We must be seen as partners in crime."

"It won't work here," she grumbled.

"What won't work?"

"Partners in crime," she said. "Knowing the dynamics here, I doubt it would."

"Tell me more," I said.

"Well, many times, business teams just toss digital initiatives to our team. We only see them in the monthly reviews, where they mostly add more initiatives. The business teams have a project, not a product mindset. They think of every initiative as a discreet deliverable, with a start and end date. However, product is a journey, not a destination. We should never stop improving the experience of the customers."

I shook my head in disgust. Digital initiatives cannot be treated as projects and cannot be driven by digital teams alone. Business and digital teams must work hand in glove. But what if we turned the problem on its head?

I said, "Digital-first initiatives led by the business to deliver outcomes that are aligned to our purpose! How do we bring about that shift?"

"What? That's crazy talk!" Lisa exclaimed, laughing.

I smiled. "I know it's crazy. But we can't do the same thing over and over and expect different results. We must make radical changes in our approach and message it clearly during every interaction, right from day one."

She appeared skeptical.

"Don't worry too much. I got this." I assured her and moved on. "Next up is digital leadership & team skills."

"Our team, right?" she asked.

"Yep—digital leadership with the right digital team, like designers, product managers, etc." But having digital talent in our team alone would limit possibilities. I added, "We must do something to digitally upskill the entire organization. I know an upskilled organization is not an immediate need for the success of transformation, but it will expand the horizon of what's possible with digital."

"Like what skills?"

"I think basic digital skills—and we need a way to activate a digital mindset."

"A digital mindset?" She was intrigued.

"Yep, people with a digital mindset have the ability to unlock possibilities with digital. They are curious about digital and keep track of new emerging tech innovations. They marry business and digital elegantly, they promote experimentation and they leverage data to refine the digital solution." I paused to let it sink in. "Just imagine the possibilities if everyone at Fitness First had a digital mindset."

"Yeah, that'd be fabulous but it'd take a while to get there. In fact, upskilling in digital is a challenge itself. It's an ocean."

"I know," I said patiently. "We will provide a primer on specific topics like Design Thinking, Critical Thinking & Innovation, Human-centric Product Management, and Digital Leadership. Plus we'll orient the team with case studies on how emerging technologies were leveraged to solve customer and business problems."

She thought for a moment, "Interesting choice of topics. It touches important areas, from leading with empathy to human-centric product development and it provides inspiration through real-world examples."

I nodded and added *Digital leadership & team skills* to the list. We looked at the whiteboard intently to determine what else must exist to get the digital transformation right.

"I guess we're missing the delivery model. A Digital-first delivery model," she said.

"That's right. I have a time-tested Digital Innovation approach. I'll talk about that later." [*Digital-first delivery model will be discussed in detail in Part Three and Part Five*]

I added *Digital-first delivery model* to the whiteboard.

"What about a business plan?" I asked. "We need a well-laid-out business plan with budgets, metrics that go beyond ROI and timeline," I added.

"Yeah, that's right," she said. As I wrote *Business plan,* she revealed a shocker. "Neo, we don't have enough funding to continue with our product managers from the external suppliers."

"Are you serious?"

She nodded sheepishly.

"What the hell happened to all the funding?"

"Susan stopped new funding after Joe was let go. We are going to run dry soon."

"How much money is left?"

"Enough to keep paying our external suppliers for another month. After that, our digital team will be stretched thin."

I froze. "That's alarming. Let's crank out a solid plan and get hold of Susan." As we wrapped up, I asked my EA to invite the SLT to a meeting to align on the transformative purpose of Fitness First.

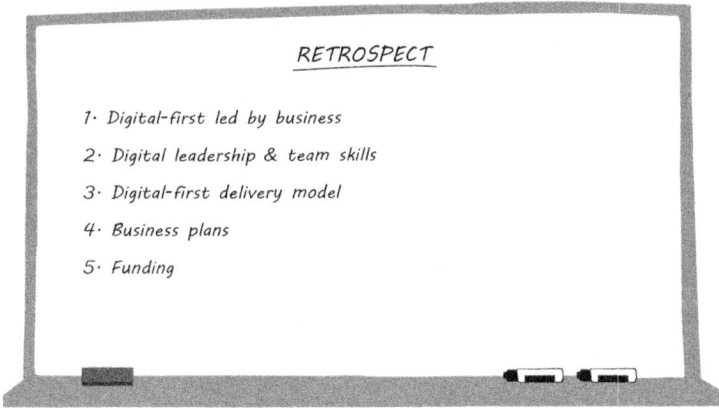

RETROSPECT

1. Digital-first led by business
2. Digital leadership & team skills
3. Digital-first delivery model
4. Business plans
5. Funding

Minimum requirements to make a transformation successful

PURPOSE-DRIVEN

After frustrating delays and rescheduling, my EA finally got the SLT together for a meeting. From the very beginning, it was clear that the SLT was not taking the meeting seriously. Furthermore, Sam declined the meeting several times and I needed to meet with her personally to secure her attendance.

I did not lose hope. I was confident that once the SLT was aligned with the transformative purpose and a focused group of digital initiatives, we would have a solid foundation to deliver results rapidly with the Innovation Pods. However, the dynamics at Fitness First were unique—Sam was authoritative, Stan was unpredictable and Tim might drag his feet. If I burned up too much time bringing each one of them along the journey, it would put at risk the main goal—identifying a strong set of digital initiatives for (a) business building with new digital business models and (b) digitizing the core business.

I decided to structure the meeting with absolute precision, visualizing every single minute of interaction with the SLT and preparing collaterals and presentations. I was confident and prepared. At least, that's what I thought until the meeting began.

The SLT assembled in the boardroom, waiting to figure out why in the world we had been hounding them. I was delighted to see that Mike was also there, sitting next to Sam. Without wasting a moment, I introduced the transformative purpose of Fitness First and asked the SLT to share their thoughts.

Be the best in the world at helping individuals and families on their path to better health

No one spoke.

Thankfully, Sam chimed in. "This is great. We help people on their path to better health. I think it will open many opportunities for us to define products and services." She turned to the SLT and said, "This is a defining moment, folks! Why we exist, what problems to solve and who we want to be to each person we touch through our work."

She paused for a moment and asked, "Questions, anyone?"

More silence.

A hand went up—it was Stan. "Why define a purpose? Don't we have a vision and mission already?" Sam looked at me.

"Glad you asked Stan," I said. "Any other questions or thoughts?"

"Why are we adding a purpose *now*?" asked Tim. "Shouldn't we be talking about how digital can help us hit our quarterly sales numbers?"

Anna went next. "The more I think about the purpose statement, the more I see possibilities. Knowing our purpose would make our marketing efforts more cohesive."

"Great," I said. "Let me talk about purpose-driven organizations so that all your questions will be answered." I was well aware that these questions would come up, so I had put together a few slides.

In the next fifteen minutes, I explained how a transformative purpose creates a deeper connection with customers, does more for communities, attracts and retains talent and in the process achieves greater results and impact. While I saw head nods and a broader alignment on the purpose, I felt that there were still some open questions.

"I am still unclear how things will change for me now that we have a *purpose*," Stan said with sarcasm. "We have real issues with our operations and I can't help but feel that this digital transformation stuff is a fad. It will come and go." And he added, "No offense, Neo."

I waved it off like it was no big deal but the worst part of me wanted to punch him in his face.

Sam then said, "Well, Neo will articulate how things will change for all of us."

Everyone was silent as I forced myself to take a deep breath. My plan was to implement one of my favorite activities—"Future Storming" a highly creative and interactive brainstorming exercise that asked participants to come up with multiple compelling ideas related to our purpose that were interesting enough to be featured on a magazine, say Forbes or HBR, and define a high-level plan to make the ideas a reality. At least that was the plan until Tim curtly asked, "Now what?" He wasn't trying to be rude; I was sure. But it stung a little, nonetheless.

Stan piled on. "Are we going to talk about any real issues at all?" Before I could say anything, he continued. "We have burning operations issues. Everything is on fire right now. Why are we even having this meeting?"

With Stan and Tim so focused on their areas, it was becoming like a reality show and I was in the spotlight. I was losing control. I thought it'd be a disaster to go with "Future Storming" given the current sentiment and mindset of the SLT. I did not want to derail the meeting, at any cost.

I quickly pivoted and said, "Okay. The next step after aligning on the transformative purpose is to identify issues in specific business areas. But bear in mind that every single issue we plan to solve must align with the transformative purpose. We will then define digital initiatives from the prioritized issues while balancing the dichotomy of digital."

"Balancing what?" asked Anna.

"Oops, sorry. Let me explain the dichotomy of digital." I went to the whiteboard and wrote *Core business* on the left and *Business building* on the right. I looked at the team and said, "Digital generates value across two continuums. One is digitizing our core business and the other is creating new businesses that are powered by digital. We must balance our investments across these two continuums without losing focus on business building."

I looked at Stan and said, "We can talk about real issues now. Do you want to go first, Stan?"

I nervously went to the whiteboard and picked up a marker. Sam was watching the whole interaction intently.

Stan went on, "We have real supply chain problems. Customers are complaining about delivery delays."

"That's a serious issue. It aligns with the purpose." I said and wrote *Supply chain issues* on the whiteboard.

Stan continued, "Customers want to come to our health clubs but they can't see how busy or crowded the gym is."

Even this aligned with the purpose; I wrote *Free/busy information at Health clubs.*

Anna raised a contentious topic. She said, "We focus on selling to our customers rather than helping them. Our sales approach needs an overhaul to align with our purpose."

Tim became territorial and questioned Anna, "How so?"

"Our salespeople are tasked to sell health club packages based on the customer's affordability. Instead, the focus should be on picking the right package that helps customers on their path to better health. For that, we must reinvent our sales approach. We must educate and influence customers on the right thing to do for their health." She paused and added, "And of course as the head of Marketing, I have a big role to play in educating them too."

I wrote *Marketing and Sales approach & alignment with purpose* on the whiteboard.

Tim didn't seem to agree but he let it go for the moment. He added an issue. "Customers are willing to pay premium membership fees for fresh towels but many customers complain that towels are never available."

Stan rolled his eyes in an apparent disgust. He said, "That's not true. We've always had fresh towels."

Tim replied, "I hear this from my salespeople all the time. Let's get some data to determine the truth."

We agreed to add the issue to the white board—*Unavailability of fresh towels.*

Anna's hand went up. She said, "Customers are buying workout equipment to use at their homes but they lack guidance from fitness experts—the kind of guidance they get at our health clubs. We have an opportunity to create a product or service to fill the gap, leveraging our abilities in gym equipment and our expert consultation businesses."

Finally, an opportunity under business building—*At-home workout equipment with guidance* made it to the whiteboard.

Susan brought her financial prowess to bear by highlighting churn in the supplements business. "Going by the nature of the supplements business, we should see customers buying supplements regularly and therefore we should have a steady stream of revenue. But what we are actually seeing are spikes and drops in revenue. The past couple of quarters have been good though. We must build on that momentum to get a steady stream of revenue from the supplements business."

It did align with our purpose, because supplements were critical in helping customers on their path to better health. I wrote *Churn in Supplements business.*

Mike, who had been silently observing, said, "We have four business verticals. We have an amazing opportunity to get a holistic view of the customer as he or she interacts with one or more business verticals. Right now, data for each business is siloed. Just imagine the possibilities if we could get a 360-degree view of the customer by combining the data. It'd help us identify opportunities to help our customers on their path to better health."

360-degree view of customers across 4 business verticals was added to the list.

Mike's comment seemed to spur Neel into participating. He looked up from his laptop and quietly said, "We have legacy tech architecture—tech debt if you will. We'll need a better architecture to be cloud ready for the transformation. A lot of our systems just aren't suited to deliver customer-facing digital experiences."

Tech architecture is critical to power the digital transformation journey. *Cloud architecture & upgrades* was added to the list.

After a short break, we regrouped to prioritize the issues. I drove the prioritization exercise, keeping in mind two questions:

1. Does the issue, when solved, contribute directly or indirectly towards personalization?

2. Does the issue, when solved, contribute directly or indirectly to increasing cash or releasing locked up cash?

I also coached the team on how to think about personalization. Many successful companies personalize experiences during different parts of the customer lifecycle—for example, during the sales process where the sales rep tailors the experience to meet the customer's needs. However, forward-thinking companies adopt a hyper-personalization approach—moving up or down the value chain and creating individualized experiences at every step along the customer's journey.

The goal of prioritization was to invest limited dollars in those digital initiatives that had a direct or indirect relationship to benefitting our customers and/or optimizing cash flows. The next hour was intense, exhausting, and difficult. I argued with the SLT. I challenged them. I changed my mind twice during prioritization. I made mistakes. I learned about the fitness industry. Finally, we ended with a prioritized list.

Lisa and I left the meeting feeling exhausted. When I had envisioned the meeting beforehand, I'd imagined us assimilating as *one team,* unified around achieving our purpose. Instead, I'd felt mostly apathy, if not active resistance. The only saving grace was that the SLT was aligned on the prioritized issues.

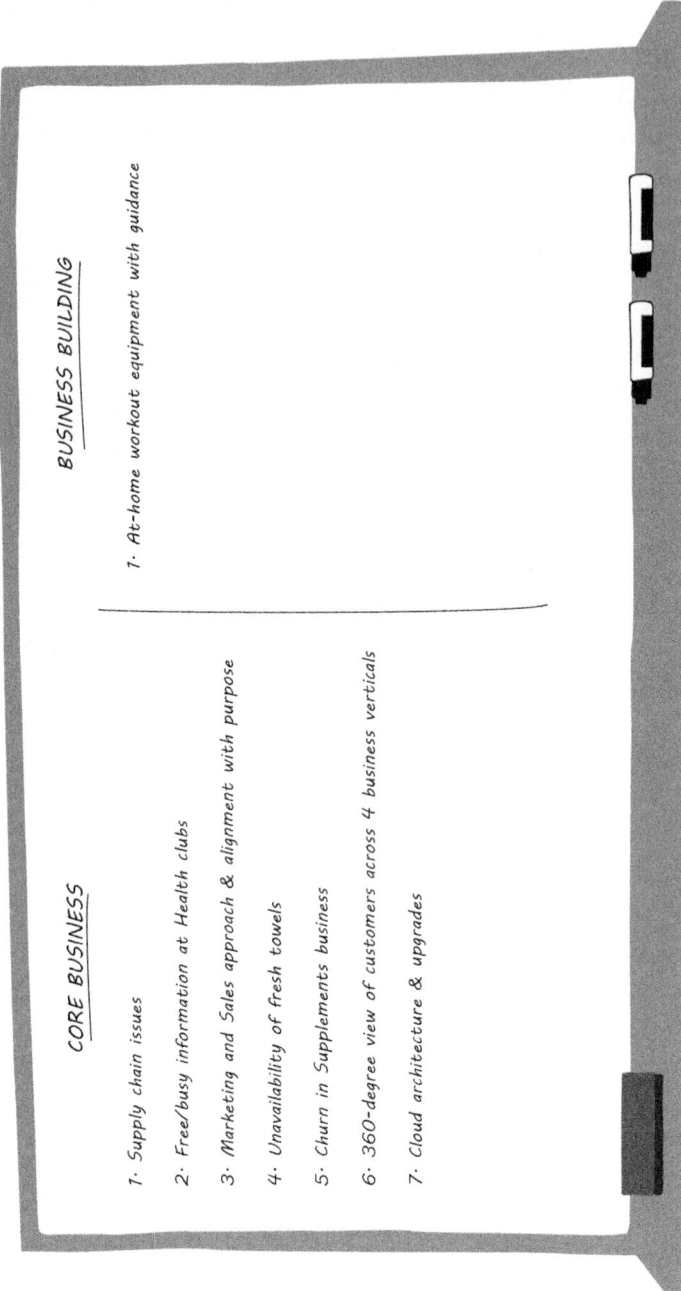

CORE BUSINESS

1. Supply chain issues

2. Free/busy information at Health clubs

3. Marketing and Sales approach & alignment with purpose

4. Unavailability of fresh towels

5. Churn in Supplements business

6. 360-degree view of customers across 4 business verticals

7. Cloud architecture & upgrades

BUSINESS BUILDING

1. At-home workout equipment with guidance

Digital initiatives

DR. NO

Lisa and I worked until 3 am that night to pull together a business plan. We felt we had a strong case and that we had a good chance to convince Susan to continue our funding. Lisa had been extremely dedicated—a true personification of a second-in-command.

We were back in the office by 8 am with coffees in hand to meet Susan, aka "Dr. No."

"Good morning, folks," said Susan. We shook hands. After some small talk about how I had been ramping up in my new role, we spoke about the transformative purpose.

"Thanks for your contribution yesterday," I said with excitement. "I strongly feel that we have a great potential to add a broader set of products and services that will strengthen the financial position of Fitness First."

"Hmm," she said. "Anna's idea of 'At-home workout equipment with guidance' could bring in some new revenue."

"Absolutely. I was thinking that we have the potential to create an ecosystem of fitness trainers. We can add fitness trainers from anywhere in the world to our digital platform and let customers pick trainers to achieve their fitness goals. Customers could pay for individual sessions or get access to classes through a monthly subscription. In fact, customers can also be anywhere in the world." I paused. "I see us building a global digital fitness platform."

"That's interesting. I haven't thought about a global digital fitness platform."

"In fact, I've identified a couple of collaboration partners to make the ecosystem a reality." I took a deep breath and said, "Why don't we walk you through our business plan and overall timeline?"

"Sure. Go ahead."

Over the next thirty minutes, Lisa and I shared the details with excitement. While Susan asked clarifying questions, not even once did she appear to acknowledge or align with our thinking. I pulled myself together and asked, "What do you think about the business plan and budget ask?"

After thinking for a minute, Susan said, "Look, Neo. The transformative purpose, business plan, digital ecosystem and the potential to add new revenue streams…all are okay." There had to be a "but" coming. And there was.

"But at this point, I don't know whether digital transformation at Fitness First is a good idea."

Then why am I even here? I wanted to ask.

She continued. "I have seen two previous CDOs fail to deliver the ROI." Without the slightest hesitation, she asked, "Do you even know what the ROI on our digital investments has been in the past 3 years?"

I shook my head. I was in disbelief that we were looking backward instead of looking forward.

She pulled up the reports and turned her monitor towards us. If the numbers were real, it looked unbelievable. She said, "ROI of digital investments so far has been nothing but a disaster. Most of the funding was used up by Bert and Joe."

Lisa looked at me, stunned and speechless.

I stammered, "But Susan, I just took the job two weeks back. Moreover, digital transformation can take a long time and requires massive investments upfront. We've got to be …"

She cut me off and said, "Neo, I get all that but we've spent $82.3 million already and all we have is a disastrous ROI. It's way too early to even talk about new initiatives and new investments unless we can show some return on previous investments." She paused for a moment and fired the last salvo. "My suggestion to you is before you start dreaming up a bunch of new investments with digital, you'd better do an inventory of the work done already and use what you have. Till then, I am unwilling to invest any further."

It was very painful to hear that. I felt angry at Bert and Joe for setting a bad precedent for ROI. And I was angry at myself for not thinking enough about my audience ("Dr. No") and tailoring our story to what Susan cared about the most.

I sighed, feeling disappointed. "Okay, we will get back to you after taking stock of prior work." I knew we'd be better off not pushing Susan at that point but instead try to convince her in the next meeting. We shook hands and exited her office.

I really wanted Susan on our side but I had failed miserably. As we walked back, all I was thinking about were the numbers Susan shared and if anything could be salvaged at all. Lisa wanted a smoke break, so we stopped at the smoking zone.

"What do you think, boss?" she asked.

"I don't know." I thought for a moment. "Do you think we can repurpose anything from the previous digital initiatives?"

She gave a wry smile and puffed on her cigarette. "You're kidding me, right?"

"Seriously? Nothing?" I asked. The situation turned from "somewhat hopeful" a few minutes back to "completely hopeless."

"Yeah. Mainly because we wasted a lot of energy chasing the latest technology that the business wanted." She thought and said, "We might be able to repurpose portions of the products and services we developed but I bet we won't get much value there. Let me confirm by tomorrow, though."

"Okay, let's plan to reconnect with Susan the day after. I will think of a plan to onboard Susan," I said. I wanted to show Lisa that I was still hopeful and didn't want to give up easily, but I had no idea what to do.

"Hey, do you have any gum?" asked Lisa.

"Yeah, I do."

I dug through my coat pocket and pulled out a pack of gum. What came along with the pack puzzled me—a crumpled business card. I unfolded it and saw that it was Charan's card, with his details barely visible. I carefully unfolded it and saw that his contact details were still intact.

"I should call him and ask for advice!" I exclaimed, pointing to the business card.

Lisa looked confused. "Who?"

"Charan!" I said.

She looked even more confused.

"My professor at Wharton. He is an expert in digital transformation with a special focus in transforming traditional organizations."

Her eyes went wide. "You should totally call him."

"Yeah…I'll talk to you later." As I walked, I read the number from the half-decimated business card and dialed Charan. It went straight to voicemail.

"Hey Charan, it's Neo. It's all going wrong here at Fitness First. I need to talk to you. Please call me."

WISDOM

After reviewing the previous CDO's digital strategy and approach, I decided to get some sleep and try to forget about the meeting with Dr. No. Before hitting the bed, I checked my smartphone one last time—no calls or text from Charan. I set my ringer on high so I would wake up if Charan called. After a few hours, my phone rang.

"Neo?"

It was Charan.

"Yes, Charan," I said sleepily. "Wait, what time is it?"

"I don't know about you but it's 5 pm here in Mumbai. I got your message that everything is wrong. And I presume you have something to tell me now."

"Right." I turned on the lights and sat up. "Well…I started at Fitness First two weeks back. These two weeks have been a grueling experience of seeing firsthand how they've been running digital transformation. It's all broken here. It's like—"

Charan cut me off. "Well, it's for you to fix it now, Neo. You'd better pull up your socks."

"Yeah, I know. Digital transformation is quite different in a large traditional organization like Fitness First. There are too many issues. I'm confused and not sure which one to tackle first."

"Let me help you with the most important ones to solve. Do they start with technology and force fit it wherever possible?"

"That's right."

"Do they have very few people aligned on their long-term vision? And the CEO is not one of them?"

"Yes. Sam is short-term focused. Numbers to the street matter a lot to her these days," I answered.

"Are they siloed and fraught with layers of bureaucracy and interminable processes? And because of that delivering at speed is wishful thinking?"

"You can certainly say that but I have a solution there."

"Good for you." He paused and added, "How about budgets and metrics? Do you see any issues with success measures in digital?"

Charan continued to amaze me with his insights—it was as if he saw everything happen. If he could predict all these things, I was sure he knew how to solve my problems.

"That's precisely why I wanted to talk to you," I said.

"Go on, I am listening. You will need to make it quick though."

"Okay. Our CFO, Susan, doesn't believe that digital transformation of Fitness First is a good idea."

"That's terrible. Why does she say that?"

"The two previous CDOs have failed her expectations."

"And those expectations are?"

"*Return on Investment.* Everything is measured in ROI. Whether to approve new digital projects or to infuse new funding or to scale back funding. Most of the time performance is assessed way too early. As a result, digital initiatives are partially completed or don't see the light of day at all."

"What's the problem now?" he asked.

"She wants us to show ROI on the digital investments made by the previous CDOs. Until then she's not keen to discuss new funding."

"Neo, you've got to fix that first. If it is not sorted soon, everything else is going to fall apart. Is that clear?"

"Yeah, but how? I know up in the boardroom they've got metrics like net profit, ROI and cash flow which they apply to the entire organization to check progress."

"Yes, go on," he said.

"But where we are, down at the digital initiative level, those metrics don't mean much. I don't think those metrics are really telling the whole story."

"Yes, I know exactly what you mean," he said.

"It was quite different at my startup. We tracked metrics beyond ROI. We never really worried about ROI. Not like Susan. If we did, we'd have never done those experiments in the first place." I took a breath and asked, "So how can I know that our digital transformation is truly delivering the right ROI to the organization?"

"Neo, you hit upon something very important. I have a few minutes to talk. Let me suggest a few things that might help you. You can try to relate it to your startup experience and what you are seeing at Fitness First."

"Sure."

"The metric Susan cares about is ROI. She wants better returns. In other words, more money than what was invested originally. Understand that there are more than a few terms that mean the same thing as that acronym—ROI."

"Okay," I answered. "So, I can say that an increase in Customer Lifetime Value is equivalent to having a positive impact on ROI. The same would be true if I could decrease customer acquisition cost."

"Exactly," he said. "One expression is equivalent to the other. But as you discovered, establishing a relationship between relevant digital metrics and ROI is key. It also requires a shift in the leadership team's mindset. Especially that of Susan, who needs to reinvent her role as a CFO for the digital era. You need to help her."

Me? Helping her? God save me.

He added, "Conventional measures used in the past do not lend themselves very well to evaluating the progress made in digital transformation. In fact, that's why I developed a set of focus areas to define the true measures."

"Fantastic—what are those?" I was curious.

"They're the areas that express the goal of ROI well, but which also permit you to develop measures to drive digital transformation," he said. "There are three of them: business building, reinventing the core and time to market."

"I remember you talking about business building and reinventing the core at your conference in London. In fact, I aligned our first set of Fitness First initiatives to those two categories," I said.

"Very good, Neo. You must know that business building and reinventing the core define *the what* you are transforming with digital."

I jumped in. "Time to market defines *the how* efficiently we are transforming with digital. Right?"

"Exactly. All three focus areas have critical measures that paint a picture of the progress you are making in digital transformation."

"Would business building include mergers and acquisitions as well?"

"Absolutely. Actually, let me explain the three focus areas to you first. You may want to write them down."

I flipped to a new sheet of paper and wrote *Business building.*

"Business building includes any new business, organic or inorganic, whose revenue is generated through business ventures that are powered by digital."

I wrote it down word by word.

Then I asked, "Can the underlying digital technology be powered, let's say, by a startup or a third party?"

"Why not? The necessary condition is that digital must be powering the business model," he clarified.

"Okay."

"The next focus area is reinventing the core," he said. "This focus area includes digitizing the existing business across the customer experience with special attention to personalization, across operations with special attention to optimization and releasing cash and across employee productivity with special attention to doing more for less and everything in between."

I thought personalization, releasing cash, and doing more for less in itself would likely have a substantial positive impact on ROI.

"And the last focus area?" I asked.

"Time to market," he said. "It concerns the speed at which you are able to respond rapidly to opportunities or issues and translate ideas into digital products and services, without compromising on usability and functionality.

Overly long times to market can mean the organization is losing to competition and that it is failing to institutionalize best practices like rapid experimentation and agile delivery."

"Time to market seems rather a simple measure."

"What is it at Fitness First?" he asked. "I bet it'd be nothing less than 12 months."

"Yeah, you're right. It's about 12 to 15 months. It was about 12 weeks at my startup."

He went on. "It is a simple measure but don't underestimate the impact of having shorter times to market and the complexity involved in getting to a shorter cycle time. It requires radical shifts—both in digital product management and deployment practices as well as managing the change with the people involved."

"Okay," I said warily. "But how do I use these focus areas to define measures that matter during a digital transformation journey?"

"Everything you manage in your digital transformation is covered by these focus areas," he said.

"Everything?" I asked. I didn't quite believe him.

"Yeah!"

"Okay. Going back to our original conversation, how do I use these focus areas and measures to evaluate progress?"

"Well, obviously you have to express the expectation of ROI in terms of measures relevant to each of these focus areas," he said, adding, "Just a second, Neo." Then I heard him tell someone, "I'll be there in a moment."

"So how do I express the metrics in these focus areas?" I asked, anxious to keep the conversation going.

"Neo, I have to go. I know you are smart enough to figure it out on your own; all you have to do is think about it and list the measures in each focus area," he said. "Just remember, you must define a threshold for the expected outcomes of each measure and use that to prioritize and approve digital initiatives that have a potential to deliver up to the threshold. For example, if customer acquisition cost is $50 per customer, you could set a threshold at 10% and approve digital initiatives that have a potential to reduce the cost by 10%. You must also be ready to abandon the initiative if the measures are not met."

"But Charan, this isn't enough. Even if I define the measures in each focus area, I won't be done. It requires a shift in the mindset of leadership. Especially for Susan, our CFO. Remember?"

"Yeah. You've got to help her transform her role as a CFO for the digital era. You must collaborate with your allies there. Preferably someone from the board. Do you have any?"

"I guess."

"Okay, Neo, I really need to go now."

"Okay, thanks—" I heard a beep and I was talking to myself. I stared out the window as the bitter-white moon hung in the sky and the smoke from the dying embers in the fireplace lingered in the air. The note pad with the three focus areas looked daunting as I thought about the most difficult task—transforming Dr. No's role for the digital era. I flung myself onto the bed, feeling restless and anxious.

THE REAL MEASURES

When I woke up, it did not feel like my usual morning—very few birds were chirping and the streets were noisy with traffic. Did I miss my alarm? I crawled from the bed and picked my phone. It was 10 am—I had missed my morning meetings. Flustered and angry at myself, I called my EA.

"Mr. Ray's office?"

"Hey, it's me," I told my EA.

"There you are. Where have you been? Is everything alright?" she asked.

"Yeah, I had something unexpected come up. It's okay now."

"Glad to hear. By the way, Mike was looking for you. Are you coming to work today?"

"Yes. Yes. I will be there by noon. Please clear my day and find the first available time with Mike. And have Lisa join us."

"You bet."

"Alright. Bye for now."

I was tired and exhausted. I wondered why Mike was looking for me. Whatever it was, I would need to deprioritize that. I needed his time to sort things out with Susan first. My phone buzzed. It was my EA.

"Hey, I got Mike. He can meet in thirty minutes."

"Thirty minutes?" I looked at my watch. "Uh, yeah, go ahead. I will be there." I took a quick shower and headed straight to work with notes from last night's discussion.

By the time I arrived, Mike and Lisa were already in my office. I quickly settled in and for the next thirty minutes, I went over it all with Mike—our discussion with Susan, her apprehensions and Charan's insights. I went to the whiteboard and wrote the three focus areas.

"We need to define measures in these focus areas."

Both were quiet. Just when Lisa was about to speak, we heard someone knock at the door.

"May I come in?" It was Stacy, my lead product manager.

"Come on in, Stacy." I glanced at Mike and said, "Stacy is one of our star Product Managers. I invited her to join the discussion."

I quickly brought Stacy up to speed on the focus areas.

"So, Charan says everything we manage in our digital transformation is covered in these focus areas," said Stacy.

I nodded.

Mike went next. "Has he shared any examples?"

I shook my head and said, "Let's start with *the what* first, beginning with reinventing the core and doing a deep dive into two areas: customer experience & operations."

"What's your plan to define measures?" asked Mike.

"Let's analyze the outcomes of a few digital initiatives. It might give a good head start to identify measures and establish a relationship with ROI."

No one objected or had a better idea, so I went to the whiteboard. As I wrote *Unavailability of fresh towels*, I said, "Remember the issue that Tim was vocal about? We should pick that. I believe unavailability of fresh towels impacted renewals."

"Now let's think about what would happen if this issue was fixed? What difference would it make to the customer and the company?" asked Mike.

"Churn would go down," said Lisa.

"Premium members would be happy because they get fresh towels when they need them. So, the Net Promoter Score (NPS) will go up," Stacy added.

"A positive NPS helps in reducing customer acquisition cost because new customers would be acquired through word of mouth," I said.

Mike went on. "Exactly. More customers mean more sales. Higher margin and reduction in costs due to efficient customer acquisition. All of these will have a positive impact on ROI." He paused for a moment. "There you go, we have a few measures already."

I went to the whiteboard and wrote the measures under *Customer Experience*. "Let's focus on operations now. What's the impact of the fresh towels problem on Operations?"

Lisa chimed in. "There's quite a lot of operations cost involved in offering fresh towels to our members. We need on-site industrial washing and drying machines and staff to manage the towels. And of course, the cost of the towels themselves, which get worn out and need to be replaced periodically."

"Do we offer the fresh towels option at every club?" asked Mike.

Stacy nodded. "Yes, I believe so. And not every club has enough customers paying the premium subscription price to justify the cost."

"So we have a couple more metrics," I said. "Cost savings optimization if we can find a solution that reduces the cost of offering fresh towels and release of cash by turning off the fresh towels option at those clubs where it doesn't make financial sense."

Mike spoke again. "Makes sense. More throughput or output of fresh towels for the same cost and releasing cash by turning off the fresh towels option—all these have a positive impact on overall cash flow and therefore, on ROI."

I went to the whiteboard and wrote the measures under *Operations*.

The next one was business building. After explaining the meaning of business building, I said, "Let's pick Anna's idea—at-home workout equipment with guidance. We've refined the idea to include a digital ecosystem of fitness and health experts. And we could explore a partnership with a startup working in the AI space."

"This is rather simple. Isn't it?" said Lisa. "Measures should be monthly active users, revenue per user, total revenue growth and market share."

"Well, I think the first measure should be the percentage of total budget allocated to business building. With Digital Giants doubling down in the health and fitness space, we must focus on new business opportunities while reinventing the core business," I added.

"That's true. How many business building initiatives are we actively working on now?" Mike wanted to know.

"None." Lisa's response was instant and curt.

"In the past two years?" I asked.

Lisa shook her head.

I sighed in dismay. "We are not pushing enough. We must—"

Lisa cut me off. "Why would we, when we're afraid of failure?"

Mike turned to me. "This really worries me, Neo. If there is a fear of failure, we hesitate to experiment. That means we can't find breakthrough opportunities."

I nodded in agreement. "We should continuously evaluate new ideas, conduct experiments and low-impact tests, build upon winners, and quickly discard losers. The beauty of digital is that it generates data. Good or bad doesn't matter. What matters is how well we harness the data to scale from our successes or pivot from our failures. That's the unique power of the virtuous digital feedback loop."

"What if we celebrate failures?" asked Stacy.

"We should," I said. "In fact, if we measure the number of initiatives pivoted or abandoned based on early test results and then recognize the teams, it may push the team to try new opportunities, test them and iterate rapidly."

"But for that, we need business building initiatives and budgets," said Lisa with a slight tinge of sarcasm.

Mike and I both nodded, as if to say, *We will get the budgets.*

"We need one more measure—time taken from commercial launch to scale," I added.

"Great. Those are good measures for business building," said Mike.

I updated the whiteboard and moved to the last focus area—time to market.

Stacy spoke. "I guess we can measure time to market in two terms: cycle time from opportunity assessment to proof of concept (POC) to commercial launch—measured in weeks or months. And second, release frequency to update IT products—measured in the number of releases during a given period."

"What's our current cycle time and release frequency?" asked Mike.

"It's terrible," said Stacy. "We may take around 12 months to get an idea to market. As for release frequency, it's 4 releases every quarter."

I saw by the look on Lisa's face that she was annoyed. I asked her what was bothering her.

"This is crazy. It got worse than before." Lisa complained.

"We will get it better," I said to cheer her up.

I updated the measures on the whiteboard for each focus area and wrapped the discussion. I asked Lisa to define a threshold for each measure based on her prior experience and provide it for my review.

As Mike was about to leave, I said, "We need to talk about Susan."

"Okay. I wanted to chat with you about something else but you go first." He looked at his watch and said, "Can we walk and talk?"

I walked along with Mike as he was checking his smartphone for details of his next meeting.

"Charan says we need to help Susan reinvent her role as a CFO for the digital era. It'd be wise for both of us to have a dialogue with her."

Mike glanced at me. "What areas does she need to reinvent?"

"We already spoke at length about measures. The other area is that she must ask the right questions," I said.

"Like what?"

"The most pertinent questions relevant for digital transformation. For example, what are we testing in digital initiatives? How will we measure outcomes? What will we learn? And how will our findings suggest whether we should double down?"

"Sounds like having *a learner's mindset* will help her?" he asked.

"Exactly."

He thought for a moment and said, "What about competitive insights? Especially the growing group of incumbents that are reinventing themselves with digital. They could be far more destructive than digital startups."

"Yeah. And the macroeconomic impacts on our industry due to digital. Industry lines are getting blurred and profit pools are shifting overnight. We must keep track of these too and Susan is an expert in that," I added.

"That's right. Susan is in the best position to provide those insights."

I was glad to see that Mike and I were in agreement. But the bigger alignment we needed was with Susan. I wondered how Mike planned to approach our discussion with her.

Mike shook my hand and said, "Alright, let's talk with Susan tomorrow. Get your EA to find time for us."

WINNING DR. NO

As I approached Susan's office, she saw me through the glass panel of her office and opened the door.

"Mike spoke to me at length," she said. "So did Sam. You will have a fresh start for our digital transformation with no baggage and no strings attached. Would $10 million be fine to get started?" Lisa and Stacy were in Susan's room with wide smiles. My EA brought me a cake with the words "For a Fresh Start" stenciled in red icing across the chocolate top. Everyone around was clapping and cheering for me.

Of course, that's not what happened. I woke up smiling from the dream and realized that I needed to meet Susan that day. As I drove to work, I had a sudden eerie feeling that we would fail again in winning Susan over and that we wouldn't get further funding for digital transformation. And that my career and life would be doomed.

Dismissing it as paranoia, I looked for Lisa's email with the measures and thresholds defined for the three focus areas. A little note in the email stated that none of the prior digital investments could be repurposed. It was disappointing and I knew Susan wouldn't be happy to hear that.

I arrived at Susan's office ahead of Mike, so I took the opportunity to get to know Susan better. As we settled in, I saw souvenirs from London that piqued my interest. We spoke about Susan's childhood in London and my recent trip to the Digital Unplugged conference when Mike arrived.

Mike seized the opportunity. "You missed the Digital Unplugged conference. It was very enlightening for me."

"Fill me in," requested Susan.

"Some of the statistics were startling. Especially the one about how every disruption in the past has wiped out 80% of incumbents. And guess what? We are barely in the early stages of digital disruption," Mike said.

Susan's mouth twisted cynically. She did not comment. She didn't need to.

"The question on my mind is, are we doing enough to avoid destruction?" asked Mike, looking at Susan.

"That's what I want to know too. Neo?" Susan cleverly punted the question to me.

Mike quickly intervened. "Susan, this is for us to reflect on because we have a better view of the past and the horizon."

She looked at Mike and said, "We're in the top 10 in our industry. Our balance sheet is strong. Aren't we fine if we stay where we are?"

"Top 10 would be suicidal, Susan. We must aim to be in the top 3," Mike said without hesitating.

I intervened. "The past two years of digital transformation at Fitness First have hardly moved the needle. Most of our past digital investments created small amounts of incremental value." I tried to sound friendly but I wasn't sure it came out that way.

Susan frowned at me. "I'm well aware that the ROI is poor. That's why I'm reluctant to spend more money."

Mike jumped in. "Neo's predecessors decided how to spend that money and they are long gone, Susan. We need to work our way forward now."

An awkward moment of silence.

Mike went on. "The conference and the discussions I've had with Neo gave me new insights and fresh perspectives. It makes me rethink how I, and in fact all of us, must approach digital transformation."

I took a deep breath and said, "Thanks, Mike. I'm here to make us all successful in our roles. In fact, let's talk about the things that need to be done differently in the financial management of digital transformation."

It took Susan a few seconds for my words to sink in. She had been a star CFO with an impressive track record, taking Fitness First through the IPO, driving M&A twice, managing the board and Wall Street expectations successfully. Getting a lesson in finance from a brand-new digital executive was the last thing she expected.

She looked perturbed. "Wait a second—do you mean I need to unlearn the financial management practices I have always known and relearn a new way?"

Without the slightest hint of sarcasm or defensiveness, I nodded my head and said, "To some extent…yes."

"You're going to explain that to me, Mr. Ray."

It was the first time in a while someone had called me Mr. Ray. It felt like the discussion was becoming contentious. Mike started to look uncomfortable.

I dove in. "Digital requires us to play a long game. But since Wall Street, therefore our board, expect to realize quick benefits, we must negotiate a roadmap that allows us to pursue long-term goals while also demonstrating short-term value. Sorry to say but ROI is not the true measure needed to assess short-term value."

"What is *the true measure,* then?" she asked.

"A new set of measures under three focus areas. They express the goal of ROI well." I projected the slide Lisa had sent. For the next fifteen minutes, I explained the focus areas, measures, and thresholds for each measure.

She looked interested. "So, you are saying any digital initiative that meets or exceeds the predefined thresholds and can deliver these measures, is worth considering?"

"Exactly. We deliberate, select and measure the performance of digital initiatives using these measures," I replied.

Mike chimed in. "Who defines what outcomes can be expected from a digital initiative?"

"We will have small autonomous teams called Innovation Pods, to drive each digital initiative," I said. "These teams define the measures and the time horizon. They kick off the work, after approval from the leaders."

"And we review and monitor their progress frequently?" Susan asked.

"Yes. While prioritizing the initiatives, we must strive to get a good balance of initiatives in *reinventing our core* and *business building*."

Susan leaned forward. "How do we strike the right balance? And who calls the shots?"

"If there is anyone who is capable of doing that," I paused for dramatic effect, "it's you, Susan."

She looked puzzled.

"CFOs are reinventing their role for the digital age. You are a critical leader in creating the architecture that can provide the right market insights, measure performance and ask the right questions." As I said the words, I realized just how much I needed that to be true. The CFO was truly critical to our success.

She pushed on. "Explain."

Mike jumped in. "With your expertise, you can keep the SLT informed about how the economics of our businesses are changing due to digital, how profit pools are shifting and how new opportunities are emerging. Further, you need to be our eyes watching the competition, especially the incumbents that are reviving with digital."

She reacted. "Yeah. With all their brand equity, loyalty and customer reach, incumbents will be a real threat."

"Potentially a much bigger threat than digital startups," added Mike.

Susan looked thoughtful. "You said that CFOs need to ask the right questions. What did you mean?"

"A learner's mindset," Mike said. "It helps us ask the right questions."

"Like what?" she wanted to know.

"What are we testing in digital initiatives?" I answered. "How will we measure? What will we learn? How will our findings suggest whether we should double down?"

"So, learn quickly and double down wherever it makes sense to move faster?" she asked.

I clarified, "Exactly. Digital Giants make twice bolder moves with four times faster speed. There is a ten-time differential between them and the rest, which makes it very difficult for others to compete."

"Look Susan," Mike said. "You are in the best position to evangelize digital with the SLT and the board and place bold bets. Not just to make us resilient but also to make us future-ready."

Susan slowly nodded. There was a palpable agreement in the air.

He continued. "You are the only person that can credibly talk about the negatives and point to the board or the SLT that if we don't invest more money, that profit pool is going away."

Susan laughed softly. "I was waiting for when you were going to ask for money again. I guess this all boils down to funding Neo's big ask?"

"Not just that." I said. "We need you on board with everything we do to become a digital-first organization. I know we can't do this without you."

"And with Neo here, we'll get digital right," added Mike with a reassuring tone.

Susan turned to her computer and pulled up a spreadsheet. She tapped in a few numbers. "Okay, Neo, let's see what you can do. I'm extending your funding for the next six months." After a moment, she added, "But that's all I'm willing to do until you can produce some tangible results. I'm not sticking my neck out any further. I still don't know which is the bigger threat to the company—digital disruption from our competitors or burning money to make Fitness First a digital-first organization."

"The new measures and the Innovation Pod Model are sure to deliver results fast," I promised recklessly.

"And I'll support you with the rest of the board, Susan," said Mike cheerfully.

THIRD DIGITAL-FIRST REALIZATION

The Real Measures

Measurement and metrics must focus on what you are transforming with digital – core business vs. new business – and how quickly are you transforming with digital. Not just ROI.

Conventional measures do not lend themselves very well to evaluating the progress made in digital transformation. The real measures that can accurately evaluate the success of digital initiatives can be categorized into three areas: Business building, Reinventing the core and Time to market.

Business building and reinventing the core define *the what* you are transforming with digital. And time to market defines *the how* efficiently you are transforming with digital. These areas express the goal of ROI well and also permit you to develop measures to drive digital transformation. However, establishing a relationship between relevant measures in these areas and ROI is the key.

Business building: Includes any new business, organic or inorganic, where revenue is generated through business ventures that are powered by digital. Example: measures included but not limited to—percentage of digital transformation budget allocated, time taken from idea to proof of concept (POC) to scale, percentage of R&D spend that translated into new product sales and percentage of gross margin contributed by new product sales.

Reinventing the core: Includes digitizing the existing business across customer experience with special attention to personalization, operations with special attention to optimization and releasing cash, and employee productivity with special attention to doing more for less. Example: measures included but are not limited to—Customer Lifetime Value, churn, Net Promoter Score and increase in throughput.

Time to market: Refers to the speed at which you are able to respond rapidly to opportunities or issues and translate ideas into digital products and services, without compromising on usability and functionality. Overly long times to market can mean that the organization is losing to competition and that it is failing to institutionalize best practices in digital innovation and agile delivery. Example: measures included but are not limited to—cycle time from idea stage to commercial launch (measured in weeks/months) and release frequency to update IT products (measured in number of releases during a given period).

For each measure, a threshold must be defined for the expected outcomes. These thresholds can be used to prioritize and approve digital initiatives that have a potential to deliver up to or beyond the threshold. For example, if customer acquisition cost is $50 per customer and if the threshold is set at 10%, any digital initiative that has a potential to reduce the cost by $5 can be prioritized.

In addition, while evaluating digital initiatives, it's important to go beyond the metrics defined above. A learner's mindset helps in looking beyond the obvious. Ask the right questions relevant for a digital transformation. For example:

- What are we testing with each digital initiative?
- What did we learn?
- How will our findings suggest whether we should double down?

It's also important to track macroeconomic impacts due to digital in your industry. Finally, insights into competitors, especially incumbents that are reviving with digital, must be monitored closely. They can be far more destructive than digital startups.

All these add up to *The Real Measures.*

Ideas to remember

- A tech-first approach is a perfect recipe for disaster. In this approach, tech is force fit to bring digital into the fold. A customer-first approach will increase the probability of success and adoption of digital interventions. When you are obsessed with the customer, whether internal or external, you'll lead with empathy and identify relevant digital interventions to address the unmet and unarticulated needs of the customer.

- Digital must be led by business. The digital team is an enabler, working to achieve the business goals that are aligned with your purpose. Business and digital teams must work hand in glove.

- Like you saw at Fitness First, a mix of personalities will likely exist in every organization. It's important to align all of them in the crucial journey of digital transformation. Remember, aligned and committed teams deliver game changing outcomes.

- People with a digital mindset have the ability to unlock possibilities with digital and believe that business problems can be solved efficiently with digital. They are curious about digital and keep track of new emerging tech innovations. They marry business and digital elegantly. They promote experimentation and leverage data to refine the digital solution.

- Five foundational elements must be taken care of to ensure success of digital transformation. Take one thing out and the transformation is guaranteed to fail. These are:

  1. Digital-first led by business

  2. Digital leadership & team skills

  3. Digital-first delivery model

  4. Business plans

  5. Funding

Let's take a look at Toys R Us. In 2000, instead of building its own online presence, it entered into a 10-year partnership with Amazon to be an exclusive seller of toys on Amazon. When Toys R Us finally launched its e-commerce site, it was too late to make any difference and it was riddled with technical errors, which frustrated customers. A decade of missteps in developing its own e-commerce presence played a big role in the 2017 bankruptcy and 2018 liquidation of what once was the largest U.S. toy retailer.

It appears that Toys R Us management lacked a digital mindset. They believed that Toys R Us was at the center of the toy industry and that nothing bad could happen to the company. This same mindset contributed to the downfall of other giants like Blockbuster, Circuit City and Kodak. Now, Toys R Us is just a brand name that is available for licensed partnerships designed to leverage the value of an iconic retail name and its beloved mascot Geoffrey.

Digital-first must be led by business executives but if business executives lack a digital mindset, disasters like these are bound to happen.

- "Future Storming" is a creative and interactive exercise that asks participants to visualize a compelling future that would go on a magazine, say Forbes or HBR, on a future date. Once the future state is envisioned, the team defines what success looks like, potential challenges, what needs to be done differently to achieve the future state and KPIs to measure the outcomes.

- When you have limited dollars, invest in digital initiatives that can directly or indirectly deliver personalization or in initiatives that can directly or indirectly increase cash or release locked up cash. If possible, go one step further with personalization and adopt a hyper-personalization approach – moving up or down the value chain and creating individualized experiences at every step along the customer's journey.

- The CFO must reinvent her role for the digital era. She must monitor macro and microeconomic indicators and the way business models will evolve with digital. Further, she must have the courage to talk about the negative and point out to the board that if investments are not made, a specific profit pool is going away. Finally, she must build required instrumentation to perform data analytics and present accurate, concise, and relevant financial data to support business decisions in a timely manner.

PART 3
WIN SOMETIMES LOSE SOMETIMES

PERSONAL
REALIZATION

I was home by 10 pm that night, feeling relieved that Vitamin M was taken care of. Rummaging through the refrigerator, I attempted to find dinner but had to settle on leftover pizza from the previous night. Wolfing it down with some beer, I dined in and felt content.

I missed Tina and Riya. Since the day I joined Fitness First, my calls to them had been quick check-ins to see if they were doing fine before I jumped back into the craziness. Nothing beyond that. I just hoped Tina wouldn't be mad at me.

I called Tina. She answered.

"Hi," I said. "Guess who's been having crazy days?"

Tina smiled wanly. "Sounds like you are. It's also been crazy here."

"Okay. We're both having crazy days." I told her. "I'm sorry for the short calls. I just wanted to make sure you're doing fine."

"We are doing okay. How did it go with the CFO?"

I was happy to share the good news with Tina. "We got our funding. Sorry I was so distracted, figuring things out." I tried to coax some empathy from Tina. "It's been a lot harder than I thought it would be. I should have spent more time on our calls. I really am sorry!"

Tina shrugged. "I know you are doing your best, love. No need to apologize to me but Riya is having a tough time. She really misses you and she's too young to understand why her Dad's not around."

"Is Riya near you? Can I talk to her?"

Tina shook her head. "Mom took Riya out. Can you call back in a couple of hours? I know it is late there already but she'd love to see you."

I hesitated. "I can try. It's getting late and I've got a 7 am meeting."

Tina's smile wavered. "Riya really misses you. She asks me when you are coming home almost every day. But I understand that you have your priorities."

"Please don't say that. You don't understand the pressure I'm under."

Tina's lips tightened. "I understand enough. I spent my time in the corporate world too. Neo… I knew who you were when I married you. That your career and work would always come first and I would get whatever was left. And I'm fine with that. But your daughter needs you."

"Look, I put the hours in because I have to, not because I want to," I tried to justify. "It'll all be fine soon. I promise I will make time for us."

"Neo, don't make promises you won't keep."

"I just have to get everything moving. And then maybe I can come for a visit."

Tina was quiet for a moment and then she said. "You've got to get some sleep, right? Let's talk tomorrow."

"Tina! Don't end the call when you are angry."

She sighed. "I'm not angry. I'm crazy about you. You're just so far away and it feels like we're not in your life anymore. Like we're slipping away."

"Of course you're in my life! You are everything to me!"

Tina looked resigned. "Go to sleep, Neo. And call us when you can." And she hung up.

I mulled over what Tina said about my work and priorities. Maybe she was right—my actions or inactions made it seem like I'm taking Tina for granted. But I love her and I do care for her.

She knows that. So why did I feel like I'd betrayed her?

After thinking for a few moments, I realized that I was failing to bring *harmony into my work-life*. My passion for work had inspired me to focus too hard on my connection to work and it had burned me out. I had to keep the flame going while also bringing harmony with my family by *being present.*

With that personal realization, I resolved to wait for a couple of hours and then call back when Riya was home. I lay on the couch and pulled up an article on my tablet and set an alarm in case I accidentally fell asleep.

MOVING FAST

The next morning, I felt tired but better. The late-night call with Tina and Riya was a step in the right direction and I was glad to see Mom as well. As soon as I got to the office, I sent a note to my EA to call for an emergency meeting with my team. Now that Susan was aligned, I wanted to move fast and earn a chance to become the permanent CDO much earlier. I started to write a list of actions.

The emergency meeting started at 9 am in my office.

"I'd like you all to know that we have a go-ahead from Susan, our CFO, for funding our digital initiatives." Everyone cheered.

"We have a lot to do. First, we need a working model of the Innovation Pod. Which digital initiative should we pick to shape the model?" I asked.

"Why don't we pick the digital initiative I just defined the scope for and planned out?" asked Stacy.

"Go on."

"We currently require our customers to interact with staff members when they enter the club, if they are premium members and want fresh towels or if they want to sign up for a class. And the authentication system is a bar-coded card, which requires them to line up and interact with a machine. It requires a dedicated employee to monitor the customers. The cards also get worn out or lost, which adds cost and additional overhead to process new bar-coded cards. We want to make all authentication contactless and built into our app."

"What's the strategy to build and scale the contactless experience?" I wanted to know.

"We're testing at two health clubs first. After that, we'll roll it out across 400-plus clubs."

I felt a Pod model would accelerate the delivery. Since Stacy said she had a plan already, I decided not to shake things up by talking about my Digital Innovation approach. "Great. Let's form an Innovation Pod to test and iterate at these two health clubs," I said.

Some of my team seemed confused.

I explained. "The Pod model helps in accelerating delivery. Each Pod will have a Product Manager who plays the role of Pod Lead, a Business Designer who understands customer needs and conceptualizes the solution, a Visual Designer to bring the concepts to life on a digital canvas and Full-stack Developers to make it real and live."

Lisa chimed in. "I will form the team right away."

"And don't forget to define the measures and identify representatives from key functions so the Pod Lead has everything they need to move with full force."

"You bet," said Lisa.

As we were discussing the next steps, I saw Sam walking towards my office. She entered my office and stood near the door. I waved my hand and told her I would be with her in a few minutes.

I continued to address my team. "Look, guys. We have the digital initiatives, our budgets are approved, Innovation Pods will drive the initiatives and the measures will keep us true and help us deliver outcomes. I want us to move fast. Now go deliver, team!"

"To new beginnings," said Lisa, followed by the team in chorus. They looked excited and energized.

As the team went back to their desks, Sam approached me. "Nice pep talk, Neo."

I smiled.

In the next fifteen minutes, I brought her up to speed on the initiatives, budgets and measures, Pod model, etc.

Sam seemed pleased with the update. "Good job with Susan. She's a tough nut."

I smiled and nodded in agreement.

"By the way, we need better results in our health clubs' business next quarter. I want you and your team to focus on this," Sam said. It sounded like an order. And then it got worse. "Double down or work round the clock. Whatever it takes. We need results."

I was startled. Perhaps Mike had wanted to caution me about this.

Hesitantly, I said, "Let me look into this."

She gave a thumbs up and headed out.

———

The next eight weeks passed in a blur. We launched two more digital initiatives and two more Innovation Pods. The roadmap was starting to come together. However, I was starting to get worried because the contactless experience initiative was still ongoing and it was only supposed to last five weeks.

I called Lisa, Stacy, and the Pod team in for a review.

"How are we doing?" I asked.

"No problems with the two new initiatives we just we kicked off," said Lisa. "But we have to talk about the contactless experience initiative."

"What's the latest?" I asked.

"We are about 70% complete and—"

"And we took almost twice the time already?" My irritation and impatience bled into my tone.

No one spoke. That silence troubled me even more.

"I want to know why the Pod model couldn't deliver results at speed." I could sense that the team was hesitant to share. I took a deep breath and spoke carefully. "Look guys, please do yourself a favor. Be candid. We must shape the Innovation Pod model based on what we've learned. I want to know why the Pod model failed."

"Actually, *we* failed the Pod model," said Stacy.

"What do you mean?" I wanted specifics.

"Most of the team in the Pod are part-timers. If we want to run full steam, we need full-timers dedicated to the Pod and the initiative," she said.

"Part-timers, as in playing multiple roles?" I asked.

The Business Designer from the Pod team opened up. "I've been working in shifts—20 hours every week as a functional consultant on the HR Management System project and another 5 for weekly reporting. All the while being part of the Innovation Pod."

I was shocked. "Is that true for all of you?" I asked.

They nodded.

"Unbelievable. I will sort this out in a couple of days," I expressed my apologies for not taking care of the team. Since I didn't want to leave any loose ends, I asked, "If we have a dedicated team, will the Pod be in a position to deliver results at speed?"

Silence again. I was losing patience.

Stacy raised her hand. "As you know, we are dependent on the rest of the organization to deliver our desired outcomes. However, we don't see a sense of urgency from other teams to solve problems for the customer."

"As in, you don't feel the other parts of the company are invested in our mission?"

"That's right. Not everyone cares about contactless customer experience as much as we do. They don't know why and how we plan to deliver the experience," she clarified.

I looked at the Pod Lead. "Walk me through the customer experience."

"Sure. Our concept for the contactless experience was to integrate all authentication and sign ups into the Fitness First Mobile app. We leverage all the security, biometric fingerprint and facial recognition features built into our customers' phones. Customers will be able to access all health club facilities, classes, and services in their membership package. Our customers don't have to wait in line or interact with the staff. It will improve our data and we can decrease our operational cost," said the Pod Lead.

"That's a neat concept. You leveraged existing digital assets and introduced low-cost authentication mechanisms." After hearing the solution concept, I was even more confused why it'd take more than a few weeks. "Did you involve anyone from the interdependent functions while brainstorming the concept?"

The Pod Lead shook his head.

I was startled but I didn't let my frustration show.

"Go on. What happened next?" I asked.

"We put a project plan in place listing the tasks for each of us and the interdependent functions."

"What are the functions?"

"The Mobile App Team for adding the new features. The Facilities team for identifying the physical access and authentication requirements. The IT Infrastructure team to activate authentication through the app and cloud setup. The Commercial team for procurement. And finally, the Health Club Operations team for training," the Pod Lead answered.

"I guess you oriented them about what was expected of them. Right?"

"Yeah."

I could see where the story was going. "And you followed-up with them and tried to influence whatever you could? And if that didn't work, you escalated with their bosses, right?"

"That's correct."

I lost it. "Of course these functions don't have a drive or sense of urgency! Why would they? They were never part of the solution." I stressed the last sentence to drive home the message that we must bring everyone along for the journey. I paused for a moment to let the message sink in.

"So, you're saying we shouldn't treat them like *task takers*. Instead, we should make them *co-creators* of the solution concept?" Lisa inquired.

"Exactly! Only when they become part of the solution will they have visibility into customer actions during the contactless experience, the problem we are trying to solve and how their efforts play a key role in stitching the whole experience together."

It felt like a light bulb moment for the team.

I added, "You must include only those interdependent functions that play a key role in defining the future state of the solution concept."

"So, does that mean it might be efficient for the Commercial Team to just be a task-taker?" Stacy asked.

"Yes. The rest of the functions—the Mobile App Team, the Facilities Team, the IT Infrastructure Team and the Health Club Operations Team—must be co-creators," I clarified.

Lisa intervened. "We need to test this new approach. But before that, we need a mechanism to bring all these teams together—like a framework."

"Hmm, I'll give it some thought. Let's regroup in a couple of days." I wrapped the meeting, assuring the team that we would find a way.

I wondered what kind of framework would work at a large organization like Fitness First. I had never faced these issues at Digi Gate. Of course, at Digi Gate we worked like a small family, having a unified view of the customer journey. Should a new customer scenario come up, we quickly huddled and pulled in relevant functional representatives to brainstorm the future state of the customer journey. We always took a team approach to defining who needed to do what so we could deliver a seamless customer experience.

Here, the Pod Lead was trying to bring clarity but at a task level. The Lead hadn't anticipated the disconnects nor delays from the interdependent functions. And to top it off, the whole team was overworked. No wonder the first Innovation Pod was failing to deliver at speed.

I had to think of a proactive way to make the interdependent functions be co-creators of the future state customer experience. We had to get absolute clarity—a unified view of the customer journey across the organization and an understanding of how the experience would be stitched together.

CHECK-IN

The next day was a drag—I had my regular check-in with Sam at 3 pm. Lately, Sam had been erratic—sometimes she was positive and encouraging, sometimes she would be impatient or distracted. The last thing I wanted now was another problem. As I drove to work that morning, I got a text from Sam '*Waiting in your office!*' But my meeting with her was scheduled for 3 pm. Why did she want to meet earlier? And *an exclamation* point? What did it even mean?

As I walked to my office, my adrenaline was pumping. I wondered why in the world Sam wanted me to meet early. I'd lost any hope of getting work done that morning—I usually went in early to catch up on the stuff I'd be too busy to tackle once the day started. That day was even more important—I needed to figure out a way to make the Innovation Pods more efficient.

The door of my office was wide open. I walked in and there she was, sitting behind my desk.

"Hey Sam, what's going on?"

Sam looked livid. She said, "We've got things to talk about. Sit down."

"Sure, but you're in my seat." Perhaps the wrong thing to say but I felt I was losing respect.

She became even more furious.

"You want to know why I'm here first thing in the morning?" she asked. I nodded.

"To talk about your speed boats," she said with sarcasm.

Speed boats? She must have been referring to the Innovation Pods. But I still wanted to confirm.

"You mean the Innovation Pods?" I asked.

"What else?" She paused for a moment. "Are they changing the direction of the ship or are they lost in the abyss?" she screamed.

"Well Sam, the Pod model worked well at my startup. It hasn't worked quite as expected here. I'm exploring ways to—"

She cut me off. "You are here to implement time-tested practices. This is not a place for you to experiment."

I was flustered. I needed to salvage the situation and address the Innovation Pod issues.

I gathered myself and said, "If you want outcomes, then I need enough people dedicated to the Pod!"

"You've got enough people! Look at your efficiencies, for God's sake! You're taking ten weeks to complete a project that was planned for five weeks. You've got a lot of room for improvement," she said. "Don't come crying to me about not having enough people until you show me you can effectively use what you've got."

"But the root cause we discovered is that the Pod team is overworked. Everyone is playing multiple roles. That's not sustainable, Sam."

I was about to add more details when she held up her hand to shut me up. She stood up and went to close the door.

Oh shit, I thought.

She turned by the door and told me, "Sit down." I had been standing the whole time. I took a seat in one of the chairs in front of the desk, where a visitor would sit.

"We don't have time. I told you already—quarterly results are important," she said.

I put on a reassuring tone. "I understand this is a top priority but we've got to address the root—"

Sam exploded. "Damn it, I am not here to listen to your problems. I want results. You better get it right before it's too late. I can't afford any further delays." She stormed out of my office.

I sat there, speechless. Sam was getting worse. She just didn't want to hear about problems. I was glad that I didn't share the bigger problem: unifying the organization on the future state. I thought for a few minutes and sent a note to Charan explaining the situation and asking for his guidance.

The rest of the day was full of meetings and it went by quickly. The next thing I knew, I looked out of the window and it was dark outside. The sun had set and I was in the middle of my eighth meeting of the day. After everyone was gone, I called Mike and told him about the Innovation Pod and my conversation with Sam.

Mike suggested that I bring up the issue of overworked Pod teams at the next SLT meeting. He assured me that it'd be resolved. He said that Sam had been under tremendous pressure and that it'd all be okay after our next quarterly results.

As I packed my things to go home, I heard my phone buzz. It was a text from Charan. It said *Service blueprint.* Nothing more.

What in the world is a service blueprint? I was sure if I were to call Charan to tell me more about it, he would say, "Neo, you are smart enough to figure it out by yourself."

I sent a note to my team to look into service blueprints and asked them to join me for lunch the next day.

LEARNING THE ROPES

That night was a personal crash course for me on service blueprints. I realized I had implemented bits and pieces of a service blueprint at Digi Gate already.

A service blueprint is a tool used to analyze the current state or to define a future state by visualizing the relationship between people, processes and physical and digital touchpoints tied to a specific customer journey. It functioned as both a communication tool and a collective empathy tool. It was a communication tool because it aligned the interdependent functions by clearly defining what each one of them is expected to do. It was a collective empathy tool because a service blueprint helps teams understand how the customer sees or experiences a product or service.

The next morning, I had my EA order lunch for our meeting. As the clock struck 12:30 pm Lisa, Stacy and the Pod team walked into my office.

"Good afternoon, team. I think we've found a breakthrough for our issues," I said with excitement. Over the next thirty minutes, I went through everything.

"So, a service blueprint is like a simple process flow diagram created from a customer perspective?" asked Stacy.

"That's right."

Lisa went on. "And the process flow defines the specific actions performed by the customer as they go through the journey and how we orchestrate our efforts to deliver the experience, right?"

"Yeah. Every single effort that is relevant—directly or indirectly, visible or invisible—to delivering a delightful experience to the customer will be detailed in the service blueprint," I added.

I went to the whiteboard and started drawing.

Physical
evidence

Customer
actions

Front stage
actions

Back stage
actions

Support
systems &
processes

Tech

Staff

Tech

Process

Line of interaction

Line of visibility

Line of internal interaction

"Let's create a service blueprint. We'll use an example from outside our business so that we can think freely." I thought for a moment and said, "During the pandemic, a new feature was launched by an eCommerce app to alleviate pandemic fears. Let's look at that." I wrote *Visibility of a service person's temperature or vaccination status.*

"First, let's focus on the actions a customer would take to check the temperature or vaccine status of a person coming to provide in-home services, like plumbing or installing a new appliance. Can anyone tell me the flow of customer actions?" I asked.

The Pod Lead went first but with a bit of skepticism. "First of all, if it's a new service, customers need to be aware of the service. Maybe customers saw a banner ad on the homepage of the app?"

"Great."

Stacy added, "After the service person is assigned with the task, relevant details of the service person will be updated on the My Service Orders page of the app where the customer tracks their work orders. Details such as name, temperature and history of temperature or vaccination status may be provided."

"Perfect. Let's put that on the whiteboard."

"Now, let's talk about front stage and backstage actions. We need to talk about actors or teams from different interdependent functions. What actions are critical to delivering a seamless experience every time the customer goes through the journey? Anyone?" I asked.

"The website or app should be updated with content and ads announcing the availability of service personnel's health details. These are front stage actions that must be driven by the Mobile App Developer. The text and creative for the banner ads are…backstage actions driven by the Creative Team?" shared Lisa with hesitance.

"Right on." I encouraged Lisa.

Stacy went next. "Perhaps service personnel are given a wearable that sends live temperature data? And they are expected to wear the wearable while on duty?"

"I like the idea. What team or function should be involved in this?" I asked.

Physical evidence	Website or app	Website or app	Website or app	Website or app	Website or app
Customer actions	Learns about safe service delivery	Places a service order	Goes to My Service orders to track	Views service provider details with a green tick	Taps on the pic & sees live temperature & history

Line of interaction

Front stage actions Tech Staff

Line of visibility

Back stage actions

Line of internal interaction

Support systems & processes Tech Process

"The IT Infrastructure Team to configure the wearable and send the data to the cloud, the Service Provider Management team to set expectations with the service personnel and the Commercial Team to buy wearables," added the Full-stack Developer.

"Remember, we involve only the critical functions for a service blueprint. In this case, the Commercial Team will be a task-taker," I clarified.

"What could the backstage actions be?" asked Lisa.

"Hmm. Let's see… I bet the Operations team would need to get the wearables to each service person," added the Business Designer.

Lisa jumped in. "If the service person is vaccinated or if they get boosters, vaccination status should be added. Integration with a vaccination status database and the eCommerce app is the backstage action."

"Great." I added the details to the whiteboard.

"Perhaps, service personnel training? If the service people are doing what they are expected to do, I'd think the details of temperature should *automatically* go to the cloud and update the website or app," said the Pod Lead.

"Who would do the training?" Lisa asked.

"I guess the Service Provider Management team," answered the Pod Lead.

I updated the front stage and backstage actions on the whiteboard. I felt confident that the people in the room were getting a hang of the service blueprint.

"Okay, we also have to detail the systems or processes that are critical to delivering the features. What would those be?" I asked.

Lisa weighed in. "As for systems, eCommerce systems and modules like My Service Orders and the Service Personnel page. APIs for wearables to get access to the real time feed of service personnel's temperatures and one more—the vaccination database."

"As for processes, I guess the agile approach to deliver the tech," shared the Business Designer.

Stacy highlighted, "Operations staff and service personnel Standard Operating Procedures (SOP) are required as well."

The Pod Lead closed the discussion with the creative design and approval process. I updated the whiteboard to complete the service blueprint for

Physical evidence	Website or app	Website or app	Website or app	Website or app	Website or app
Customer actions	Learns about safe service delivery	Places a service order	Goes to My Service orders to track	Views service provider details with a green tick	Taps on the pic & sees live temperature & history
Line of interaction					
Front stage actions — Tech	Website/app updated with banner ads	Not relevant	Not relevant	Website/app updated with service provider's details & health status	Website/app updated with service provider's temperature & history
Staff					Service provider continues to wear the wearable
Line of visibility					
Back stage actions	Creative & copy for the ads			Creative & page designs for health status. Operations team provides wearable sensor to service providers	Creative & page designs for health status
Line of internal interaction					
Support systems & processes — Tech / Process					

providing visibility of service personnel's temperature and vaccination status.

"That wasn't as complicated as it sounded. We could do this for each one of our initiatives," said Lisa, staring at the whiteboard. The rest of the team agreed.

"Yeah," I said. "We have implemented some of these elements already. But we haven't been as structured and stitched together compared to a service blueprint. We need the Pod team and the interdependent functions to come together to collaboratively define the service blueprint for each digital initiative—and it's the Pod Lead who must drive it."

I paused to let it all sink in.

"Guys, this is it. We have what we're looking for. If a service blueprint is created collaboratively, we will have set a solid foundation for the digital initiative. And we will shift the focus to what matters the most—customer experience. We will see the gaps we need to address so we can deliver the future state experience. And most importantly, we will gain alignment with the interdependent functions."

There was a great sense of relief among the team, except for the Pod Lead.

I looked at the Pod Lead and asked, "What do you think?"

"It's great. But I was wondering what will happen with the gaps we identified. Will they be translated into work streams that must be delivered through the Innovation Pods?" asked the Pod Lead.

"Exactly. You hit the nail on its head. Don't forget that we deliver the future state experience in collaboration with the interdependent functions. The Pod Lead chalks out a weekly plan and conducts a daily standup with the team to discuss three topics: what was done yesterday, what is the plan for today and any blockers that might hinder progress. This helps the Pod Lead to monitor progress and address roadblocks, if any, before it's too late."

I could see little light bulbs glowing over the heads of my team. It was comforting to see that we had a way forward. "Now, let's get into real action with one of our initiatives. I will be actively involved this time around. I'm going to teach you a five-step Digital Innovation approach that includes a

Physical evidence	Website or app	Website or app	Website or app	Website or app	Website or app
Customer actions	Learns about safe service delivery	Places a service order	Goes to My Service orders to track	Views service provider details with a green tick	Taps on the pic & sees live temperature & history
Front stage actions — Tech	Website/app updated with banner ads	Not relevant	Not relevant	Website/app updated with service provider's details & health status	Website/app updated with service provider's temperature & history
Front stage actions — Staff					Service provider continues to wear the wearable
Line of interaction					
Back stage actions	Creative & copy for the ads			Creative & page designs for health status / Operations team provides wearable sensor to service providers	Creative & page designs for health status
Line of visibility					
Support systems & processes — Tech	eCommerce system		My Service orders module in core system	Service provider module in core system	Wearables integration for auto update
Support systems & processes — Process	Creative review process	Agile dev process	Operations & Service provider SOPs	Creative review process	Agile dev process
Line of internal interaction					

technique called 'Cover Stories'—where we start with an end vision for the customer and work backwards to make that vision a reality."

The team was intrigued and excited. For the next thirty minutes, we worked to identify the right digital initiative and the team for the Innovation Pod. We decided to solve *Unavailability of fresh towels*, assuming that Tim and Stan both agreed it was a real problem to solve. I had a hunch that it was indeed a real problem. It must be denting sales and therefore sales incentives.

We decided that Stacy would lead the Pod and Lisa would be the Business Designer. I felt that with a strong team leading the Pod and supported by Full-stack Developers and a Visual Designer, we would surely deliver results at speed. This time, I wanted to hear nothing but positive feedback from Sam.

SOLVING FOR FRESH TOWELS

Lisa, Stacy, and I took care of the pre-work—we wanted everything to be tightly controlled. I braced for what I was sure would be a bit of friction, if not fireworks.

Lisa appeared concerned. She said, "Hey Neo…it might be hard dragging me to work tomorrow."

"Oh, come on! What's worrying you now?"

"It's hard to believe that lack of fresh towels is really negatively impacting our sales. And yet Tim highlighted it as a major concern? And on top of that, improving towel management means we must collaborate with Stan, and he is…"

"Incredibly arrogant?" Stacy winked.

Lisa nodded.

I said, "I think you need to leave your doubts behind and listen to Tim with an open mind. Getting the head of sales on our side is critical. And if we can also figure out how to save money in Operations and maybe make Stan's life easier, why would he push back? In fact, he'd love us."

Lisa didn't seem completely at ease. She was probably uncomfortable with the political aspect.

I continued. "One thing I want us to be very clear on is that we're not here to convince anyone. You always said, we have to focus on the customer and how we can work together to deliver a delightful experience. Just be customer obsessed."

"Yeah, you're right."

"Moreover, you are going to learn how to use cover stories—you've got to be looking forward to that. Right?" I asked.

"Of course I am." She smiled and got back to her pre-work.

The next day, I kicked off the meeting with my team, Tim, Stan and one of Stan's team members, Nicholas. Nicholas was the Operations Manager responsible for towels.

"Okay," I began. "We discussed during the workshop that unavailability of fresh towels is one of our prioritized initiatives. We need to—"

Nicholas was astonished. "Wait a minute. You guys had a workshop on digital-first initiatives and you picked *towels* as an issue? You've got to be kidding me!"

That was harsh. I looked at Tim and asked him to share the data he had dug up, that went beyond customer complaints.

Tim pulled out printouts with numbers and handed them around. He looked directly at Stan when he spoke. "Look, guys—the situation is bad and we've got to solve it before it becomes worse. 20% of our revenue at health clubs is from premium subscribers. Fresh towels are one of the driving factors for whether our customers keep their premium membership. Since this issue arose, we've been losing premium customers a lot more."

In the short time I had been at Fitness First, I'd learned that Tim was a numbers guy. His statements were always backed with solid data. He knew his business from top to bottom and it was probably one of the reasons he always delivered the sales targets.

Stan went first. "How much lost sales are we talking about?"

"$140 million per year," said Tim, looking at Stan and Nicholas.

Stan and I were surprised. Nicholas' face turned red.

I jumped in. "Gentleman—we have a unique opportunity to use digital-first practices to solve this issue, *with speed*. We'll introduce our new approach, which will soon become the new way of doing transformation at Fitness First. All you have to do is follow along and contribute. You guys with us?"

Tim and Stan nodded in agreement.

"Great. Can we look at the current process for towel management?" I asked.

Nicholas walked to the whiteboard and wrote *Towel Management*. He drew the process flow visually and explained the steps. I was stunned to see that the entire process was highly manual and judgment based—from determining how many towels were required, when to replenish them, where to find soiled towels, to the laundry cycle. To top it off, the entire process wasn't standardized across all 400-plus health clubs.

I went to the whiteboard and drew a box in the upper right corner. "Okay. Let's get started with our new method for transformation. We have a five-step Digital Innovation approach. I'm going to write each step in this box and we will go through them one-by-one."

I wrote:

- *Frame the Challenge*
- *Know the Customer*
- *Ideate to Solve the Right Problems*
- *Envision a Cover Story*
- *Create a Service Blueprint*

I turned back to the group and looked at both Tim and Stan. "Some of these steps are going to feel familiar and some of them are going to be new. I'm asking everyone to keep an open mind as we go through the process. Can we all agree to that?"

Stan glanced at Tim, who was nodding eagerly. Stan muttered, "Yes, I'll keep an open mind. For now." Nicholas gave a thumbs up.

I grinned. Maybe we might get somewhere. "First step is to *Frame the challenge*. For that, let's put ourselves in the customer's shoes and explain the challenge from their perspective. Specifically, we should clarify who the customer is, what they're trying to do, why they're facing the issue, how they feel and what the outcome is."

Lisa thought for a moment before jumping in. "Premium subscribers (*who*) want to get fresh towels but many times end up with no fresh towels (*what*) because towel management has been manual and reactive (*why*). This makes our subscribers feel annoyed (*how they feel*) and less motivated to renew their subscription (*outcome*)."

"That's great. Do the rest of you agree with the challenge?" I asked.

"Yeah, that's a good summary," Tim added. Stan and Nicholas agreed.

"The second step of the Digital Innovation approach is *Know the customer*. We need to understand the customer's persona, demographics, and psychographics. Most importantly, the *context* of the customer and their needs," I explained.

In the next ten minutes, Tim projected a number of fancy slides and explained the details of the customer's persona, demographics, and psychographics. He also shared data analytics of the premium subscription business and insights generated from trends, including customer feedback.

After he explained the details and addressed questions, I shifted the focus to the most important area—the *context* of the customer and their needs. Context and challenge would provide a clear view of the customer's jobs-to-be-done. As Clayton Christensen, a famous Harvard Innovation professor, referred to in his book, *The Innovator's Solution*, "job" is shorthand for what a customer really seeks to accomplish in a given circumstance. Understanding a customer's jobs-to-be-done helps us design human-centric digital interventions.

"We must understand the context and circumstance of the customer as they experience our product or service. In this case, servicing the customer with towels. It helps us to empathize with the customer and experience the situation from their lens," I explained. "Anyone want to take a shot?"

Nicholas went first. "Usually, customers freshen up at the health club after a workout so they can continue their day without needing to go home. If towels aren't available, it disturbs their plans and that's annoying."

"Good start."

"If the customer is willing to pay extra for fresh towels," Tim added, "it's likely that they don't want the hassle of managing their own towels."

"Quite possible," I said.

Stan jumped in. "Some customers literally drench themselves with sweat while working out. They may feel embarrassed if they can't wipe the sweat off and they might just skip their workout if towels aren't available."

"Great points," I replied. "In fact, as part of the pre-work for this workshop, Tim helped my team connect with a few customers to better understand their context. We heard something similar from them." I asked Lisa to share additional insights.

Lisa projected her slides and said, "Customers care about hygiene. They use towels while working out and to clean the equipment after use. They expect others to do the same."

Stacy went next. "A few customers stated that the experience of picking up the towel is a bit annoying."

"What do you mean?" asked Nicholas.

"Half the time, the authentication mechanism for picking up towels doesn't work. Customers were asked to make a manual entry in the register," Stacy replied.

"Furthermore, customers often reported seeing that the bins for soiled towels were full while the bins for fresh towels were empty," added Lisa.

"Hmm…," Nicholas said. Stan was listening intently.

The contextual details of the customer painted a clear picture of their journey and how we were serving them.

"Now that we understand the customer's context, the third step of the Digital Innovation approach is to *Ideate to solve the right problems*," I shared.

"How do we know which problems to solve?" asked Tim.

Nicholas chimed in, "Would breaking down the towel management process help?"

"Yeah," I said. "Since the process is largely manual right now, breaking it down should help identify the process steps and problem areas." I tossed the marker to Nicholas.

Nicholas wrote 4 areas on the whiteboard.

Nicholas pointed to the fourth focus area. "Our laundry cycle times are the best-in-class range. We should spend our energy on the first three areas."

"Okay." I took a closer look at the remaining focus areas. "Is the collection of towels really the right problem to solve?" I asked.

"Yes," Nicholas clarified. "Our health clubs are massive; 40,000 square feet with 2 levels. Members leave towels everywhere. It requires two employees to walk around the health club collecting towels—more during rush hours. Despite looking around carefully, the Operations Team discovers towels during regular maintenance. In some cases, after a few weeks."

Estimate

Manual estimation of the number of fresh towels to stock

Initiate

Health club staff determines when to initiate replenishment

Collect

Manual collection of soiled towels from across the Health club

Launder

Cycle time – sort, repair, launder, fold and replenish

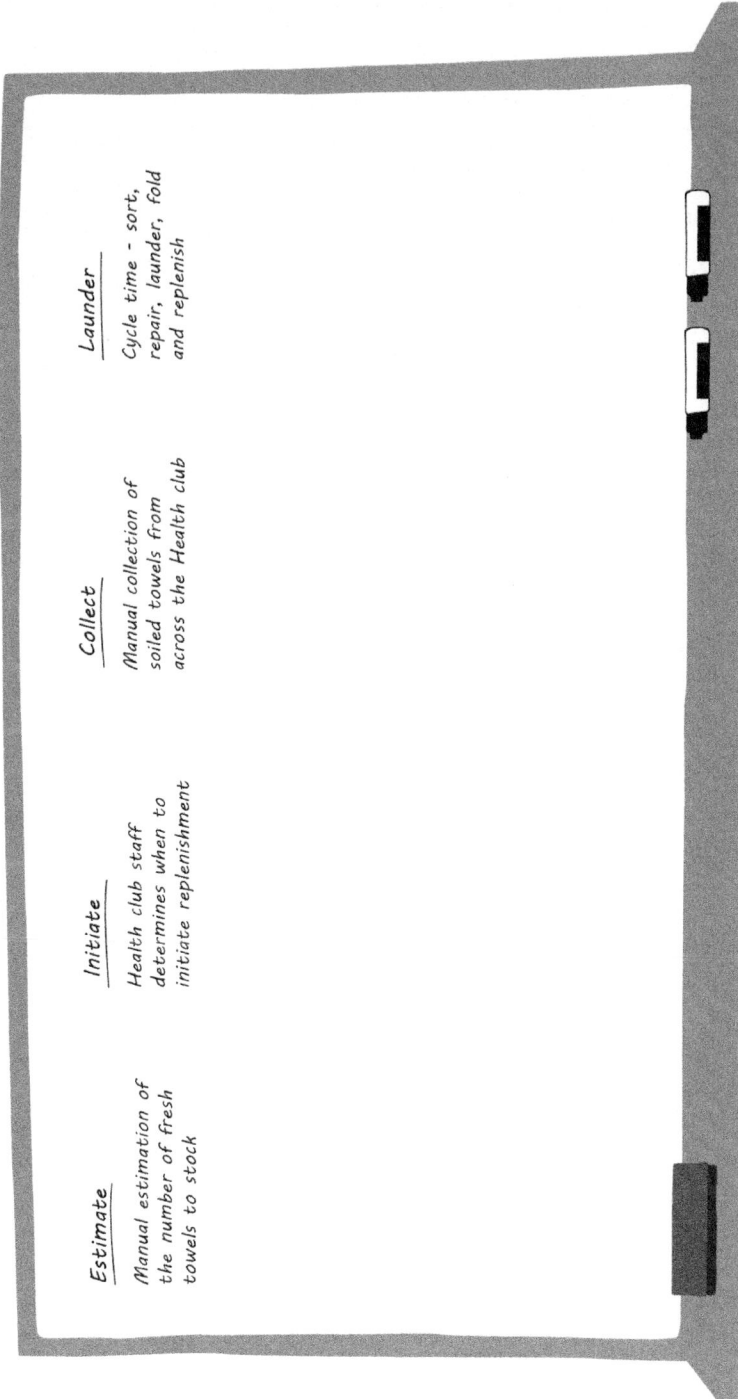

Towel management – Focus areas

"And those towels can't be used anymore?" asked Stacy.

"Sometimes."

"Okay," I said and introduced a new concept to get to the right problems. "We have a few opportunities to bring in digital and streamline the process but before we do that, let's define HMW questions."

"A *What* question?" asked Stan.

"Let me explain. HMW stands for *How Might We*. These questions force us to look for opportunities in challenges instead of getting bogged down by problems. It forces us to think about how we can deliver a future state outcome by looking at the 'Art of the Possible' with digital."

"Are there any guidelines?" Lisa wanted to know.

"Yeah." I went to the whiteboard and wrote the guidelines.

- Start with the problem areas or insights uncovered
- Focus your How Might We (HMW) questions on the expected outcome
- Never state the solution in the HMW question
- Keep your HMWs narrow enough to know where to start yet broad enough to give room to explore wild ideas

"Let's pick the first problem area," I said, looking at Lisa.

She thought deeply. "Well…our expected outcome is that no premium customer should ever be denied a fresh towel."

"Good. Go on. Construct a How Might We that is narrow, yet broad enough to get interesting ideas."

"Okay.…How Might We estimate the right number of fresh towels needed at all times so that no premium customer is ever denied one?" she said.

"Let's see. Since you mentioned '*estimating the right number,*' I don't think the question is too narrow, as we know where to start. It's broad enough since you want a solution that'd work *at all times*," I said.

We spent the next fifteen minutes defining the remaining two HMW questions. Nicholas enthusiastically took the lead. [*If the questions are complex or critical, a Rapid Innovation Sprint can be activated. Details regarding Rapid Innovation Sprints are covered in Part Five*]

Estimate

Manual estimation of the number of fresh towels to stock

HMW estimate the right number of fresh towels needed at all times so that no premium customer is ever denied a fresh towel?

Initiate

Health club staff determines when to initiate replenishment

HMW kick off the replenishment at the right time so that towels are always available?

Collect

Manual collection of soiled towels from across the Health club

HMW efficiently find soiled towels in the Health club so that the collection process is streamlined?

Launder

Cycle time - sort, repair, launder, fold and replenish

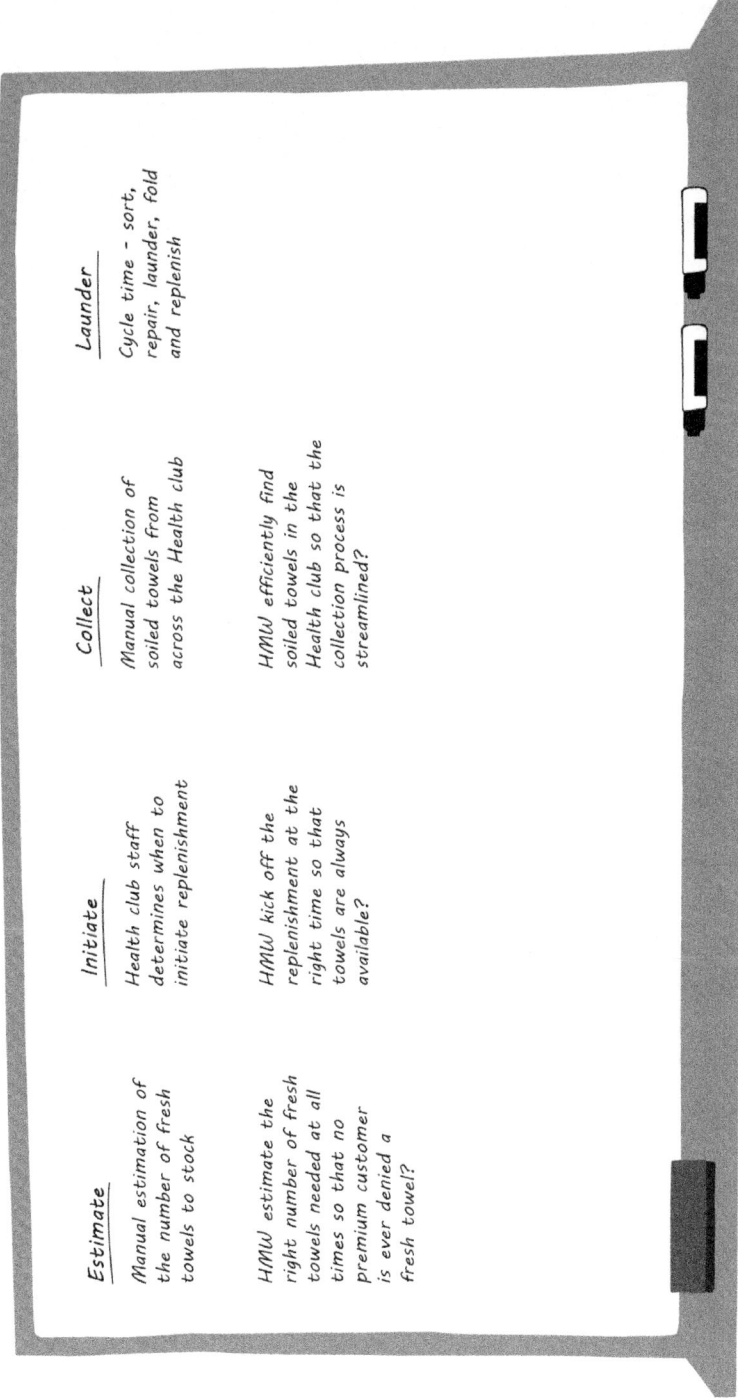

Towel management – HMWs aligned to the problem areas

"We've made great progress so far. Let's take a thirty-minute break. The next session will be exciting—we will ideate solutions for the How Might We questions," I said.

During the break, Stan and I discussed the Innovation Pod and how it would drive the initiative to fruition. Hearing me emphasize the importance of having dedicated full-time teams, he spoke to Nicholas and identified additional staff members from the Operations Team to join us for ideation and to become a part of the Pod. I was impressed at how seriously Stan was taking the process.

After ten minutes, the additional people from the Operations team arrived. I asked Lisa to bring them up to speed with the details of HMWs and what we were up to.

As the team settled in after the break, I pointed at the whiteboard and the list of steps for the Digital Innovation approach. "We are in the third step: *Ideate to solve the right problems.* The fourth step is to *Envision a cover story* and the last step is to *Create a service blueprint.*"

Before anyone could ask a question, I added, "I know half of you don't know what I'm talking about, so just follow along. I'm going to divide you into two teams."

I formed two teams, one led by Tim and the other by Stan. Then I introduced "What If" statements for ideating solutions.

"Now that we have the right problems to solve in the form of How Might We questions, we will focus on ideation using a technique called 'What If statements.'" I explained the concept. "'What If' statements help us define the future state that elegantly addresses the How Might We question. When we define the future state, we tap into our digital mindset and identify opportunities to bring digital to bear."

"Are there guidelines for these, as well?" asked Stacy.

"Yeah. The quality of 'What If' statements goes up when we follow a set of guidelines," I clarified.

I went to the whiteboard and added the details. "When you're stuck, ask yourself these seven questions. It will push you to think further."

GUIDELINES

1. Defer judgment. Because there is no right or wrong answer

2. Go for quantity over quality. More the merrier

3. Look beyond the obvious and consider possibilities. Push beyond the boundaries

4. Have a healthy disregard for the impossible

QUESTIONS TO ASK WHEN YOU ARE STUCK

1. How would a startup solve this?

2. How would a Digital Giant solve this?

3. Have you seen this problem addressed in any other industry? How did they solve it?

4. How would you solve this if you had extremely constrained resources?

5. How would you solve this if you had unlimited resources?

6. How would you solve this problem with zero human touch?

7. What is the most ridiculous way to solve this problem?

Guidelines and Questions

"The guidelines and questions will force you to look at the 'Art of the Possible' with digital and define a digital future, without getting bogged down in execution challenges," I added.

After explaining the guidelines, I asked the team to spend ten minutes working silently to come up with "What If" statements for each HMW question. After that, I asked them to deliberate with their teams for fifteen minutes to evaluate the "What If" statements, refine the statements as a team and prioritize them. After that, we worked as a group to finalize the "What If" statements.

How Might We estimate the right number of fresh towels needed at all times so that no premium customer is ever denied a fresh towel?

After ten minutes of silent ideation and fifteen minutes of discussion at the team level, both teams were ready to share. Ideas like mathematical modeling for estimating and predicting the number of towels were presented. However, Nicholas knew that any mathematical model would work only when we had data, which was not the case in all health clubs.

Nicholas said, "Let's just stock 10% more towels than the number of members attending the health club at any given time slot." He wanted to convince the team to go with an easier solution.

The Operations Manager jumped in. "That would lead to inefficiencies and additional cost. First, member numbers spike during rush hours. It would mean overstocking during off-peak times. Second, I ran the cost for purchase and maintenance per towel recently. If we overstock, we'll need to shell out more."

Tim asked Nicholas a pointed question. "What's the problem with going with the mathematical model?"

"Well, for one, data availability and data quality," said Nicholas.

"What about it, Nicholas? We have a lot of data," said Stan curtly.

"We need *quality data* to build the model," Nicholas emphasized.

"Like what kind?"

"Member footfall during different times and the number of members who would use towels," said Nicholas. "It's worth noting that even non-premium members can rent a towel."

Stan looked thoughtful. "And we would need to tie member traffic data to our laundry cycle times in order to replenish towels."

"We need historical data to predict these. But while the cycle time data is available at most health clubs, it may not be consistent," said Nicholas.

Stan rolled his eyes. "What do you mean by not consistent?"

"We don't have a common taxonomy for the cycle time data because we've been using the data to generate the metric, not for connection to anything else. So, the data labels and formatting are different at different health clubs. Some use spreadsheets and some are using legacy software for towel management."

Tim had been watching quietly as the Operations people debated back and forth. "We just opened Pandora's box. Didn't we?" Tim said with mild sarcasm.

Stan was fuming with anger. He clearly didn't appreciate how the discussion highlighted a problem in his Operations department.

Just when it was about to get dramatic, Stacy came to our rescue. "So, we have data at most health clubs...right?"

Nicholas nodded.

"In that case, we might have a solution." Stacy paused. "We just need to create a data lake where we can map data from different sources and normalize it to make it consistent. We can then extract data from the data lake."

"Can it be done quickly?" I asked.

"It's a bit complex but it's a solvable problem." Stacy gave us all hope.

We summed it all up and wrote the "What if" statement.

What if we build a Predictive Model that uses advanced Machine Learning techniques to estimate the right number of towels needed at all times?

We moved on to the next HMW.

> ### How Might We kick off the replenishment of towels at the right time so that towels are always available?

We followed the same drill—ten minutes of silent ideation, followed by fifteen minutes of deliberation within the team. Both teams worked intensely to arrive at a consensus.

Tim stood up to present. He and his team were enthusiastic to share their "What if" statements.

"Go ahead, Tim," I said.

"One idea we discussed was using a proximity sensor to solve our towel problem. The sensors placed in the bins notify the operations staff when it's time to initiate the laundry cycle."

Stacy chimed in. "We also talked about the need to experiment to get it right."

I smiled. "So, you're using IoT and artificial intelligence to solve the problem. Great! What about you and your team, Stan? What's your 'What if' statement?"

Stan, not willing to be outdone by Tim, also stood. "Well, we took inspiration from Waze—our members will help notify us when towels reach a predefined mark."

"Why would members be motivated to inform us?" asked Lisa.

Nicholas replied, "Each health club is a community of like-minded fitness enthusiasts. Through gamification, we create a sense of belonging. When a member sees a 'notify us' mark on the towel bin, which will be painted halfway down, they inform us through the app. By doing that, members can earn reward points that can be redeemed later for 1-on-1 classes, etc. We can have a leader board to inspire others."

Stacy asked, "All that will be through the Fitness First app?"

Stan nodded. "Yeah, that's the idea."

Stacy shared a glance with Lisa. "You know, it'd take a lot of time and effort to bring gamification into the Fitness First app. We don't have that luxury right now." She looked at me, inquiringly. "Or do we?"

I pivoted the idea. "What if we built something similar for the Operations Team? It's the Operations Team who has to initiate the laundry cycle. Let's center our focus on improving the productivity of the Operations Team. We could create a solution that does four things. One, show the availability of towels. Two, inform the team when to replenish them. Three, initiate the replenishment cycle. And four, notify when towels are ready for stocking up. We can layer up gamification elements at later stages. We'll leverage low-code/no-code solutions to build it fast. The focus must be on usability, not on making the app look classy."

I looked at Lisa and Stacy, who seemed concerned. "Let's take this idea offline with Neel. I feel confident that we can find a faster way to solve this using available off-the-shelf app building tools."

Stacy nodded.

I went to the whiteboard and wrote the "What if" statement that remixed both the team's "What if" statements.

What if we have sensors in each towel cabin and set thresholds to notify health club staff to initiate the laundry cycle?

"Let's solve the third and final How Might We."

How Might We efficiently find soiled towels in the health club so that the collection process is streamlined?

The teams followed the same drill. After silent ideation and team discussion, Stan's team wanted to go first. But this time, it appeared that there was a lack of consensus among the team.

Stan said, "We discussed tagging each towel with an RFID and using a scanner to identify towels so the Operations Team can collect them fast." An RFID is a chip that uses a radio frequency to identify itself or the object it is attached to.

Lisa probed, "How many towels are we talking about here?"

Nicholas clarified, "8000 per health club, give or take a few hundred."

"And the cost of each towel would be around $3 to $5, right?" asked Lisa. Nicholas confirmed.

"What's the cost of one RFID?" I asked.

"Around $2, including sewing it into the towel. If we buy in bulk, we might get them for less than a dollar," said Stan.

Nicholas did the math. "The cost of a towel is around $3. It needs to be replaced every three months. We cannot spend $2 to tag the towel with an RFID. It will increase the overall cost of each towel too much."

"Yeah, the idea is commendable but the solution isn't viable unless we can figure out how to make the costs work," I said.

Tim went next to share his team's "What If" statement. "We took inspiration from the sensor-based solution. We want to have a smart towel collection bin placed at different strategic points in the health club. They'd look attractive and noticeable. When a member drops a towel in, the bin would be programmed to clap and say, 'Thank you.'"

"A proximity sensor would notify the Operations Team when the smart bin is full," added Lisa.

We deliberated further on how to conceptualize a smart bin for soiled towels. Tim took the marker and wrote on the whiteboard.

What if we create a smart soiled bin to inspire members to drop in soiled towels and to notify the ops team when the bin is full?

Looking at the whiteboard, we felt a sense of accomplishment. We decided to take a break and regroup after fifteen minutes. As the team walked in after the break, I wrote *Cover stories* on the whiteboard.

I said, "The fourth step is to *Create a cover story*. It's just like a cover story of a magazine."

"Like what you see on Fortune?" asked Tim.

"That's right. Let's hear from you guys. What would be the typical contents of a cover story?"

Lisa went first. "A headline written in plain simple English?"

"Right. And not just the headline—the whole cover story should be in plain simple English," I responded.

"Details of whatever accomplishment is worthy of a cover story?" said Stan.

"That's right! A cover story must include details of the problem and how the solution elegantly solves that problem."

Tim went next. "A quote from an interviewee. Something that gets the reader excited."

Estimate	Initiate	Collect	Launder
Manual estimation of the number of fresh towels to stock	Health club staff determines when to initiate replenishment	Manual collection of soiled towels from across the Health club	Cycle time - sort, repair, launder, fold and replenish
HMW estimate the right number of fresh towels needed at all times so that no Premium customer is ever denied a fresh towel?	HMW kick off the replenishment at the right time so that towels are always available?	HMW efficiently find soiled towels in the Health club so that the collection process is streamlined?	
What if we build a Predictive Model that uses advanced Machine Learning techniques to estimate the right number of towels needed at all times?	What if we have sensors in each Towel cabin and set thresholds to notify Health club staff to initiate the laundry cycle?	What if we create a smart soiled bin to inspire members to drop soiled towels and to notify the Ops team when the bin is full?	

What if statements mapped to HMWs

Title

Short compelling description [update at the end]

Date of Launch
A future date when the initiative shall be launched

Innovation Pod Team
List the Pod team with the right composition

Focus area
Business Building/Reinventing the Core/Time to Market

Business Vertical
Name of the Business Vertical

Summary

Elevator pitch of the Cover story, assuming no one reads past here.

Opportunity/Problem Statement

Describe the opportunity & problem for the customers or internal stakeholders that your solution or tool is likely to address. Describe each problem briefly and talk about the impact and how painful it has been for the customers or internal stakeholders. Use data to describe the impact of the problem or opportunity.

Solution/Idea details

Describe how your solution or tool elegantly solves the problem. Give a brief overview of how it works, and then talk through how it solves each problem you listed above. Go into sufficient detail to give confidence that your solution actually solves the problem.

Customer quote "

Create a fake quote by a customer or stakeholder of your solution, but one that sounds like it could be real. The customer should describe her pain point or the goal she needs to accomplish, and then how the tool you launched enables her to do so.

Metrics to track for progress

Measures under Business Building/Reinventing the Core/Time to Market

Optional

Potential annualized benefits
Approx. annual savings/benefits

Timeline
Approx. timeline to complete initiative

Investments required
Approx. Amount to be invested

Digital technology required
Tentative details of digital technology required for project execution

Cover story template

"Right on. In our cover story, we must have a quote from the customer. This can be an external customer or an internal customer. I hope you know who the internal customer is?" I wanted to know.

"I guess the Operations Team would be the internal customer for our smart soiled bin, right?" asked Nicholas.

"That's right. In addition, we'll have mockups wherever required and a Q&A to clarify the most frequently asked questions."

I projected the cover story template and summarized: "A cover story must effectively convey the Desirability, Feasibility and Viability of the idea. The cover story will be written with a future date, for when our success has been realized. It must have a clear headline. It conveys Desirability by clearly describing the problem, why it is important to solve, and how the customer experience will improve. It must state with clarity how the solution elegantly solves the problem with digital and include a hypothetical quote from a satisfied customer. Feasibility is described through the assessment of what technology will be required and describing the operational aspects, where necessary. It must have mockups, wireframes or prototypes of the future state experience along with a Q&A to provide additional details of the digital intervention. Lastly, Viability is articulated by providing investments required and measurable results, including financial, operating, or market share.

"Who writes the cover stories?" asked Stan.

"For now, Stacy and Lisa will write the first draft. We'll regroup in a few days to review and refine it as a team. After that, we'll have a few customers review the cover story. We will then refine it to include customer feedback," I answered.

The team looked physically exhausted but mentally energized. A break would let the lessons sink in.

PRESENTING THE COVER STORY

As I stepped into the office a few days later, I got a text from my EA saying that we would be meeting in the boardroom to review the cover story. *Why the boardroom?* As I walked in, I was startled to see senior leaders from the Health Club Business Team and from the enabling functions. I was even more surprised to see Mike.

Mike came over to greet me and got right to the point. "Okay, we'll have your team present your work from the front of the room. You've got thirty minutes."

"To do what, Mike?" I asked. "What are you even doing here?"

"We're all here to hear about the steps you guys implemented early this week, especially the cover stories."

I was confused. "And what's the goal here?"

He gave me a puzzled look, as if I were a fool about to reject a great opportunity. "Neo, word spread that the steps you guys implemented are refreshing and effective in bringing multiple teams together for a common goal. You want to embed digital-first practices within Fitness First, right?"

"But Mike, you've got to have a hands-on experience to appreciate the five-step Digital Innovation approach."

Mike thought for a moment. "I get it. Just introduce the five steps and give a primer to the cover story you guys created. Keep it to the point," he concluded.

At that moment, Sam entered the room and took a seat at the head of the table, where the Chairman usually sat. My mind was spinning but I had to pull myself together because at that point Mike turned to the executives sitting around the table and announced, "Neo is going to introduce the five-step Digital Innovation approach and give a primer on the cover story they created for one of the digital initiatives."

I was smiling but inside I was thinking *this is crazy.* It's an understatement to say that I was nervous. I turned to the whiteboard to write the five steps—and then it hit me.

Show it. Don't tell.

I decided that it'd be wise to *begin with the end in mind* by giving a preview of the cover story first and then talk about how we got there. I asked Lisa to project the cover story and get printouts. And then I dove in.

"Okay. Some of you know that we formed an Innovation Pod—it's like a SWAT team—to solve an operations problem that costs us $140 million in annual sales for our health clubs business." Sam looked intrigued by the sales number and the potential to increase the topline. "We took a new approach to solve this issue. We have not implemented any solution yet but we are off to a great digital-first start."

Lisa distributed the printouts of the cover story, mockups, and Q&A. "To set the context," Lisa said, "a cover story was written with a future date in mind where our success has been realized. It's a unique innovation technique where we define a future state *with the human in mind* and work backwards to make it a reality."

As the leaders scanned through the printouts, I said, "I'd like each of you to spend ten minutes silently reading the cover story." And then I sat down.

One of the executives had been skimming the papers and said, "About these sensors, do you really expect…"

"Sorry," I interrupted. "Let's hold all questions and comments for the next ten minutes. Please review the material in silence. This is an important part of the process."

Sam cleared her throat and everyone looked at her. She was staring at me from across the room. Then she very deliberately looked down at her papers and began to read. I breathed a sigh of relief.

Those ten minutes felt like defining moments for me. I was nervous—I could hear my heartbeat in my head pounding like a huge drum. I could hear everyone's heartbeat. No one was moving—everyone was reading the cover story.

After ten minutes, I said, "As you can see, we defined the digital interventions and a future state to address the operations problem."

"And this was done after intense discussion," added Stacy. "With this end goal and customer experience in mind, we made a plan to deliver the digital interventions."

"Why write a cover story?" asked a senior leader.

"It creates a shared vision of what matters most—*customer delight*. We start with the customer, see the world from their lens and solve their problems. It provides clarity of the end goal and accelerates the path to build," I answered.

Sam went next. "Who reviews and approves the cover stories?"

"I have yet to put a formal structure in place. For now, the core team, Tim, Stan, Susan and I will review and approve it."

Sam raised an eyebrow, looking unimpressed. Sensing her irritation, I shifted the focus to the five-step Digital Innovation approach. I went to the whiteboard and listed the steps.

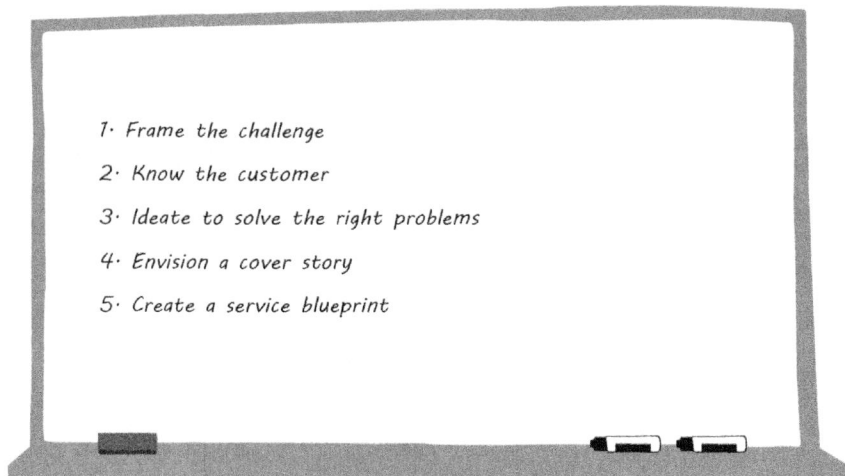

1. Frame the challenge

2. Know the customer

3. Ideate to solve the right problems

4. Envision a cover story

5. Create a service blueprint

Digital innovation approach

Over the next fifteen minutes I went through the details of the first four steps. I explained what we did in each step and showed the outcomes to provide context. Most of the people in the room listened intently and appeared intrigued.

"We are at step four right now. In step five, we will create a service blueprint—it's a process flow diagram detailing the future state experience from a customer perspective. It provides clarity to the relationships between people, functions, technology and processes."

"What happens after that?" asked Neel.

"The Innovation Pod drives the digital initiative to make the cover story a reality," I replied.

"Quite interesting," said Mike. He looked at Lisa, Stacy and me and said, "Thank you for walking us through the five-step approach." He turned to the leaders in the room. "Okay. I know thirty minutes isn't enough but I wanted you guys to get a primer of what will hopefully become the new normal at Fitness First. Stay tuned for more details from Neo as he plans to make it second nature for all of us."

As the leaders walked out of the room, a few came to us and asked how they could collaborate to implement the five-step approach on some of their initiatives. It was quite encouraging for me and the team.

As the leaders left the board room, I wondered why Mike, a board member, was around so often. But whatever he was doing would likely help during the transformation, so I didn't care.

"Were you aware of this?" asked Tim, referring to the impromptu meeting with senior leaders.

I shook my head and smiled.

"Good show," he said.

"Yeah. Thanks to Lisa and Stacy." I gave a thumbs up to them. "Let's review the cover story, mockups and Q&A as a team and determine if we need to refine the details."

The working team reconvened.

Nicholas went first. "I have an issue with the metrics."

"What about it?" asked Stan.

"Savings of twenty hours per week seems quite aggressive," Nicholas replied.

Title

Fitness First launches smart solutions to better serve its Premium Members

Innovation Pod Team
Lisa, Stacy, Jim, Diane, Chad, Bryan

Date of Launch
01ˢᵗ Mar 2023

Business Vertical
Health Clubs

Focus area
Reinventing the Core Business

Summary

Premium members, who were once terminating their subscriptions due to the towels issue, are now referring their friends and family to join Fitness First. They are experiencing smart solutions for towels management at Health Clubs that ensure no premium member is ever denied a fresh towel. These are helping increase NPS and plug revenue leakage due to churn, to the tune of $ 140 M in subscription sales.

Opportunity/Problem Statement

Premium subscribers pay a fee every month to get access to fresh towels. However, many premium members complained about the unavailability of fresh towels. The experience of picking up towels is annoying because the authentication mechanism doesn't work half the time. Customer plans are disrupted if fresh towels are unavailable. Further, they feel towels help to maintain hygiene. These issues result in increased churn of premium subscribers, with a top line impact of $140 M.

Solution/Idea details

The towels management process is heavily manual, so we will bring three solutions. 1) A predictive model to predict the right number of towels based on members' needs; 2) A Smart towel bin to notify the Ops team via a productivity app for initiating laundry cycles at the right time; 3) A smart soiled bin to inspire members to drop the used towels and notify the Ops team when the bin is full. All these cumulatively ensure no premium member will ever be denied a fresh towel.

Customer quote “ I am a premium member at Fitness First. I never knew if a towel would be available when I arrived. I used to see full bins of soiled towels and empty bins of fresh towels most of the time. But now, it's different. Fitness First has created some great solutions for managing towels. I always have fresh towels now.

Metrics to track for progress

Reinventing the core — Top line impact — $140 M | Hours saved – 20 per week per Health Club | 5% improvement in NPS

Optional

Potential annualized benefits	Timeline	Investments required	Digital technology required
$140 M top line	$12.5 M worth of team hours repurposed	3 months for soft launch & 9 months for roll-out	$2 M	IoT based solutions; Advanced analytics & AI; Low code/no code-based productivity apps

Cover story for the unavailability of fresh towels

"What do you propose?" asked Stan.

Nicholas appeared to be doing mental math for a few moments. "Ten hours seems reasonable," he said.

We deliberated on what was reasonable and agreed to ten hours.

Tim went next. He suggested that we change the NPS improvement to 10%.

With these changes, the cover story, mockups, and Q&A were ready for customer feedback. We invited our internal Operations Team and external customers to review the materials. After getting their feedback, we refined the details and moved to the next step—creating a service blueprint.

I went to the whiteboard and created sections for the service blueprint. For the next hour we discussed, deliberated, and detailed the customer journey and created a service blueprint from a customer's perspective.

We identified four workstreams: (1) Smart towel dispensing bins, (2) A low-code/no-code app for the Operations Team, (3) Smart soiled bins, and (4) A predictive model. We kicked off the Innovation Pod.

The next ten weeks went by quickly, with a few pleasant surprises. The Innovation Pod got great support from the Health Club Business and enabling functions, thanks to Mike's impromptu session with the senior leaders. Our digital initiative gained popularity and garnered priority.

Our CTO Neel assigned a dedicated team, including a data scientist, a low-code/no-code expert and a technical expert on sensors. The Commercial Team expedited procurement. The Product Design Team helped design and embed the sensors in the smart soiled bin.

We progressed quickly toward a soft launch at ten health clubs. However, the month during the soft launch was a roller coaster ride with mixed results. We got pushback from two health clubs, who complained that the model did not predict accurately and there were still instances of stock out. One club reported that the model slowed them down—apparently, customers never complained about stock outs at these clubs. The rest of the seven clubs reported positive results.

Physical Evidence	Health club lobby	Health club lobby	Towel cabins	Health club	Soiled towels bin
Customer actions	Customer sees ad for Premium membership	Customer enrolls for membership	Customer picks towels	Customer uses towels	Customer returns towels in soiled bin
— Line of interaction —					
Front stage actions — Tech		Membership details updated	Low/no code app for Ops	Towel cabins with sensors	Smart soiled bin & towel cabin with sensors	Low/no code app
Front stage actions — Staff	Place ads	Assist customer with package & enroll	Check towels availability, wait time etc on the app	Notified about time to initiate laundry cycle	Place clear instructions to return towels	Notified to clear the bins and place fresh ones in the cabins
— Line of visibility —					
Back stage actions	Package details & pricing; Creative & copy for the ads (one time)			Collect soiled towels & initiate laundry cycle	Laundry cycle is started; Copy for instructions (one time)	Laundry cycle completed
— Line of internal interaction —					
Support systems & processes — Tech	Not relevant	Membership module, predictive model	Towel management - modules	Sensor data collection & processing	Algorithms & thresholds for notifications; Sensor data collection & processing	Algorithms & thresholds for notifications
Support systems & processes — Process	Creative review process		Towel estimation & notifying process		Towel replenishment process	

Service blueprint for the unavailability of fresh towels

Neel and the data scientist identified an additional problem with data labels as the root cause of inaccuracy at the two clubs experiencing stock out issues. The two clubs were still using spreadsheets and furthermore, staff members were sending different versions. After fixing the issue by standardizing the spreadsheet, the model was tested for two weeks, this time with better results.

After the soft launch, the Innovation Pod, Tim, Stan, Nicholas, and I regrouped to debrief and plan for roll-out.

"Not bad," said Tim.

"Not bad? It's a lot better than not bad," said Stan.

Tim smiled and nodded. He was excited about the results.

"We must be doing something right," said Nicholas, feeling relieved.

"Yeah. But it isn't enough," I muttered. "We've got 400 more health clubs." Their enthusiasm was justified but we had a long way to go.

"Yeah, right. That's when we'll see the needle move," said Tim.

Lisa chimed in. "I suggest an opt-in approach for scaling the model."

"What do you mean?" asked Nicholas.

"Not every health club is facing towel issues, right Tim?"

Tim nodded.

Lisa went on. "Let's not shake things up at health clubs that are doing fine. Let them opt-in if they want to."

"That makes sense," I said.

During the rest of the meeting, we discussed the roll-out plan and finalized high-level details. All of it seemed sound to me. I told Stan and Nicholas to proceed with full speed and keep us informed.

As I drove back home that day, I reflected on the past few months. I felt proud that I got things back under control. A few more digital initiatives and successes like this and I would be set. I could bring my family to the US. I called Tina to share my excitement.

"Hey."

"Hi…what's up?" she said shortly.

Tina hadn't been her usual self lately. She sounded formal, distant.

"Nothing much. Just wondering what you're doing," I said.

"The usual stuff."

"I have something to tell you," I said, excitement creeping into my voice.

"What is it about?"

"We just had our first success."

"Oh. Good for you."

"No actually, it's good for *us*." I paused. "I figured it all out. A few more successes like this and I should be set."

"Great," she said, a little muted. "That's good news."

"It's great news. It's just a matter of time now. Soon you can all come to the US."

No answer. Tina just looked at me over the video, her face still.

"Tina?" I asked, "What's wrong?"

"Neo, I told you before. Don't make promises you won't keep."

"What do you mean? I'm killing myself over here to make this work."

Her lip quivered. "Maybe this was a bad idea. I thought I could manage everything, but…"

This wasn't how I wanted the conversation to go. "Tina, I have to work. And it was your idea that I take this job."

"I don't have a husband anymore. Riya doesn't have a father. Do you even love us?"

"What are you talking about? I'm doing everything for you, for our family. This is crazy."

"Your work is your family. Your career and work have always come first and everyone else gets whatever is left." She started to cry. "Don't forget—I gave up my career as well. I'm the one living in India while you are in my hometown."

"Tina…please stop."

She looked away from the phone as her crying continued.

"Look, I put the hours in because I have to, not because I want to," I tried to justify. "It'll all be fine soon. I promise things will get better."

Tina was quiet for a moment and then she choked out, "You said all that before. I can't trust you anymore. Here, talk to your daughter." She disappeared from the video.

"Tina!" I called after her. "Come back! Let's talk about this."

I heard Riya scream in the background. "Hi Daddy!"

I calmed my emotions and smiled at Riya. "Hey honey, you will be here soon. I promise."

"Yay! I'm going to the US! I just can't wait, Daddy."

"I can't wait to hold you in my arms, honey."

"We miss you Daddy," said Riya. "Mamma is sad."

"Can I talk to Mom?"

Riya glanced at Tina. "Mamma says she doesn't want to talk to you."

Long pause.

"Did you have a fight again?" asked Riya.

My eyes teared up.

"Mamma says she will talk to you later. I gotta go, Daddy. Bye."

Riya hung up before I could say bye. I tried calling back but there was no answer.

I needed to make things right with Tina. And I knew everything would be good again once I became the permanent Chief Digital Officer.

FOURTH DIGITAL-FIRST REALIZATION

Innovation Pods

Deploy small, autonomous teams composed of customer-obsessed intrapreneurs to deliver digital initiatives.

An Innovation Pod is a small, autonomous team that is on a mission to make cover stories a reality. They set priorities, experiment rapidly, learn, fail and pivot as needed to deliver the future state experience. Key benefits of self-reliant and self-directed teams include fostering ownership, increasing the velocity of decision-making, and improving the ability to deliver initiatives rapidly.

Each Pod will have a Product Manager who plays the role of a Pod Lead, Business Designers who understand business needs and conceptualize the solution, Visual Designers to bring concepts to life on a digital canvas and Full-stack Developers to develop the solution and go-live. In addition, representatives from the business are added based on the cover story. For example, if the cover story is to increase oil production with predictive analytics in Reservoir Management, a Reservoir Engineer is required in the Pod.

Each member of the Pod should demonstrate intrapreneurial skills—they should have an entrepreneurial mindset and be willing to take risks, break the status quo and look at the problem holistically. Furthermore, the team should have a digital mindset.

In digital-first transformations led by the business, each Innovation Pod is driven by the business, guided by the hub and championed by the whole umbrella of the organization. Business led transformation ensures financial resources are available, the Pod has access to the customer base, issues are rapidly resolved through a Management Committee and the Pod can leverage the best talent across the company. Innovation Pods must be ring fenced and empowered with the right tools, support and capabilities to focus on one cover story from inception to launch. Focusing sets the Innovation Pods up for success. [*The Management Committee and its constructs are discussed in detail in Part Five*]

Amazon is highly focused on just a few aspects of the customer experience. At a press conference after the announcement of Alexa devices, Jeff Bezos was asked what new technology he would be focusing on ten years from now. He said, "I always get the question of what's going to change in ten years. I almost never get the question: *What's not going to change in the next ten years?*"

Focusing on what matters most to customers in retail, he said, "I know that customers want low prices; they want convenience and fast delivery; they want vast selection. And I know that's going to be true ten years from now." These are also known as "customer promises."

He jokingly added, "It's impossible to imagine a future, ten years from now, where a customer comes up and says, *Jeff, I love Amazon; I just wish the prices were a little higher.* Or *I love Amazon; I just wish you'd deliver a little more slowly.* Impossible."

Amazon's priority has always been to invest in the most important elements of the customer experience and to remain focused over the long-term. When you have something that you know is true over the long-term, you can afford to put a lot of energy into it. Let's pick one customer promise—*customers want convenience and fast delivery*—and see how Amazon has continued to innovate on that promise.

Amazon started as an ecommerce retailer and later expanded into physical stores. The in-store buying experience is fraught with friction: no ratings of the products, no clarity on the total cost of products added to the physical cart and long checkout lines. These become even more apparent when you are used to buying online.

Through a game changing innovation called Amazon Go, customers can use the Amazon app to enter the store, take what they want from the selection of products after reviewing the ratings and go!

Amazon Go is powered by Just Walk Out Technology, which automatically detects when products are taken from or returned to the shelves and keeps track of them in a virtual cart. When the customer is done shopping, they can just leave the store. Shortly after, Amazon charges the customer's Amazon account and sends a receipt.

However, in this experience customers are expected to authenticate themselves with the Amazon Go app, for which they need to take their phone out.

Source: Shutterstock

Source: Shutterstock

To make it even more convenient for customers, it wouldn't be a surprise if Amazon integrates Amazon Go with another game changing innovation called Amazon One, a fast, convenient, contactless identity service that uses your palm—just hover to enter, identify, and pay.

All these innovations were made possible because of an autonomous approach to developing new products, grounded in what Amazon calls the "two-pizza team." "We try to create teams that are no larger than can be fed by two pizzas," said Bezos. "We call that the two-pizza team rule."

The two-pizza team is a small, decentralized team designed to foster autonomy and ownership. Amazon believes that the smaller the team, the better the communication and collaboration. Small, autonomous teams are self-directed and ensure speed and quality of iteration. They have a single threaded focus. This shifts their perspective, allowing them to look at digital interventions as an end-to-end experience. The teams have autonomy within their area but are supported by corporate frameworks and resources. It's like having tons of little startups powered by a behemoth.

FIFTH DIGITAL-FIRST REALIZATION

Digital Innovation Approach

Solve customer problems rapidly with the five-step Digital Innovation approach: 1) Frame the challenge 2) Know the customer 3) Ideate to solve the right problems 4) Envision a cover story 5) Create a service blueprint

The five-step Digital Innovation approach starts with the customer and solves their problems. A customer can be an external customer or an internal customer (i.e., an employee). This approach defines unmet and unarticulated needs, clarifies the right problems to solve, rigorously examines ideas, aligns interdependent functions, and fosters a shared vision for the future state experience. Customer-centric innovation and co-creation are at the core of the five-step Digital Innovation approach.

1. Frame the challenge

Put yourselves in the customer's shoes and explain the challenge from the customer's perspective. Specifically, clarify who the customer is, what they're trying to do, why they're facing the issue, how they feel and what their outcome is.

2. Know the customer

Understand the customer's persona, demographics, and psychographics. Most importantly, understand the *context* of the customer and their needs. This will provide a clear view of a customer's jobs-to-be-done and their unmet and unarticulated needs. "Job" is shorthand for what a customer really seeks to accomplish in a given circumstance. Contextual details of the customer paint a clear picture of the customer's journey and how customers are served.

3. Ideate to solve the right problems

There are two sub-steps.

A. Defining the right problems:

The first step is to define the problems in the form of HMW questions. HMW stands for How Might We. Problems defined in this form force us to look for opportunities and challenges instead of getting bogged down by problems. It's like forcing us to think about how we can deliver a future state outcome by looking at the "Art of the Possible" with digital. Below are the guidelines for writing HMW questions.

- Start with the problem area or insights uncovered
- Focus your HMWs on the expected outcome
- Never state the solution in the HMW question
- Keep your HMWs narrow enough to know where to start yet broad enough to give room to explore wild ideas

Once the list of HMW questions are defined, evaluate whether the HMW questions, if addressed, will solve the unmet and unarticulated needs of the customer. If the answer is yes, it is the right problem to solve.

B. Ideation:

"What if" statements help us come up with ideas to define the future state in a way that elegantly addresses the HMW question. When we define the future state, we tap into our digital mindset and identify opportunities to bring digital to bear. Below are guidelines for defining "'What if" statements.

- Defer judgment. There is no right or wrong answer
- Go for quantity over quality. The more the merrier
- Look beyond the obvious and consider unorthodox possibilities. Push beyond your boundaries
- Have a healthy disregard for the impossible

When you are stuck, ask yourself the following questions. These will push you to think beyond and generate new perspectives and ideas.

- How would a startup solve this?
- How would a digital giant solve this?
- Have you seen other industries address this problem? If so, how did they solve it?
- How would you solve this if you had extremely constrained resources?
- How would you solve this if you had unlimited resources?
- How would you solve this problem with zero human touch?
- What is the most ridiculous way to solve this problem?

These guidelines and questions force you to look at the "Art of the Possible" with digital and define a future state without getting bogged down with execution challenges.

If you are hard-pressed for time, a Rapid Innovation Sprint can be activated to create new concepts or to answer critical business questions through prototyping and testing the ideas with real customers. It's a 5-day rapid innovation process that involves business strategy, innovation, behavioral science, design and more.

Day 1: Frame the challenge, understand the customer, pick the most important areas to focus on and define the How Might We questions.

Day 2: Sketch competing ideas and solutions on paper.

Day 3: Make difficult decisions and turn ideas into testable hypotheses.

Day 4: Hammer out a realistic prototype.

Day 5: Test the prototypes with real customers and decide whether to tweak the concept or abandon it.

[*Rapid Innovation Sprints will be discussed in detail in Part Five*]

4. Envision a cover story

Prioritized "What If" statements or product concepts need to be articulated through cover stories. A cover story creates a shared vision of what matters most—*customer delight*. Start with the customer, see the world from their lens and solve their problems. A cover story provides clarity of the end goal and accelerates the path to build.

A cover story must effectively convey the Desirability, Feasibility and Viability of the idea. The cover story will be written with a future date, for when our success has been realized. It must have a clear headline. It conveys Desirability by clearly describing the problem, why it is important to solve, and how the customer experience will improve. It must state with clarity how the solution elegantly solves the problem with digital and include a hypothetical quote from a satisfied customer. Feasibility is described through the assessment of what technology will be required and describing the operational aspects, where necessary. It must have mockups, wireframes or prototypes of the future state experience along with a Q&A to provide additional details of the digital intervention. Lastly, Viability is articulated by providing investments required and measurable results, including financial, operating, or market share.

5. Create a service blueprint

After the cover story is approved, create a service blueprint. A service blueprint is a tool used to analyze the current state or to define a future state by visualizing the relationship between people, processes and physical and digital touch points tied to a specific customer journey.

It is both a method of communication and a collective empathy tool. It is a communication tool because it aligns the interdependent functions by clearly defining what each one of them is expected to do and brings them on the same page. A service blueprint is a collective empathy tool because it helps teams understand how the customer sees or experiences a product or service.

Every single effort that is relevant—directly or indirectly, visible or invisible—to delivering a delightful experience to the customer must be detailed in the service blueprint. Gaps between the current state and future state experiences are identified as workstreams and are created to address these gaps. These workstreams are led by the Innovation Pod and are delivered in collaboration with the interdependent functions.

Ideas to remember

- To get the most out of an Innovation Pod, make sure the team has sufficient bandwidth to lead an initiative. It's highly recommended to staff Pods with dedicated full-time resources.
- Identify interdependent functions or cross-functional teams that play a key role in the future state experience. Make them co-creators of the future state solution right from the get-go. Interdependent functions must have a clear, unified view of the customer journey across the organization and how the experience will be stitched together.

A good example of a company taking a customer-first approach and using the co-creation process is Yulu Bikes, a micro-mobility startup disrupting the last-mile commute in India. Yulu was launched by Amit Gupta in 2017 with a vision to provide the common Indian an affordable, accessible, and easy-to-handle commute solution, without needing to purchase a personal vehicle or to have a driver's license.

Yulu followed a customer-first approach and iteratively co-created its signature Yulu bikes: Yulu Move, Yulu Miracle and Yulu DEX. Yulu's in-house R&D team led the bike concept design in collaboration with customers and with cross-functional teams acting as co-creators. They kept in mind the urban needs of the customer, challenges like theft, vandalism, the condition of the roads and their goal to be sustainable yet affordable. Customers' feedback influenced the bike's no-nonsense design.

Yulu Move, Yulu Miracle and Yulu DEX

The target customer of Yulu is dynamic. While Yulu began by targeting white-collar customers, their target audience evolved over time to cover young adults, elder citizens, college goers and grey-collar workers. As their scope changed, customers with different personas were engaged during the co-creation process.

The process resulted in an ergonomic, unisex two-wheeler electric vehicle that is designed to be anti-theft, anti-vandalism and prone to low or no damage because of its sturdy materials and design. Users welcomed this commute solution but another challenge emerged—driving adoption of the new way of moving around.

Keeping in mind the customer's needs, Yulu established Yulu Zones near IT parks and bus and metro terminuses, which helped people adopt Yulu bikes for their last-mile commute. As demand increased, the zones were diversified to include colleges and similar locations. Not only did the cross-functional team make the entire

process of carrying out operations more efficient, they also contributed to the holistic development of the infrastructure while the bike
was being developed in parallel.

Yulu Zones

"A customer-first approach and co-creation process helped us understand customers as humans and their goals. In addition to designing
the bike ergonomically, the need for seamless pick-up and drop-off
points, maintenance and charging hubs became very evident. The technology to connect vehicles, provide real-time visibility of the bikes and
the Yulu Zones have been received very well by the customers," said
Amit Gupta, Founder and CEO of Yulu Bikes.

Amit Gupta with Yulu bike

What's unique about Yulu Bikes is the need to operate the bike without a driver's license: a requirement for many urban migrating commuters. This issue was addressed by limiting the maximum speed of the bike to 25 km/hr, above which the customer would need a driver's license.

After a successful launch in Bengaluru, Yulu expanded to other major cities. With a registered base of four million users, Yulu increased its monthly active users from 5K in March 2019 to 170K in March 2021. Also, Yulu witnessed a 2.6X growth in Yulu bikes deployed during the same period. All of this would have been impossible if not for the customer-first approach and co-creation process.

PART 4
DRINKING FROM THE FIRE HOSE

DEFENSE

Sam called a meeting with everyone who directly reported to her—essentially, the Heads of the four businesses and the senior leaders of enabling functions. The meeting, we were told, was to begin promptly at 8 am.

It was strange that Sam didn't say what the meeting was about. She had instructed us to be in the conference room by 8 am and to bring with us a thorough assessment of business performance and numbers. It seemed that this would be a pre-meeting before announcing the quarterly results. The rumor was that Sam was going to use the meeting to deliver some news to us about how badly the businesses performed in the second quarter. Then she was going to hit us with some unachievable targets and a new performance drive for each business.

By 7:45 am, I had parked my car in the designated spot for the Chief Digital Officer—interim for now but hopefully permanent soon. I got out of the car and picked up my laptop case and printed copies of my accomplishments—mostly in the health club business, as Sam had asked me to put a special focus there. Though I was worried about the overall state of Fitness First, I was feeling confident about what we were doing with digital. I started walking to the elevator.

"Neo!" I heard from behind me.

I turned; it was Lisa. She was stubbing out a cigarette. I wondered if she had been waiting for me. "Good morning!" I said. Lisa fell in step with me and we walked toward the entrance of the building.

"I'm glad I caught you," Lisa said. "Have you heard the news?"

"What news?" I asked.

Lisa stopped suddenly and looked around. We were alone. "About Sam as the CEO," she said in a low voice.

I shrugged and said, "I have no idea what you're talking about."

"Last night I had drinks with Sam's Chief of Staff. He let some things slip and I wondered if you knew. This quarter's results are not good. Sam has been struggling. The board has given her an ultimatum," she said. "She's got till the end of the year to show results."

"Are you sure?"

Lisa nodded. "Apparently the board has been coming down on her hard. And they might not just replace her. There has been some talk about really shaking things up. Cleaning house."

My first reaction was that it was no wonder Sam had been acting erratically. Her ruthless push to increase performance in the health club business with digital was starting to make sense—it was a $1 BN business, contributing to 60% of Fitness First's overall revenue. But would she succeed? Would she have a job in six months? *Would I have a job*? Suddenly I thought about Tina and her accusation that she couldn't trust my promises. How would she react if I failed?

Lisa whispered. "Neo, you're a good boss and I really want you to succeed. I think we are really close to getting it right this time. But I worry that nothing we do will be able to turn things around."

I swallowed. All my confidence drained away. "Thanks for telling me. I really appreciate it."

Lisa nodded. "If you hear anything more, will you let me know? I don't want to be caught unaware." She gave me a half smile and rushed off.

I felt lost, not knowing where I was supposed to be. Suddenly I remembered the meeting. I made my way to the conference room—the meeting started promptly at 8 am. Sam went through the performance of one business after another, starting with the health club business, followed by workout equipment, supplements and fitness experts. I no longer knew whether I should feel confident about the progress made in the health club business.

The health club business contributed 60% to overall business; I wondered how the remaining three businesses had performed.

"…the supplements business is growing…" "…churn in old customers…" "…fitness experts business…" "…disastrous performance…" "…customers are preferring home workouts…" "…should explore…" "…not able to meet the demand…" "…supply chain constraints…" "…not tried new ways…"

I tried to focus but I just couldn't concentrate.

"Have you done anything with digital here?" asked Sam.

Suddenly, I realized I was in the spotlight.

"I'm sorry…what are you asking?" I said.

Sam looked perturbed. I looked around to see if someone could fill me in.

"Supply chain…to meet growing demand in the workout equipment business," Stan said reproachfully.

I shook my head.

Sam frowned. "Why not?"

"Well…I just focused on the health club business as per—"

"Why in the world would you focus only on one business?" she yelled.

"Wait a minute, Sam —"

"I don't have a minute!" she roared. "Are you a Chief Digital Officer for the health club business or for Fitness First? God damn it!"

That hurt. She paused for a moment, as if she had to let that message sink in. And then…BAM! She pounded her fist on the table and glared at me. "If you can't act like the Chief Digital Officer of Fitness First," she continued, "I've got no use for you."

"But you were—"

Stan intervened. "Sam—Neo has been quite good at solving the issues in the health club business." I was glad he was taking my side. And then he rubbed salt in my wound. "But perhaps he can't deal with the digital transformation of four businesses at the same time. We are a large company, you know?" And he looked at me.

It took me a few seconds to realize what he was doing.

"I guess Neo is startup worthy…and not meant for a large organization like us," Stan added, putting the last nail in the coffin.

I thought I had brought Stan around. I was in disbelief. The room went quiet. I was speechless.

Sam brushed it off as if she didn't care what Stan said. She walked to the far end of the table and addressed everyone. "I don't want to hear explanations. I don't have time for excuses. I need performance. I need digital to add value. And I need to see improvements to the bottom line!"

Everyone nodded. She made her point and stormed out of the room. With little solace left, I gathered myself and walked to my office.

If you can't act like the Chief Digital Officer of Fitness First, I've got no use for you. You are startup worthy…not meant for a large organization. That's all I could think of as I walked back. It was reverberating in my ears. I tried to calm down but couldn't. What I thought would be an easy discussion turned into a disastrous excoriation. And I had to listen to Sam's public outbursts, despite doing what she asked me to?

The rest of the day was full of meetings. I was hardly paying attention. All I was thinking about was that it had been six months since I joined Fitness First. I had been limping along month after month and it never got any better. It just got worse.

What was the matter with me?

I told myself I had to stop wallowing. I tried to calm down, to think rationally. I was all by myself in my office. There was no one around. It was late. No more meetings. No more interruptions. I analyzed the situation.

Okay, we had good people. For the most part, yes, we did. We had buy-in for the prioritized initiatives in each business. We had the five-step approach. It might be new to the team but I felt confident that the momentum we created with the last initiative should help us push things forward across Fitness First. All I need is to activate the Innovation Pods and make the five-step approach second nature within each Pod. So, what the hell was I sulking for?

I simply needed to double my efforts. I knew that if I worked hard, with the right intentions, I could move mountains. I had done it before. I sweated my way through Wharton. I built Digi Gate from the ground up. Fitness First was no different. There was no way I would let doubt bog me down.

RISE AND FALL

For the next two weeks, Lisa, Stacy and I worked round the clock, meeting with the stakeholders from all four businesses, as well as the enabling functions. A lackluster response from the business stakeholders worried me but I realized that everyone was being distracted by the urgency to deliver outcomes. They didn't want to think about the future, even though digital would help them.

We activated twelve additional Innovation Pods. Lisa and I conducted a two-day training on the five-step approach with the Innovation Pods to kick them off properly.

I walked into the conference room for our first weekly sync with the twelve Pod Leads. I saw Lisa standing near the window and savoring the view of Mount Rainier from the large window of the conference room. She probably hadn't noticed me.

I walked to the window and asked her, "Have you ever been to Mount Rainier? I drove there with my wife when we lived here before."

"Hey…didn't see you coming." Lisa looked at the mountain again. "I've actually climbed it."

"Really? How was it?"

She brightened at the memory. "It was about 10 years ago. By far the most extreme challenge I've ever tackled. It was very scary, very hard and it was the adventure of a lifetime." She barked a short laugh. "I don't think I could do that now. Too worn out."

For a moment I felt that every single word she shared sounded like my journey at Fitness First. The big question was, would I make it to the end and be able to call it an adventure of a lifetime?

Lisa saw me thinking. "Are you all right?" she asked.

"Yeah…kinda."

She didn't believe me. "What's bothering you, Neo?"

I took a long breath. "To make Fitness First a digital-first organization, change is inevitable—change in thought, change in approach and a change in how we work as a team. It's a new way of doing business. The question is, is the team ready yet?" I felt a mix of excitement and anxiety. Excitement because the trajectory had been set and the ball was in motion. And anxiety because I couldn't afford to drop the ball, at any cost.

"We did everything we could. Let's hear out the Pod Leads and guide them as they move forward," she said.

I nodded in agreement.

Just when we were about to start the meeting, I got a video call from Tina. It was unusual to get a call from her at that time of the day—it was the middle of the night in India.

I answered.

She was carrying Riya in one hand and holding her phone in the other. It looked like she was in a hospital.

"Hey…Mom fell in the bathroom an hour ago. I think she broke her leg." Tears filled her eyes.

"What?" All the color drained out of the room.

"I'm in the Emergency Room waiting for the doctor now."

"Oh no…how bad is it?"

"She's holding up. The paramedics arrived quickly. They immobilized her, stabilized her and transported us to the hospital."

Tina tried to angle the camera so that I could see Mom. And then she abruptly said, "The doctor is here. I'll call you back." And she hung up.

I collapsed in the chair, feeling helpless. Tina and Mom needed me more than ever. But we had just activated not one but twelve Innovation Pods. Who would guide them if I were to go to India?

Lisa walked towards me. "I'm sorry to hear about your mom," she said. She paused for a moment. "You should go. Family has to come first. We'll keep the flag flying while you're gone."

Lisa was right. I told her to keep me informed and rushed back to my office. As I stepped out of the room, I saw Stacy and the rest of the Pod Leads walking to our first weekly sync. She looked worried. I wanted to talk to Stacy but at that moment what mattered most was my family. I called my EA to get me on the first flight to Bengaluru and went home.

I sent Tina a text: *I'm getting on a plane. See you in 28 hours.*

Forty-five minutes later, I was backing my car out of the garage to head to the airport. It was a strange feeling, as if I was leaving the battlefield and letting my team fight on their own.

RECOVERY

Before taking off, I video called with Mom at the airport. Mom was happy to see me even though she was in pain. The doctors said she broke her tibia and fibula. They said she needed surgery but that she would be normal in six months—the exact amount of time remaining for me at Fitness First.

The surgery was complete by the time I got to the hospital, 28 hours later. The doctors had made an incision through her knee. A metal rod was inserted alongside her tibia, with screws inserted to the side of her knee and ankle to keep it in place. I slept in a chair in Mom's room.

After a week of inactivity post-surgery, Mom was assessed by the physios, who said she had a long road to recovery. But just two days later, she walked for the first time with crutches. The tiniest of milestones became like conquering Everest for her. But she never gave up easily. She was discharged from the hospital after ten days, a few days earlier than usual due to her speedy recovery. I was glad that I was around to take care of Mom, while Tina took care of the rest.

When we got back home, Tina had everything set up for Mom—a helper, crutches, rehab classes, strength training, etc. I decided to spend a few days at home with Tina and Riya before I headed back to Seattle. Tina spent most of her time with me. It felt just like old times.

The day before my flight, Tina suggested we go for a walk. As I was stepping out, Riya whispered in my ear, "Daddy, when are we all going to Seattle?"

"Real soon," I stammered.

Riya's question didn't go away. I couldn't respond to her with confidence. In fact, I hadn't been keeping track of what was happening on the twelve Innovation Pods. It had been two weeks. I just hoped that the team was making progress.

Tina and I walked in the park in our neighborhood. It was a nice, breezy evening. We sat down on a bench by the large water fountain in the park. We sat without saying anything for a while. She asked me if something was wrong. I told her about Riya's question.

"She asks me that all the time," said Tina.

"She does? What do you tell her?"

"I tell her we'll be going to Seattle real soon."

I laughed. "That's what I said to her. Do you really mean that?"

She was quiet for a second. Finally, she smiled at me and said, "You've proved that your work isn't the only priority. Thanks for coming to India. You were there just when we needed you the most."

"Of course. You are so important to me."

She thought for a moment. "I know you said you'd figured it all out with your job. But...I'm still worried about coming to be with you."

"Why?"

"If and when we live together, you know what's going to happen, don't you? Everything will be fine for a few days. And then a week later, your work will take priority. We'll be having the same arguments. And it'll be the same story all over again."

I sighed and said, "I was having problems at Digi Gate. And now at Fitness First, I really have to get it to a stable state. But what did you expect from me, Tina?"

"Neo, you're not like the others who go to work and come home at regular times."

"Yeah...I'm not like that. I want to be ambitious. I want to have a big career. What's wrong with that?"

"Do you even know why you want the things you do?" she asked.

"Because that's how I grew up. Setting big goals and working towards them. And what about you?"

"Does it even matter to you?" she said.

"Yes, it does. It puts things into perspective."

She paused for a second and said, "Look where we're heading again. Another fight?"

Tears started rolling down her cheek. I reached to wipe them away but she brushed my hand aside.

"I'm sorry," she murmured. "I just don't know if I can do this."

"Tina…this isn't fair!"

She turned to me and said, "It doesn't feel fair to me either or to Riya." And she walked home without looking back.

When I got back home, I started packing my bags and spent the last few hours with Riya. My flight was early in the morning.

"Daddy, you have to see this."

"What is it?"

"My report card," she said. "You must see it. Now." She handed it over.

"You got all A's!" I gave her a tight hug and a kiss. "That's fantastic! I am really proud of you."

And then she started telling me how fun her pre-school had been with all the singing, dancing, and yoga, all through online classes.

Tina walked in. She said, "I'm sorry about what happened."

"It's not your fault. It's me. I promise I will figure things out and get it right, for all of us."

We both started smiling. And then we hugged and kissed each other. Riya came running, thrilled to see us happy and hugged us both.

GASOLINE ON FIRE

While waiting at the busy Bengaluru airport, I activated my email sync and downloaded my work emails. Over seven thousand emails were waiting for my attention. *Oh my goodness!* Most of them were from my team. A few were from Mike. And there was an email from Sam with a single line: *SEE ME IN MY OFFICE.* I wondered what the hell had gone wrong now. I decided to check on the emails from my team first.

After a few hours of catching up enroute to Dubai, I realized that it was utter chaos. I presumed Lisa would have called me if there was an emergency but she had decided to just email me since I was in a family situation. All along I had thought *no news is good news.* Little did I know that yet another disaster was in the making.

I tried my luck calling Charan during my layover in Dubai. It went to voicemail. I couldn't stop worrying about what Sam was furious about. I looked at the Americans sitting across from me, getting ready to board the plane back to Seattle. And it struck me—maybe Lisa knew. I called her.

She answered right away. "Hey Boss…how are you? How is your mom?"

"She's doing okay now. It's a long road ahead for her."

"Where are you now?" she asked. She sounded tired.

"In Dubai…wait, what time is it there?"

"11 pm. Stacy and I are just wrapping up a few things before we call it a day."

"You guys are still at work?"

"Yeah. It's been like that for the past two weeks. It's not going smoothly."

"Sorry I'm not there to help you guys. I thought you would call me… and I didn't check my emails at all. My fault!"

"Have you read my emails now?" she asked.

"Yeah, just finished catching up with the important ones" She hadn't said anything about Sam. "Listen—I'll be in Seattle by 1 pm. Let's meet at 3 pm."

I hung up, feeling terrible for my team. I boarded the plane and looked at my emails again. I wasn't sure whether our issues were typical for an organization scaling a digital transformation, or if the problem was specific to me. I tried calling Charan one last time before the plane took off but the flight attendant politely asked me to turn off my phone.

After a minute or so, the plane shook, the engine's noise grew and the bird soared into the sky, pushing me back into my seat and making the earth fall away. Travel from Dubai to Seattle felt the longest. I wasn't in the mood for on-screen entertainment, nor did I want to think about work issues. But Sam's email wouldn't leave my mind.

I stared out of the window as the sky darkened. I noticed bright skies on the other side of the window. The furthest end of the sky took on a surreal saffron hue as the clouds reflected the fading sun's red and bright orange glow. It was picturesque. What made me mad was that I was always running so hard that I didn't have time to pay attention to the miracles around me. Instead of letting my eyes soak in the twilight, I was worrying about Sam and why she had sent that email. The last meeting with her had stressed me out. I didn't want to let that happen again. Forcing myself to calm down, I went into a deep slumber. I woke up when the flight attendant announced that we would be arriving late to Seattle. Brilliant. Nothing seemed to be working in my favor.

On the way home, I texted Lisa to tell her that I would be a little late and requested that she meet me in my office. I got ready to go to work but all I wanted was to sleep. And the day had just started for me.

"Good afternoon, Lisa," I said as I walked into my office.

I noticed her eyes were puffy, like she wasn't getting enough sleep; I thought mine probably looked the same. I gave her some Indian delicacies I had picked up from Bengaluru airport. After some small talk about Mom and my family, we decided to spend thirty minutes per Innovation Pod looking over everything—the team, problem statement, cover story, etc.

The next six hours went by fast. As I went through the details, I could see a few patterns emerging. I said, "Let's look into the common themes and patterns of what is slowing us down."

She nodded and thought for a moment, perhaps to determine which one to discuss first.

She started with the people. "I know you inherited the team but you need to know that we have a few C players. In fact, some are wrong hires."

I went to the whiteboard and wrote *Digital talent quality*.

"Who hired them?"

"Bert—poor guy! It was when Sam forced him to hire more people to speed up the launch of the stores. He just couldn't find 'A' players."

"Okay. Let's move on. Did you like the quality of the cover stories?" I asked.

"Most were good. The decent ones made it past Susan. A few cover stories were mediocre at best. They never went past me."

"Why didn't you approve them?"

"Not much effort was made to *know the customer* and their context. And in the case of internal customers, aka employees, no time was spent at all."

I added *Customer-first* to the whiteboard. That's a difficult problem to solve. It requires a shift in mindset.

"Moving on, I've seen quite a few escalation emails. Did we not get enough support from the other teams?" I asked.

"Support? You've gotta be kidding. If I were to rate it from 1 to 10, with 10 being the best, I'd give a 2. At best."

"That's terrible! I'm sure we were clear in our expectations with the service blueprint—why weren't they supportive?"

"Very simple. Their rewards aren't linked to the outcomes of the Innovation Pods."

I was frustrated. The best reward must be delighting the customer. In startups, a lack of support becomes visible very quickly. That's not the case for large organizations.

"How would you rate it for the unavailability of towels initiative?" I wanted to know.

"Around 7—but it got high visibility because both Tim and Stan co-created the solution."

I added *Collaboration & Support* to the whiteboard. That was a complex problem to solve.

I went to the next theme. "What is the issue with delivery quality?" I asked.

She looked perturbed. "I am upset about the quality standard. Too many people are okay with mediocre quality. And that leads to rework—sometimes multiple times. It's highly inefficient and wastes everyone's time."

"And the problem exists because?"

"Again, here too, the rewards of interdependent teams are not linked to the outcomes of the Innovation Pods."

I wrote *High standards* on the whiteboard. Another difficult problem to solve in a short amount of time.

"What else?"

"Well, some of our team members, including Stacy, want to make everything perfect. I tried communicating to her that *perfect is the enemy of good*. But she just doesn't get it," she said.

"That's surprising. She's one of our best."

"Yeah—I guess it's the fear of failure. We have a culture of punishing failure. It's not you, Neo, but something that people feel," she clarified.

"Hmm…I guess success is overrated and failure is underrated here." I paused for a moment. "The beauty of digital is that it generates data—good or bad. Our goal must be to ship a minimum desirable solution and use data to iteratively course-correct."

"Absolutely," she said.

I added *Ship to learn with data* to the whiteboard.

1. Digital talent quality
2. Customer-first
3. Collaboration & support
4. High standards
5. Ship to learn with data

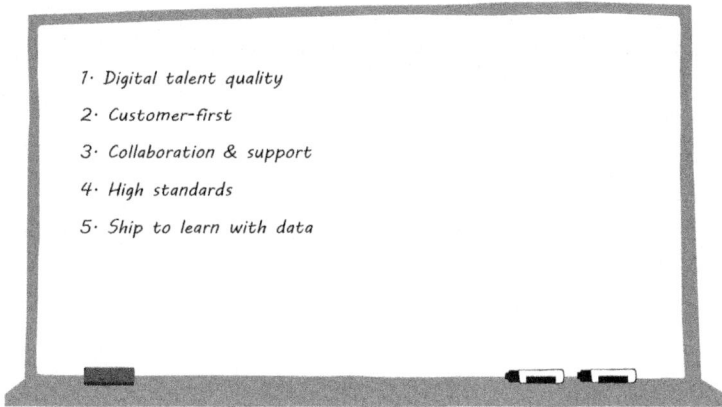

It was past midnight already. I thanked Lisa for holding down the fort and told her to take off. As I reflected on the themes, emails, and cover stories, two big issues hit me.

One, I felt the solutions in the cover stories were short-term oriented—do something fast, even if it was a band-aid solution, but deliver results quickly. We needed long-term thinking—to build for the future with a clear vision and purpose in mind. There was also a lack of agreement on how each initiative, when stitched together, would align with the business strategy and help us achieve our purpose. That alignment must and could only be provided by the SLT. The trajectory of every single digital initiative must be aimed toward the big vision and purpose of the organization.

And two, we needed an effective governance structure to manage multiple digital initiatives. Lisa could do only so much. We needed a formal one, one that would work in large organizations. While I could create and test one, I didn't have time to experiment. I just couldn't afford to lose. I needed to call Charan again.

I picked up my phone and called him and it went straight to voicemail. I checked his "last seen" status on WhatsApp. It was ten days before. I just hoped he was safe and sound, wherever he was.

CRASH

It was about 1 am. I'd forgotten about dinner. I slipped away from my office to run home and grab something frozen. Once I was in the car, I found I had lost my appetite and started feeling drowsy. I was terribly jet lagged. I thought of taking a taxi but I decided to roll down the window and let the cool breeze keep me alert. It was dark outside. Most of the city was resting.

As I drove home, I felt nostalgic about Bellevue. The city I had lived in for a decade. Everywhere I looked, some kind of memory was waiting in my mind's eye. I passed Bellevue Square Mall, where I had finished a half-marathon in record time. I saw the alley where I bought cupcakes for Tina and Riya. I drove down the street where I met my buddies for drinks on Friday nights. I knew the best places to buy things, the good restaurants and the places to stay away from. I felt a sense of ownership toward the city and I had more affection for it than for any other city. The more memories that crowded in, the more I got a feeling that was warm and uncomfortably tense.

I wanted everything to fall into place at Fitness First. And then a weird thought came to me—maybe I should just give up and use the time I had left to try to land another job. For a while, I tried to convince myself that calling a head-hunter was the best thing to do. But, in the end, good sense prevailed. A job with another company would get Tina here and maybe I'd get a better position through sheer luck. But that would mean giving up in the middle of the race and that failure would haunt me for the rest of my life. I'd feel like I ran away. I just couldn't do that.

I started feeling hazy. My eyes were closing automatically. I rubbed my eyes and continued driving.

I felt some responsibility to finish what I started. It's not like I owed my life to Mike or Fitness First but I wanted to give it my best shot during the next five months. Five months was better than nothing for *the last chance*. But that brought up the big question: what the hell could I really do? I had already done the best I could with what I knew. Doing more of the same and hoping to see different outcomes would be foolish.

I didn't have time to research. Neither could I hire expensive consultants. Plus, I was sure none of them could tell me more than what I already knew. I knew the problem and I knew that a problem defined is a problem half solved but I wondered if I could ever get myself out of trouble. I closed my eyes.

The sound of my phone ringing snapped me awake.

The guard rail of the on-ramp was rushing toward me.

I slammed my foot on the brake, jerked the wheel.

A huge BAM rocked the car on the front passenger side. Alarm bells blared in my sleep-deprived brain as the airbags to my side and in front of me exploded outward.

The car was spinning, I couldn't see.

Flashes of memories with Tina, Riya, Mom and Dad. I was seeing everything at once, staring at a lot of monitors with each screen showing a different scene. I could see their faces so clearly.

Tina, Riya. I didn't want to die. Not with regrets.

I tried to take control of the wheel but it was impossible. I pressed hard on the brakes and pulled the emergency brake. The car spun once more, moving towards the left side of the ramp before it hit the shoulder. And then the car stopped. Everything had happened in just a few seconds.

Somehow I forced myself out of the car through the jammed doors. There was fluid leaking from under the engine. I stepped quickly away— was the car going to explode? My heart was hammering, my hands shook. Slowly I realized it was brake fluid. The car was a wreck; the front was smashed on the passenger side. Looking down at the shoulder that stopped my car, I realized that, if not for that shoulder, I would have landed on the eight-lane freeway under the ramp where vehicles were going 85 miles per hour. A sick pit in my stomach opened up as I imagined what would have happened if I had landed on the freeway.

I quickly checked my arms and legs to see if they were intact. I felt the rest of my body to see if I was injured or bleeding. I could feel a searing pain in my neck but I didn't seem to have a visible injury. It was unbelievable that I came out of the accident unscathed. Honestly, had destiny willed it to happen any other way, there was nothing I could have done, except for dying a death with regrets.

I sat on the side of the ramp and some oncoming vehicles stopped and checked to see if I was doing okay and if I needed any help—humanity still exists. After a few moments, I took the risk of grabbing my phone from the car. My hands could barely hold still as I tried to dial 911. Then I saw that it was Charan who had called me, alerting me at just the right time and saving my life. And there was a text from him that read:

In Seattle tomorrow for a meeting at noon. I can meet you in the morning if it works.

In the distance I saw the flashing lights of police cars coming to the scene.

I texted Charan back*: Looking forward to it. You're a life saver!*

Ideas to remember

- Digital transformation is a long and complex journey. Often one might feel dejected and want to give up midway. It is critical to stay put and stay the course. Carve out a 30/60/90-day plan and clearly define outcomes. Small wins, as you move along, will act as a boost to push things forward.
- The majority of digital transformations fail to deliver value. Even the most successful companies suffer from digital transformation failures. Below are some of the reasons for failure. Make every effort to identify and address the issue.
  1. Lack of clarity and dedication from senior management
  2. Lack of quality digital talent
  3. Not taking a customer-first approach
  4. Rigid systems and interminable processes with layers of bureaucracy
  5. Lack of quality standards
  6. Waiting for the perfect product

Let's take a look at Nike FuelBand, the tracker that was launched in 2012 and kicked off a multi-billion-dollar industry. Nike was among the driving forces that brought fitness wearables to the mainstream. It stood alongside Fitbit and Jawbone as one of the only major players to hold a substantial share of the wearable retail market. Fast forward three years and the wearable was shut down.

What went wrong with the Nike FuelBand?

First, not taking a customer-first approach. Nike FuelBand rode the wave of the "quantified self" movement, where the user is interested in knowing about themselves with numbers. The fundamental flaw was that FuelBand bombarded users with data—steps taken, calories burned, height jumped, distance traveled, etc.—but did little to contextualize these metrics in a way that would add long-term value for the customer and create stickiness.

"We tried to put data in the consumer's hands but I don't know that we put depth in that data—a lot of it was data for data's sake at times," said Jordan Rice, Senior Director, Nike Smart Systems. "I began to ask myself a little bit, how deep is this connection that we've actually created? Are people connected to the brand and the products? Is this data actually meaningful to them? Is there depth, are they taking any insight away from this or are we really creating a gimmick?"

Second, lack of clarity and direction. The FuelBand app for Android arrived two years after launch, missing out on a major customer segment. The exclusivity with Apple cost Nike dearly. Although, looking back, it seemed to work well for Apple—setting the stage for what was to follow, raising awareness and creating a market that the Apple Watch could come along and swallow. Even Nike's deep relationship with Apple could not reignite exclusive partnerships like the Nike+iPod alliance. As a result, Nike axed the majority of its FuelBand team, some of whom joined Apple, and Nike revoked its plans for future FuelBand releases.

It wasn't just the lack of a customer-first approach or the lack of Android support or the lack of direction—Nike just didn't put the machine behind the FuelBand the way it could have. A missed opportunity!

- As the adage goes, "Perfect is the enemy of good." One must not aim for perfection in the digital era. The beauty of digital is that it generates data—good or bad. Create a Minimum desirable solution—a solution that has the features most desirable for the customer—and leverage customer usage data to course correct and refine the product or service.

- With a long-term orientation, assess how each initiative, when stitched together, will align with the business strategy and help you achieve the purpose of the organization. That alignment must and can only be provided by the senior management. The trajectory of every single digital initiative must be toward achieving the big vision and purpose of the organization.

PART 5
TRANSFORMING AT SCALE

SAGE WISDOM

Waiting at the terminal to pick up Charan, I thought about last night's near-death experience and my miraculous escape. My neck was extremely sore and stiff but otherwise I had come out of that brutal accident without a scratch. If Charan had called even a few seconds later, I don't think I would be alive. As I reminisced about last night's events, I heard someone yell my name.

"Neo!"

It was Charan. I waved my hand and pointed to the black Lincoln car I hired for the morning. The chauffeur opened the door for us and we both hopped in.

Charan looked radiant. He had a fresh and youthful glow on his face. I asked, "Your 'last seen' status on WhatsApp was ten days ago. Did you go to a retreat or something?"

"Yes!" he paused. "A ten-day Vipassana meditation," he said with a smile on his face.

"TEN DAYS?"

"That's right! I am a Vipassana practitioner."

"Tell me more."

"Well, Vipassana meditation helps you be *self-aware*. I find it extremely useful. I am much calmer, sharper and most importantly, mindful. Countless studies confirmed that a thirty-minute meditation every day improves the gray matter in your mind."

"Gray matter?"

He nodded and said, "Gray matter plays a significant role in all aspects of human life, for your executive presence, cognition, creativity and much more. You should try Vipassana."

The thought of unplugging for ten days seemed daunting. Maybe I would investigate it after I firmed things up at Fitness First.

"You don't look well," he said. "Everything alright?"

"I'm jet lagged. And I barely slept last night after a near-death experience." I paused and said, "And thank you for saving my life."

Charan looked confused.

I explained how the car hit the shoulder, the spin, the crash and how I came out unscathed.

"That's insane. You should be resting now," he said.

I waved it off. "I've been trying to reach you for the past two days. I am so glad you are here. We tried to scale our digital transformation efforts organization-wide and fell flat on our face."

He paused for a moment and said, "I want you to give me as much background about the situation as you can."

All the way from the airport I talked non-stop about our predicament. He listened intently. What he said after that was comforting. "You are facing problems that are typical for a traditional organization. The good news is that most are solvable problems. Some will take a long time, though."

"But I just have five months left."

"Five months is still enough to show progress," he clarified. Charan could read the puzzled look on my face. "You don't understand, but you will," he said as the chauffeur stopped at Fitness First's corporate headquarters.

I wanted Charan's presence to be low-key, so we met in my office. Lisa and Stacy were waiting for us. As I made introductions, I could tell my team was waiting to see if Charan really was the Messiah who had solutions to our never-ending problems.

"Neo filled me in on your recent efforts to scale your digital transformation." He looked at our last night's notes on the whiteboard. "Are these the themes of the issues?" he asked.

Lisa nodded.

He stood in front of the whiteboard and began to pace as he spoke. He looked at me and said, "First and foremost, you need to be absolutely clear about the basic building blocks for becoming a digital-first organization." He went to the whiteboard and wrote what appeared to be the building blocks—three of them.

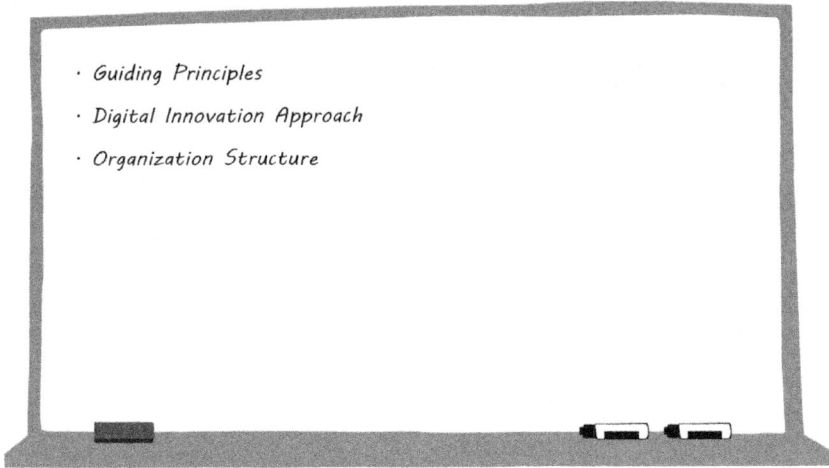

- Guiding Principles
- Digital Innovation Approach
- Organization Structure

He looked at me and said, "Neo, if what I heard about the five-step approach is true, I feel you are in good shape for the second building block. The bigger issue for you is the third building block—organizational structure."

"Okay."

He went on. "It may be cliché, but *culture eats strategy for breakfast* applies to all transformations. More so for digital transformation. Culture can be either the biggest accelerator or the biggest hurdle. To get it right, you must practice a set of behaviors."

"Guiding principles define those behaviors and set the right culture?" I asked.

"Exactly. Guiding principles are a set of values that define a framework for expected behavior and decision-making. They guide you during all circumstances, irrespective of the initiative, strategy or type of work," he clarified.

He looked again at the other whiteboard where we had our notes from last night.

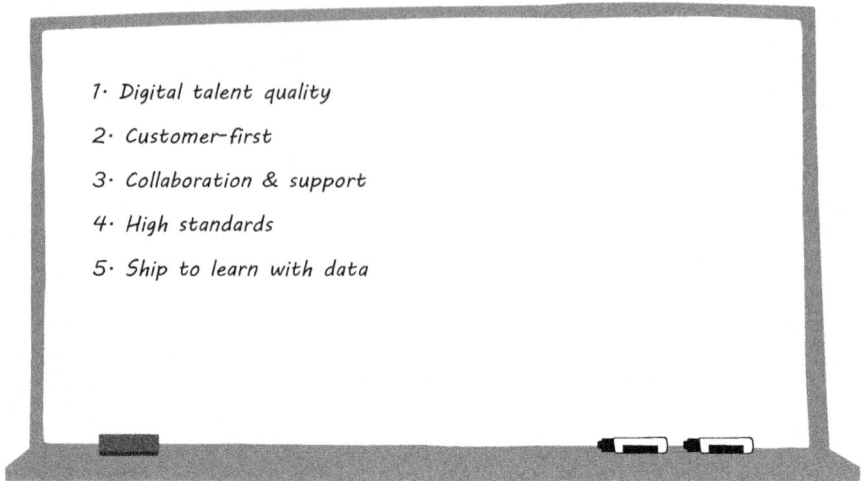

1. Digital talent quality
2. Customer-first
3. Collaboration & support
4. High standards
5. Ship to learn with data

"Let's start with these and define your guiding principles. You will find them relatable." He read the first theme and said, "Don't you think it's an expected behavior for A players to find A players, for the most part? Whereas, B players will likely not hire A players, for obvious reasons; rather, they hire B or C players. And that'd be detrimental to the growth of the company."

He paused for a moment to let that sink in. "Every hire and promotion is crucial to set a precedent and to build the foundation for the type of organization you want. You must raise the bar with every hire and promotion. You must spot high-potential leaders and create opportunities for growth. Rewards, recognitions and promotions—all must be linked to digital outcomes and metrics."

"What if we don't find the right talent?" asked Lisa.

He smiled. "You keep looking. You'd be better off not hiring the wrong person. Wouldn't you?"

"So, we shouldn't give in until we find what we're looking for?" she asked.

"Right. We want an asset, not a liability," he replied.

I thought for a moment. "Are you sure? Because finding good talent is hard. We need to move fast."

"That's exactly the point—you will be moving fast as a digital-first organization. You need the best digital talent to move fast."

I thought again. "Well, we need to relook at hiring and promotion practices. But it's a difficult one to roll out."

He nodded and put an arrow mark next to the first theme and wrote the first guiding principle: *Hire and develop Digital Talent.*

He read the next theme: *Customer-first,* and said, "Many digital transformations fail because the right problems are not solved. Understanding *the why* of every initiative is a critical first step. And *the why* should align with the customer—directly or indirectly."

"How would you achieve that alignment?" asked Stacy.

"If you are customer obsessed, you would naturally get that alignment," he said.

"Yeah—everyone in the organization must be customer obsessed. I'm thinking we should plan a series of experiential trainings on Design Thinking," I said.

"You must introduce 'First Principles Thinking' also. While solving for the customer, 'First principles Thinking' helps in actively questioning every assumption you think you know about a given problem or scenario. You must then empower teams to create new knowledge and solutions from scratch to address the unmet and unarticulated needs of the customer, directly or indirectly."

"I love it. This will help us question our age-old assumptions and look at problems with a new lens," Lisa said with excitement.

He nodded and wrote *Start with a why* next to *Customer-first.*

"Let's address the third theme while we talk about organizational structure," he said. "I will add a new theme you missed—*incrementalism.* From what you said about the quality of cover stories, incrementalism seems deeply rooted."

Lisa and I nodded in agreement.

He erased Collaboration and support and wrote *Incrementalism* and said, "Trying to be marginally better doesn't move the needle. You must constantly think differently and place big, bold bets. Combine that with high standards and you will deliver excellence."

"But how do we bring about that change?" I asked.

"It requires a shift in mindset. People who think big see problems as opportunities. They can dream and visualize what they want and do not feel constrained by the impossible. They explore new ideas. They are fearless risk takers."

"I guess we must lead with our example and reset the tone at the top."

He continued, "Don't forget that ideas are a dime a dozen. You must continually raise the bar and drive the teams to deliver high quality products and services."

He wrote *Think Big and Deliver Excellence* and moved to the last theme on the whiteboard. "In the digital era, the focus must be on speed to market so you can compete better. And in some cases, you may get first-mover's advantage. It's critical that you have a sense of urgency and a bias for action to ship the product and course-correct with data as you move along."

"Right, so I encourage the team to harness data and course correct iteratively. We plan to leverage data to *Fail fast and Pivot smart.*"

He clarified a point that was especially applicable to us. "Most legacy organizations are 'data rich'—meaning they have tons of data generated from digital solutions but they are not 'data-driven'. You must build the right instrumentation to leverage data and grow. You analyze the data to learn how customers are reacting and refine your digital solutions through growth experiments."

"Growth experiments?" I asked.

"Yeah—you leverage experimentation and data to continuously pivot with a goal to delight the customer and stay ahead of the competition. Let's take Facebook or Netflix. They have thousands of active experiments running at any given time."

We were awestruck. "When does the experimentation cycle end?" asked Stacy.

"Never." He did not hesitate. "Digital product innovation is a journey, not a destination." And then he clarified, "In your industry, you might end up running about a thousand experiments during the initial years. As you mature, you might end up with more. We'll talk more when we discuss organizational structure."

Charan looked at the four guiding principles and said, "You need to add two more."

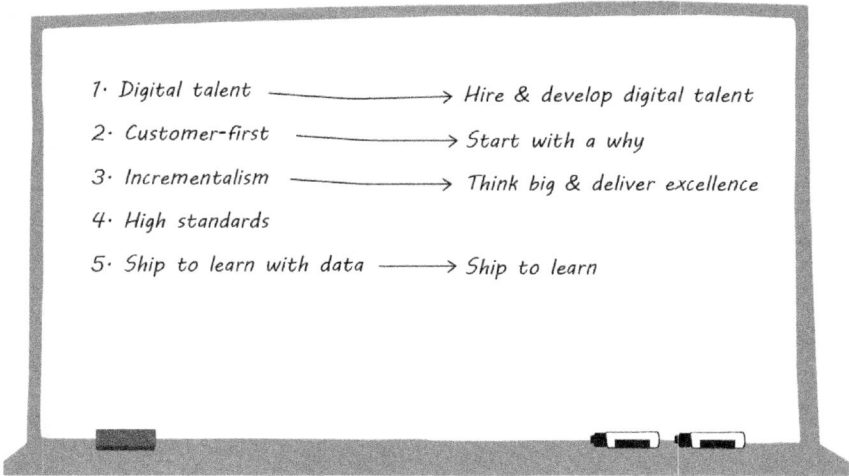

1. Digital talent ————————→	Hire & develop digital talent
2. Customer-first ————————→	Start with a why
3. Incrementalism ————————→	Think big & deliver excellence
4. High standards	
5. Ship to learn with data ————→	Ship to learn

He continued. "Lack of adoption of digital solutions has been one of the biggest reasons why digital transformations fail. And the root cause is adding tech for the sake of adding."

"Yeah. We have three digital platforms to communicate with our employees and none of them are useful," said Lisa.

"Exactly the point. Tech must be relevant and useful. Tech must be purpose-built, which happens when you humanize tech to solve the problem and address the customer's unmet and unarticulated needs." He wrote *Humanize tech.*

"And the last one is frugality. No organization has unlimited resources. Fitness First is not an exception. Embrace constraints and adopt a mindset of simplicity and being resourceful. Aim to offer smart and effective solutions without sacrificing the quality of user experience."

As he wrote the last guiding principle, Lisa asked, "How do we enforce these guiding principles?"

"Good question. Guiding principles must become a way of life at Fitness First. Your hiring, firing and promotion decisions must be based on how effectively employees live and breathe the guiding principles."

He saw a worried look on my face. He looked at me and said, "Neo, you know culture transformation is a slow process. I'm sure you are smart enough—"

"—to figure things out," I completed his thought.

We both laughed.

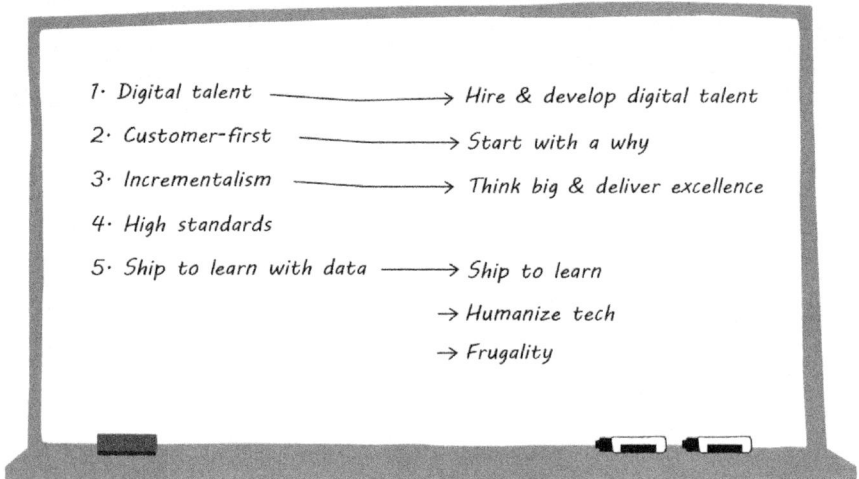

Just when we were about to discuss the next building block, Mike walked in. He greeted me and my team and went straight to Charan. He shook his hand and said, "So great to have you with us, Charan. Thank you for helping us out."

Charan smiled and said, "My pleasure."

Mike went on. "I'm sure you already know about our struggles to become digital-first. We want to leverage digital to scale big. With Neo here, we have a new hope. But before Neo, it was a mess. The past three years have been a roller coaster ride. Is it just us or have you seen something similar in other organizations?"

Charan thought deeply. "It's not unusual to get stuck during a digital transformation. In my years of experience advising clients on digital transformations, I have seen a lot of variances in the level of complexity and the time it takes to become digital-first and to scale big. To get a general idea of how complex it'll be and how long it'll take, we can look at two elements. First, overall revenue from different channels and second, how much of that revenue is from digital business models. These two data points can paint a picture of an organization's maturity and how complex the journey will be to become a digital-first organization."

"Interesting. Tell us more," said Mike.

"Sure. Let me explain with a 2-by-2 matrix." He drew it on the whiteboard. He then plotted three companies and little arrow marks pointing to the top right quadrant. "As you can see, Company A and B are incumbents—they could be medium-to-large traditional organizations or family-run businesses—Company C is a Digital Native i.e., a company born in the digital era."

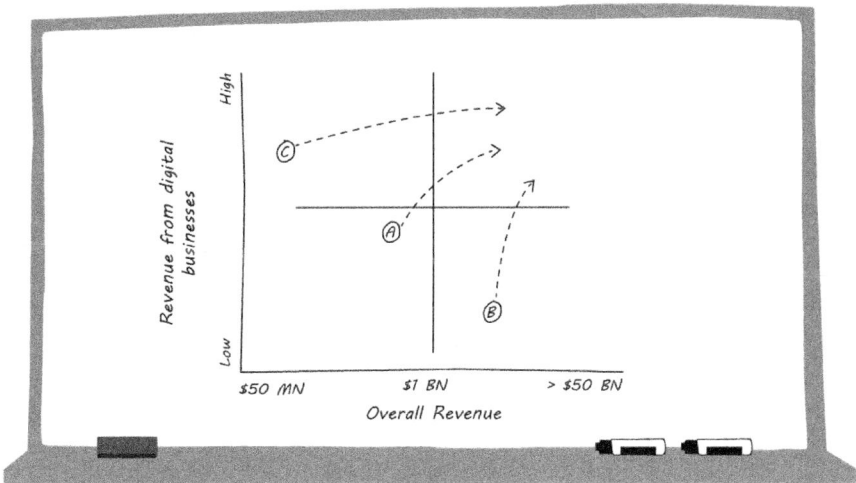

Mike looked intently and asked, "So you're saying Company A's journey to become digital-first will likely be easier…because?"

"Company A has a digital foundation and more experience in building and launching digital business models. They are also smaller, with more obvious opportunities to gain market share via digital," Charan clarified and added, "Unlike Company B, which is a very large traditional company where most of the revenue is generated from non-digital business models. For Company B, launching new digital business models and moving to the top right quadrant will be slow, as it will be a steep task."

Mike thought for a moment. "Because Company B likely won't have the experience or structure for building and launching digital business models…right?"

"Exactly, but not just that. Since it's a large company, it will likely have extensive bureaucracy and rigid systems. Most of the company will resist the change. Fundamental shifts will be needed to become a digital-first organization, which will make it a more complex, harder journey to move to the top right quadrant," added Charan.

When I looked at Company C, I could relate it to my experience at Digi Gate. I said, "Company C looks like my startup. We were already digital-first. But we had a scale-up problem."

"That's right. Building an organizational structure that can help the startups scale while retaining a digital-first culture is key to success. And that's complex, too," added Charan.

Mike reeled the conversation back to Fitness First. "Actually, we empower each business at Fitness First by assigning them a budget and asking them to identify and drive digital initiatives. Any thoughts on the effectiveness of a decentralized approach like this?"

"Well, I know a company that ran hundreds of digital initiatives at the individual department level. But since digital meant different things to different executives, those efforts were siloed and didn't add up to anything significant. Worse, it resulted in duplication of effort and waste. Remember, digital initiatives without a holistic direction at the organizational level will not be worthwhile," clarified Charan.

He went on. "In fact, digital has created more destruction for incumbents than added value because digital has been an afterthought and efforts have mostly been misaligned."

I jumped in. "Incumbents must adopt a digital-first way of life to avoid the 'Kodak moment'. Since technological advances are happening at a rapid pace, fast must be the new normal. But you are saying we need to go slow to go fast."

"Exactly. The traditional way of using digital adoption to make things faster, cheaper, and better will lead to a lipstick effect. Digital must touch every element of a digital-first organization."

"What do you mean by every element?" Lisa asked.

"Let me explain. Incumbents must look at how their business models will change by tapping into the 'Art of the Possible' with digital. They must think about how their strategy, competitive advantage and business model will change or should change with digital. How operations and value chains should change. How supply chain, logistics and channels should be reimagined and how interactions with customers should change to adapt to their quickly-changing behaviors." He paused to let the message sink in.

"This new way of life helps incumbents continue to stay relevant in a quickly-changing world. The path for incumbents must be to balance the dichotomy of digital well but sooner rather than later they must also focus on business building with digital. It requires a shift in mindset."

"Well, that's going to take a while," I said.

"That's right. Transforming a traditional organization into a digital-first organization is complex but quite possible with the right set of strategies, organizational structure, people and culture—among other things," Charan explained.

"Let's talk about the third building block—organizational structure," I nudged Charan, cognizant of the time left.

"Of course. Can you talk to me about the Innovation Pod first?" he wanted to know.

"Sure—An Innovation Pod is a small autonomous team," I replied. "They are self-directed. They set priorities, experiment rapidly, learn, fail, and pivot. More like a start-up."

"That's good. I can see how such a setup would increase the velocity of decision-making and deliver initiatives rapidly," said Charan.

"Yeah. These teams have an intrapreneurial mindset. They are ring fenced and empowered with the right tools and capabilities to focus on one cover story, from inception to launch. We plan to have multiple Innovation

Pods activated in each of the four businesses and a few at the group level for enabling functions."

Charan seemed confused and concerned. "Who is going to guide them? Who is going to monitor their progress? I'm sure this will be as new to the SLT as to the existing teams."

"We don't have a formal structure yet. Lisa has been guiding all twelve Pods while I was in India." And that's why we fell flat on our face, I thought.

He went on. "Autonomy shouldn't imply a lack of oversight or guidance. You must not let them hang out to dry. I suggest a hub and spoke model to address that."

Mike looked puzzled, as though Charan was an alien speaking an incomprehensible language. "Can you simplify that for me?"

Charan went to the board and drew a hub and spoke to explain the new organizational structure that would set the foundation toward becoming a digital-first organization. He added a title: "Chief Digital Officer."

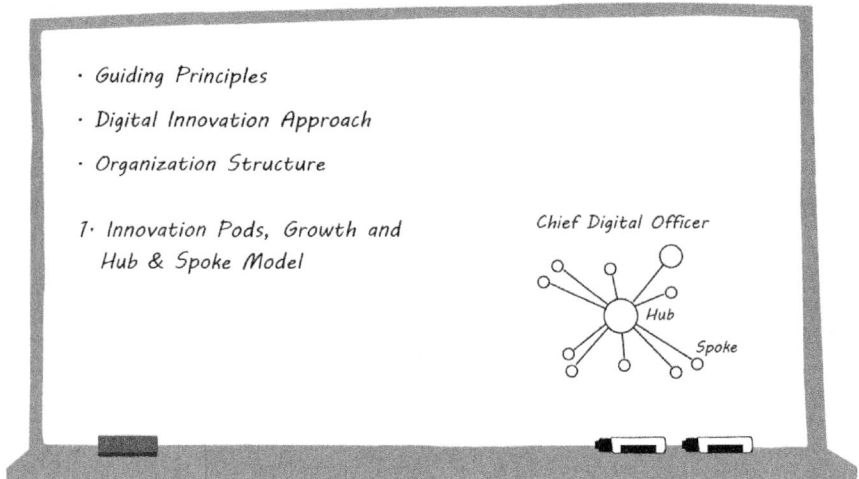

He continued. "You will likely have multiple Innovation Pods working alongside each other. These Innovation Pods must be activated by the hub, which acts as a nerve center."

"A nerve center?" asked Lisa.

"Yes—the hub acts as a delivery oversight powerhouse that guides and enables Innovation Pods at spokes—business units and enabling functions—to drive digital initiatives successfully. The *Chief Digital Officer* will head the hub."

I jumped in. "I suppose the hub, as a nerve center, churns out frameworks, methodologies and guidelines for the Digital Innovation approach, as well as a playbook with examples."

"Exactly. The hub has two goals, primarily. One is to ensure consistency in implementation and high execution quality. The other is to guide and support Innovation Pods with the Digital Innovation approach, agile methodologies, new emerging tech and solutions such as low-code/no-code development platforms, artificial intelligence and IoT, among other things," clarified Charan.

Lisa looked excited. "So the hub becomes the engine and powerhouse to fire up the Innovation Pods."

Charan smiled and said, "With the right team composition."

"Which is?" I wanted to know.

"Let me explain. In addition to the team in the Innovation Pod, you need Design Strategists—people who balance business strategy and human-centered design—and Specialists—people who have niche skills, like agile delivery or new emerging tech. Design Strategists and Specialists must operate within the hub but they collaborate with multiple Pods at the respective spokes to co-create digital solutions and unlock possibilities with digital," explained Charan.

"But the engineers in each Innovation Pod are from Neel's—our CTO's—team," I added.

"That's fine," said Charan. "Engineers are better managed by them."

The look on my face was equal parts enthusiasm about the new model and anxiety about the change. While I knew we needed to adopt a new way of doing business, I hadn't known the level of effort it'd take to get there.

Charan continued. "A growth-oriented Chief Digital Officer and his team will be the custodians of the Digital Innovation approach and growth.

They ensure Pods live and breathe the guiding principles and follow the Digital Innovation approach at the spokes."

Mike looked at the whiteboard, taking a deeper look at the hub and spoke model and asked, "What's the expectation on the *Growth* side?"

"Glad you asked. It's important that you know about a methodology called GrowthOps. Digital Giants and forward-thinking startups leverage this methodology to convert strangers into promoters. It's a discipline that sits at the intersection of product, marketing, and data science with a goal to continuously discover and continuously innovate," he answered.

"That's interesting. Tell me more," said Mike.

"Well, the GrowthOps Team's aim is to get the largest percentage of the target customer base to experience the core value of the product or service as *quickly* and as *often* as possible. As the target customer experiences the product or service, data is analyzed intently to get insights into customer interactions. The GrowthOps Team identifies friction points and implements rapid innovation and experimentation to systematically unlock strategic opportunities—i.e., to experiment with ideas, test and scale or pivot at speed," he clarified.

"I guess it promotes a culture of experimentation and pushes us to fail fast," I said.

"Exactly! Just like how you have Design Strategists and Specialists at the hub, you form a GrowthOps Team under you with data scientists and growth experts. The GrowthOps Team supports multiple Innovation Pods from the hub with the right instrumentation so the Pod can test, learn, scale or pivot," said Charan.

I thought GrowthOps was a great idea but I wanted to pivot to day-to-day execution. "Since Innovation Pods collaborate with cross-functional teams, do we need to have a steering committee?"

Charan shook his head. "Nope. A steering committee is usually viewed as a group of advisors. You don't want advisors. You need *doers*."

He went to the whiteboard and wrote *Management Committee*.

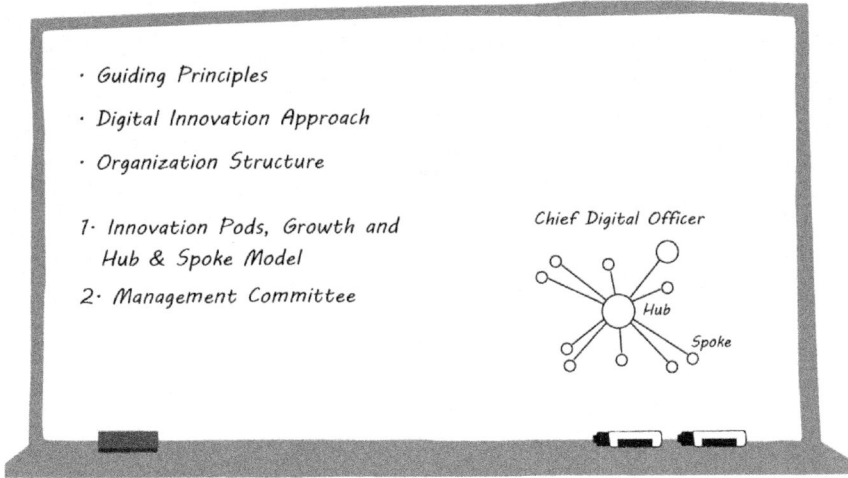

- Guiding Principles
- Digital Innovation Approach
- Organization Structure

1. Innovation Pods, Growth and Hub & Spoke Model
2. Management Committee

Chief Digital Officer

Hub

Spoke

"You must form a Management Committee that includes senior executives from all four businesses, the SLT and the heads of enabling functions. Each committee member must act like a director of a venture capital firm."

"Director of a venture capital firm, huh?" asked Mike. His brow was furrowed in thought.

I jumped in. "Interesting, so the committee must have a vested interest in the success of every Innovation Pod?"

"Exactly right! Innovation Pods are like mini startups within the larger organization. If they face any blockers, the Pod Leads are expected to surface it to the Management Committee. The committee manages by exception to bring efficiencies," he said.

"Does that mean that if the Pods don't have any blockers, it's assumed that the Pods are progressing as per plan?" asked Lisa.

"That's right. For the pods with blockers, leaders in the Management Committee are expected to take the necessary action to put the pods back on track," explained Charan.

Mike thought for a moment. "Should we link rewards and recognition of the committee members to how effectively they remove these blockers?"

"Fantastic," I shared with excitement. "That creates a drive for each committee member to go above and beyond to empower the Pod and make the cover story a reality."

"I'm okay with rewards and recognition but alignment with purpose is critical. Remember, aligned and committed teams lead to better results," clarified Charan.

Mike and I nodded.

I started to feel confident about the Management Committee and how well it would accelerate our trajectory toward becoming a digital-first organization.

"How often should the Management Committee meet?" asked Stacy.

"The committee must meet weekly to clear any blockers in the shortest time frame possible. Each committee member must have an SLA that ensures the smooth functioning of the Innovation Pods," explained Charan.

"Can you show us how the hub and spoke model and the Management Committee will come together?" asked Mike.

"Should I draw it on the whiteboard?" asked Charan.

"Yes, please."

I chimed in. "Let me take a shot at it."

I tried to make the hub and spoke model look real, with multiple Innovation Pods within each spoke—how it might look a year from now when we were firing on all cylinders.

Charan analyzed my work. "Looks about right."

Lisa intervened. "Although we had a lighter version of the hub and spoke model in place, what we lacked was the Management Committee? Right, Neo?"

I nodded.

After a few moments, Mike said, "Well, I love this model and I think this should work great." There had to be a *but* coming. And there was.

"But it will take time. Time to create the new structure and time to get it to a steady state. We can't—"

Charan interrupted Mike and said, "I do understand your apprehensions, Mike. If you want to become digital-first, change is inevitable. You must start somewhere. Start small and scale it, assuming it works. If not,

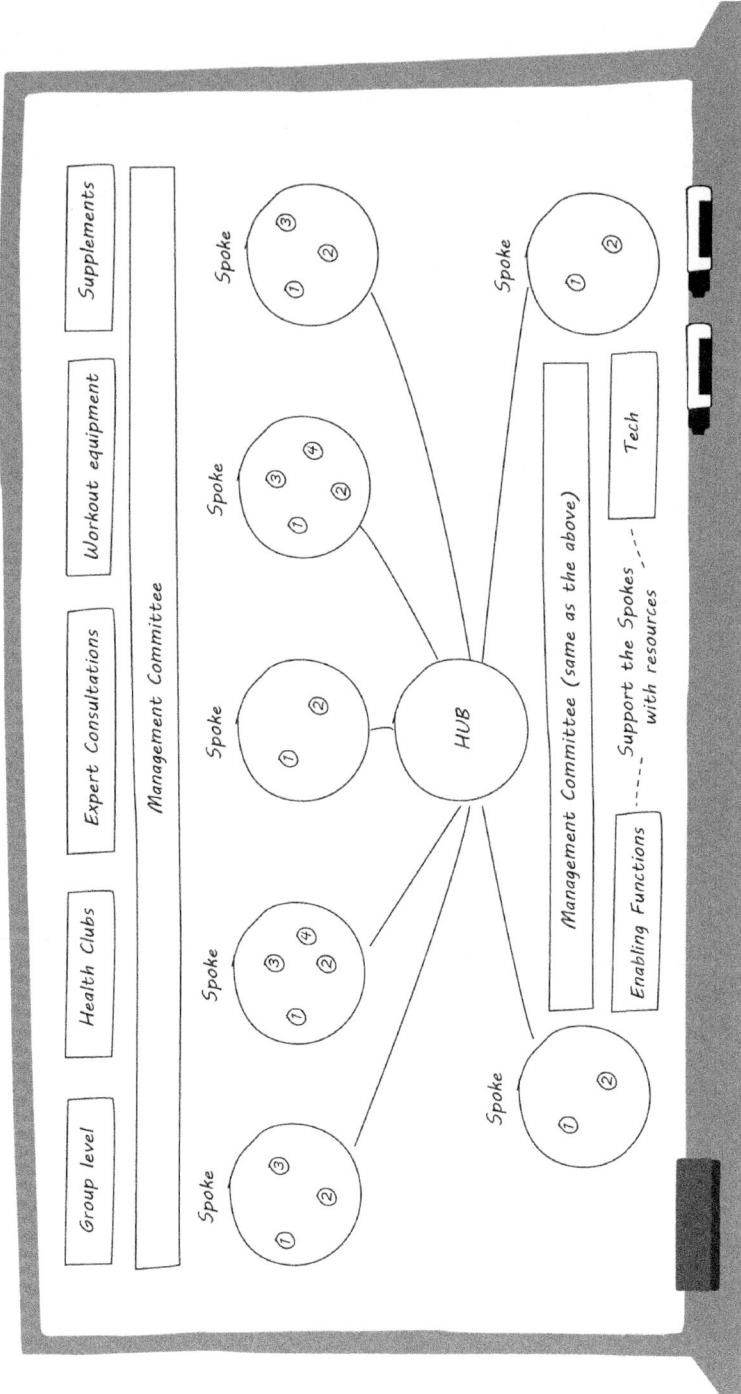

Group level | Health Clubs | Expert Consultations | Workout equipment | Supplements

Management Committee

Spoke ① ② ③
Spoke ① ② ③ ④
Spoke ① ②
Spoke ① ② ③ ④
Spoke ① ② ③

HUB

Spoke ① ②
Spoke ① ②

Management Committee (same as the above)

Enabling Functions ----- Support the Spokes with resources

Tech

we can regroup to try a different model." He looked at the whiteboard again and said, "Although, I feel confident that this model should solve your issues."

I was thrilled. Keeping in mind that Charan might leave at any time, I wanted to get every iota of wisdom from the time left. I asked, "Is there anything else in the organizational structure?"

"Yes. The Digital Governance & Value Realization Office."

He went to the whiteboard and added *Digital Governance & Value Realization Office.*

"And what's the purpose of this office?" asked Mike.

"Let me explain. First and foremost, it must function like an investment board that reviews every single cover story, funds the cover stories, and reviews the progress of each Innovation Pod monthly. The office must align cover stories with purpose, drive and ensure value creation, enforce new operating norms and methodologies and act as a proactive change agent within the organization."

"Aaah…they bring alignment across the organization and ensure the right digital initiatives are selected to accelerate the journey to achieve the purpose," I said. It was sort of a question.

"Spot on," he said and added, "they are also directly responsible for portfolio and financial management, value realization and measurement, business and technology sourcing, vendor management, change management and culture. And last but most important, building a self-reflective organizational structure." He emphasized at the end.

"Self-reflective, meaning…a mechanism to look inward and correct itself?" Lisa asked.

"That's right. In other words, the system must look at itself, evaluate and refine. For example, if it comes to the notice of the Digital Governance Office that the procurement function has been slowing things down because of its manual processes, the office must instruct the hub to activate an Innovation Pod to reimagine procurement processes and automate where necessary."

"That's like reinforcement learning…much like measure, learn and pivot. And the cycle continues forever," I added.

"Yes. To make this happen, you need the right senior leaders in the Digital Governance Office. It must be headed by the Chief Digital Officer in partnership with the CFO and have a team with cross-functional representation," explained Charan.

Mike looked like he was processing Charan's ideas. He asked, "Does value realization mean financial management?"

"That's right. I guess you've sorted out the new measures with your CFO…haven't you?" asked Charan.

"Yep. We're good there," I said.

Charan looked at all the details on the whiteboard and said, "Well, get these activated. You will be in good shape once you implement these."

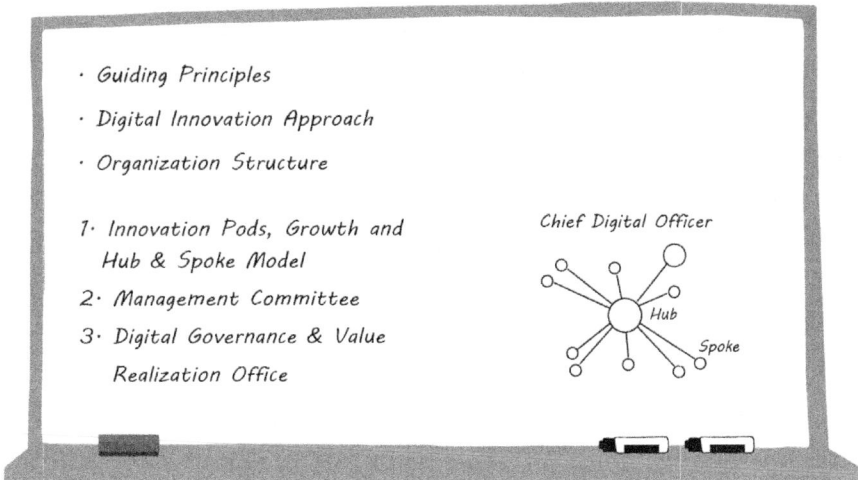

· Guiding Principles
· Digital Innovation Approach
· Organization Structure

1· Innovation Pods, Growth and Hub & Spoke Model
2· Management Committee
3· Digital Governance & Value Realization Office

Chief Digital Officer

Hub

Spoke

"That's what we hope too," said Mike.

"Alright, I have to move on to my next meeting," Charan said as he picked up his things. He shook hands with the team and wished us the best.

As Charan and I stepped into the elevator, he hinted that there was something more to becoming a digital-first organization. "Neo, I haven't touched upon grassroots innovation or innovation through startup collaboration. First, get the organizational structure right. We can talk about the other things later."

"Okay."

We stepped out to the lobby and saw a chauffeur in a black suit waiting for Charan. He gestured toward the limousine waiting at the curb. I walked Charan to the car.

As he walked, Charan looked at me and said, "One more point. Most of the cover stories you shared are designed to make things faster, cheaper, or better. Doing only those will be shortsighted." He paused and said, "Today, no matter how fast you innovate, competition catches up quickly. Focusing on cutting costs with digital will help in making existing processes more efficient but you have to look farther out—disruption could change everything about the business, making the efficient existing processes obsolete."

"I get it. We need to balance the dichotomy of digital."

He nodded.

The chauffeur opened the door for Charan. As Charan stepped in, he looked back at me and said, "Launch a new digital business. Build a digital ecosystem with partnerships. Remember, it's not the companies that compete in the future. It's the ecosystems."

And then he bid me adieu.

The chauffeur closed the door and returned to the wheel. The limousine sped off to its next destination.

TEST RUN

Driving to work the next day, I thought about our discussion with Charan and the list of actions we needed to implement. It was obvious that I needed to pull back on the number of Innovation Pods—twelve was simply too many. The most important next step was creating the Management Committee. But formalizing a Management Committee at the organizational level would be a complex ordeal. Sam would need to sign off and then I would have to get buy-in from all the leaders, followed by change management and much more. I did not have time for that.

As soon as I reached my office, I told my EA to schedule a meeting with Mike. Meanwhile, I started writing down a list of the actions Charan suggested. As I was updating my list, I heard someone knock the door.

"May I come in, boss?" It was Lisa.

I looked through the glass door and waved my hand.

She walked in, looking at the notes on the whiteboard. I could tell she was considering the way forward.

"Our discussion with Charan was very interesting—have you thought about the next steps to roll out?" she asked with genuine curiosity.

"Yeah!" I walked to the whiteboard where Charan wrote the building blocks and said, "We have some heavy lifting to do in organizational structure. We've seen that twelve innovation pods are too many if we don't have the right governance structure. But rolling out a Management Committee at an organizational level would require a lot of time and buy-in from leaders."

"I guess getting buy-in without proving the model would be tough." She sounded worried.

A thought came to me. "What if we create a lighter version of the Management Committee to *prove the model?*"

"A lighter version?" she asked.

"Yeah—if we reduce the number of pods and focus on a handful of digital initiatives, we'd need far fewer leaders in the Management Committee. It'd take a lot less time and effort to form."

"And we can determine exactly who's needed in the Management Committee for a handful of digital initiatives," she said.

"Exactly."

She kept thinking. "I understand where you're going with this. Let me pull up the initiatives and see which ones to pick."

In the next ten minutes, Lisa and I had narrowed the scope to four initiatives:

At-home workout equipment with an expert guidance ecosystem – to balance the dichotomy of digital

Churn in supplements business

Personalization with a 360-degree view of the customer

Solve supply chain issues to increase on-time delivery

My EA interrupted and said, "You can meet Mike in an hour at a nearby coffee shop. Okay?"

"Sure...thanks."

After my EA left, we got back to the next critical step—identifying leaders for the lighter version of the Management Committee.

"Let's pick the leaders, starting with the easy and obvious ones first."

"Okay."

"We need a senior leader from each enabling function—Legal, Commercial and Risk," I said.

Lisa added, "We also need Neel for Tech. Tim for Sales and Stan for Operations."

I cringed at the thought of onboarding Stan. But Operations was a critical piece in digital transformation. He had to play along so he could be part of the growth story. I decided to seek Mike's help.

Lisa went on. "Now let's look at the four initiatives. We'll need a leader from the supplements business and a leader from the workout equipment business."

"If they can't make the time to meet every week, we'll ask them to nominate their second-in-command, who must have the power to clear blockers," I added.

"What about Anna Chang, our CMO?" asked Lisa.

"Yeah, she would be part of the Management Committee...and the Innovation Pod for the home workouts with an expert guidance ecosystem initiative. It's her idea."

Lisa nodded and looked at the list again.

"I think we have a good set of leaders," she said.

"Great. I'll run this by Mike and get his thoughts. In the meantime, form four Innovation Pods to drive these digital initiatives."

I grabbed my notes and headed to meet Mike. As I walked to the coffee shop, I thought about Sam's email, the one I had deliberately ignored: *COME AND SEE ME IN MY OFFICE.* She was clearly upset about something. Maybe because of the way the twelve Innovation Pods had performed? I had to get Sam onboard to move forward. For that, I needed Mike. With Mike around, I bet Sam would behave like a sensible CEO.

I reached the coffee shop and saw Mike wrapping up a meeting and shaking hands with a tall gentleman.

"Hello," I said.

"Hey, how is it going?" said Mike.

"Hmm...hanging in there," I said. "Thanks for taking time. I need to run a few things by you before I roll out some of the recommendations we got from Charan."

"Go on, I'm listening."

"I think it's best to start small to prove the organizational structure Charan suggested. We can scale it across Fitness First once we prove the model."

"Okay."

"To start small, I handpicked four digital initiatives. We'll form a lighter version of the Management Committee to accelerate outcomes."

"What about the rest of the recommendations?" Mike asked.

"I am not too worried about it. Governance...the hub and spoke model...Guiding Principles...the Digital Innovation approach...all these will be manageable since we'll have just four Innovation Pods."

"Let me get it right—you'll still have these taken care of but not in a formal way like Charan suggested?"

"That's right, except for guiding principles, which must be organization wide." I paused and emphasized, "The Management Committee is the most important one...and I need your help there."

Mike thought for a moment and nodded. For the next fifteen minutes, we discussed the four digital initiatives and team composition for the Management Committee. He refined the list and suggested how we might bring the leaders onboard.

"Thanks for that Mike. I just need help with one of the leaders."

"Let me guess...Stan?"

We laughed. Or at least he did. At that moment, all I wanted was one less thing to worry about. I was already stressed about Sam and how to get her onboard with this approach.

I added, "Can we meet with Sam to align her with the way forward?"

"Come on—you've got to start managing your boss." He winked and smiled.

"I will. I just need you around to nudge Sam...if required."

He smiled and agreed to join me.

I thanked him and we shook hands. As I walked back, I was thankful that Mike had been kind enough to set aside time whenever I needed. It was unusual for a board member to get involved in day-to-day affairs. I wondered why he was taking that extra time to help me. Maybe he felt like he owed me because he couldn't help me at Digi Gate.

For a moment, I felt Mike would have been a great boss to work with. He had most of the qualities of a true transformational leader. He entertained new ideas, adapted quickly, listened, made difficult decisions, inspired the team, shared collective organizational consciousness, and led with a clear vision.

If only Sam had some of these qualities.

———————

The next day Mike and I met Sam in the boardroom. I suggested to Mike that we be discreet about Charan. Instead, we should keep it simple by focusing on the test run and the Management Committee. He agreed.

Sam stormed into the room, looking enraged. I took a breath and started with an apology.

"I know you're upset about the past few weeks. My team and I had a terrible misunderstanding about how to escalate issues to me when I was in India, taking care of my family situation." I paused and added, "I agree that things went out of control—and I promise that won't happen anymore."

My apology didn't seem to make any difference. As she was about to reply, she noticed Mike sitting opposite to me. She walked to him and shook his hand, then sat down. "I am losing it here, Mike. You know how the board has been the past few quarters. They're losing patience, aren't they?"

She was trying to take the board's pulse but Mike was careful in his response.

"There is still time," he said. "Neo has something to share. I saw it. Let's hear him out."

Over the next fifteen minutes, I explained the four digital initiatives and how a lighter version of the Management Committee would accelerate the outcomes of the four Innovation Pods.

She looked puzzled. "Another new thing?" she asked.

"Yeah," I said. "We need it…if we want outcomes quickly."

Mike jumped in. "Look, Sam—you should consider giving Neo a free hand. In the end, he shouldn't feel like he was never given a chance to try."

Sam kept thinking.

I went on. "I'll do everything I can to make it work. And I am confident that it will work. If it does, it'll be a win-win."

"You have Neo's neck on the line, Sam. Win or lose," Mike said, hinting to her that if I were to win after five months, she would get the credit. And if I were to lose, she'd have a scapegoat.

She nodded and gave me the go-ahead. I was thrilled to see Sam onboard.

"Now don't screw up, Neo," said Mike.

I smiled and gave a thumbs up.

Just when Sam was about to head out, I remembered the partnerships and collaborations I had created with a few businesses in India and Europe.

"One last thing, Sam. When I was in India a few weeks back, I rolled out collaborations with leading fitness clubs and their trainers in Europe and India. They might be useful for our at-home workout ecosystem of trainers."

She didn't seem to pay much attention—she was getting a call. She waved her hand…but I wasn't sure whether she meant *do whatever the heck I want* or if she was just saying goodbye. I hoped the former.

Over the next few days, I formalized the Management Committee and set the cadence, structure and expectations as suggested by Charan. I got a text from Mike that Stan understood the future state organizational structure and the role Stan must play if he wanted to be part of the growth story. Stan would play along from now on.

With all these things set, I was ready to hit a home run.

BALANCING THE DICHOTOMY OF DIGITAL

It was Friday afternoon at 3 pm. Out on the street, I saw people leaving Trinity Towers to start their weekend. I was sitting in the conference room, waiting for the teams from the four Innovation Pods. We planned a hands-on workshop on the new way of driving digital initiatives.

Lisa had added representatives from the business in addition to the standard team structure for the Pod: a Product Manager, Business Designer, Visual Designer and Full-stack Developer. As the team entered the conference room, Lisa and Stacy handed out training materials and an expectations docket with the agenda for the next three hours. It was filled with experiential, interactive, and hands-on activities. It was a crash course for the team to unlearn old ways and relearn the new way of driving digital initiatives with the Digital Innovation approach, Management Committee, governance, and guiding principles.

As we wrapped the session, Anna walked towards me. We talked briefly about the workshop, collaborations, and partnerships with fitness trainers and how an ecosystem integrated with her idea.

True to her marketing spirit, Anna was keen to get a product to the market as quickly as possible. She was more aggressive than I would have guessed. I shared the typical time taken to launch a major initiative.

She was startled. "You mean…it would take six to nine months for us to hit the market?"

I nodded.

"No freaking way!" she panicked. "Our competition is killing us. They're beating us on innovation. Their latest product announcement shows why we can't be acting as if it's business as usual. We need something here and now. We just can't afford to wait for nine months."

"I don't disagree with anything you said." I thought for a moment. "I think there may be a way out."

Anna appeared curious.

"First, let's *Frame the challenge* and *Know the customer*. How about we kick off the initiative with the Innovation Pod on Monday at 9 am?" I asked.

She checked her phone and said, "Sure…that should work."

By the time I finished my discussion with Anna, it was half past seven. I was ready to retire for the weekend. Reflecting on the events of the past few days, from a near-death experience, to turning things around, to kicking off four innovation Pods with a Management Committee, I felt the week had turned out great.

As I drove home, Anna's concerns stuck in my mind. I wondered how we could accelerate the product development cycle.

Immediately, I thought of a Rapid Innovation Sprint.

Prior to Digi Gate, I ran a Rapid Innovation Sprint with the team at Nuibi Pharma where we created a smart pill box to help the elderly take their pills without fail. We took about three months from concept to industrial design to product development. It took another month for the launch plan, marketing strategies, etc. Overall, it took four months from concept to getting the product to stores.

A Rapid Innovation Sprint should work here.

As I drove further, I tried to keep my mind off business, to clear my head. I looked at the weather forecast for the weekend. No clouds, blue skies, sunny weekend, couldn't ask for more. I decided to unplug for the weekend with some hiking, meeting up with old friends and catching up on sleep.

———————

The weekend went as planned. I was recharged for the most important week at Fitness First—all four Innovation Pods kicking off at the same time. With a packed Monday ahead of me, I went to work slightly earlier than usual. When I set foot in the office, I saw Stacy, Lisa, and most of the team busy working at their desks.

"I thought I'd be the only one early to work," I said to Lisa.

"Important day, boss," she replied. "By the way, I need to kick off the two Innovation Pods to address *Personalization* and *Supply chain issues*. I won't be able to join Anna's meeting at 9."

"That's fine. Good luck."

I walked to my office. Stacy and the Innovation Pod team for the *At-home workout ecosystem* joined me.

"Is it 9 already?" I asked Stacy.

"No, we want to clarify a few questions before Anna shows up."

Over the next thirty minutes, we discussed their questions, mostly on the Digital Innovation approach, pre-work, etc. I nudged them to think big, keeping in mind the collaborations and partnerships we had established.

"Good morning, folks," Anna said as she walked into my office. "Have you found a way to shorten the time to market?"

"Yes—but let's start with a shared understanding of the problem and a shared knowledge of the customer's context for home workouts," I suggested.

Source: Shutterstock

Personal Details		Bio Data
Name	Daisy Rogers	Daisy Rogers is a gym freak. She has a very busy schedule because she has to manage her family and her own professional life. Nearest Gym is 7 KM from her home which requires 20 mins of driving
Age	26	
Location	New York	
Profession	Developer	
Gym Freak	Yes	

Wants and Needs	Pain Points
• Wants a coach who guides with proper knowledge. • Needs a proper daily routine time table for exercise and diet charting. • Even when I am in the office, I do some exercise while sitting on a chair. • Remind me when I forget to do exercise.	• I don't find enough time for exercise, and don't have a proper diet chart to follow. • My schedule is very tight so sometimes I forget to exercise. • The gym is too far from my home; travel is very time-consuming. • The gym instructor is not regularly on time.

"I am a working mother. So I hardly find time for travelling to the gym. I wish it was in my home"

Anna projected her market research slides. They explained the opportunity and customer insights, among other things.

"With this background, let's *Frame the challenge.* For that, let's put ourselves in the customer's shoes and explain the challenge from a customer perspective. Specifically, let's clarify who the customer is, what they're trying to do, why they're facing the issue, how they feel and what their outcome is."

Stacy seemed prepared. She dove in. "There are many fitness enthusiasts *(who) that don't* have the right training or guidance to be fit in the comfort of their home *(what)*. They like the experience they get at the health clubs and want a similar experience in their homes *(why)*. This makes them feel helpless *(how they feel)* and less motivated to stay fit in the comfort of their homes *(outcome)*."

"That's great—does the rest of the team agree with the challenge?" I asked.

Anna chimed in. "Yeah, that's a good summary."

"Okay, let's move to the next step. *Know the customer* and understand their context," I said.

Anna invited three fitness trainers in for a thirty-minute discussion. We asked several questions to get specific insights into the customer's unmet and unarticulated needs and their challenges while working out at home. Contextual details of the customer painted a clear picture of what they would experience while working out at home. In addition, Anna shared market-related data and analytics associated with the workout equipment business and personal training business, showing behaviors by customer segment.

With that understanding, I went to the whiteboard to chart a high-level customer journey.

Anna spoke with resignation in her voice. "Will the customers believe that a virtual workout would be as good as an in-person session with a trainer?"

I shrugged.

She went on. "Will the customer be able to easily select from the choice of workouts based on the equipment they own?"

We wouldn't know for sure. I had to shrug it off again.

Buy

Customer learns about the virtual personal trainer network & downloads the app

Set up

Customer creates an account

Select

Customer selects a trainer and schedules a one-on-one workout or a class

Workout

Customer works out with the assistance from the trainer

"How can we move forward if we're not sure? But…" She left the sentence unfinished, waving her hand in the air. Anna wanted to go to market fast, with the right product experience that would resonate with the customer.

Hearing her apprehension, I introduced what I did at Nuibi Pharma. "A Rapid Innovation Sprint will give us the answers."

Anna's eyes went wide.

"What's that?"

"It's a 5-day rapid innovation process for creating new concepts and for answering critical business questions through prototyping and testing ideas with real customers. It involves business strategy, innovation, behavioral science, design and more."

"Great—and time to market?" she asked.

"Much faster. Say four to five months from product concept to industrial design to commercializing."

"So, you're saying that we will have answers to my questions and a product concept in 5 days that can go to engineering and development?" asked Anna.

I nodded with confidence.

"I just can't believe we'll create a new product concept in 5 days. What happens during those 5 days anyway?" asked Anna. She appeared concerned about whether we could spend sufficient time to build a concept that sells.

"It's like a hackathon," I replied. "On Day 1, you frame the challenge, understand the customer, and pick the most important areas to focus on for defining the How Might We questions. On Day 2, you sketch competing ideas and solutions on paper. On Day 3, you make difficult decisions and turn ideas into testable hypotheses. On Day 4, you hammer out a realistic prototype. And on Day 5, you test the prototypes with real customers and decide whether to tweak the concept or abandon it."

"So, Day 5 is when we get answers to the questions?" asked Anna.

"That's correct."

"How many times have you done a Rapid Innovation Sprint?" Anna asked. She wanted to be sure that we were doing the right thing.

"Many times," I intentionally kept my answer vague. "All of them were successful. Successful in that we got the right answers—whether our product concepts resonated with the customers or whether we should abandon the idea."

"Awesome!" she said, excited.

I went to the whiteboard and wrote *Team* on the right and *Pre-work* on the left.

"A sprint resembles a perfectly orchestrated heist. In addition to the Innovation Pod Team, we need a few more members to pull it off successfully. In heist terms, first we need a mastermind who guides the team during the sprint," I said.

"That must be you," said Anna.

I nodded and wrote my name, adding *Facilitator*.

"We need a captain," I continued. "Someone with the authority to make decisions. I'd call this person the decider." I wrote *Anna* and added *Decider* next to her name.

"We need a key master who can make tech work for us. And a hacker who can mockup products that look real."

"I have someone who would be a perfect hacker," said Lisa. "She's our star product and design expert. As for the key master, we already have a tech expert in the Innovation Pod."

Lisa added their names to the whiteboard.

I went on. "We need an inside man who has reach, connects with customers and provides valuable information on what works best. And then a muscle man, who takes care of logistics and operations."

"Tim will be the inside man and Stan will be the muscle man," said Stacy.

"Yep. As for pre-work, we need to recruit real customers to test our prototype on Day 5."

Anna jumped in. "I'll collaborate with Tim on recruitment."

"Great. Let's make this happen," I said and asked Stacy and Anna to align with the new team members, coordinate schedules and complete the pre-work.

We spent the next few days planning for the Rapid Innovation Sprint and bringing new team members onboard. We regrouped again to begin implementation.

Day 1

Day 1 went smoothly because Tim, Stan and the Pod Teams already had experience in framing the challenge and understanding the customer. Anna quickly got into the process. We ended the day with two clear How Might We questions:

HMW create a virtual experience to train customers at home so that customers get guidance similar to the guidance they get from a trainer in a health club?

HMW create a simple and easy way to select from a choice of workouts based on available equipment and the customer's fitness goals?

Day 2

The goal for Day 2 was to generate ideas to solve the two HMW questions that were created based on Anna's questions. During the first half of Day 2, each team member was required to define "What If" statements that were grouped, categorized, rationalized, and prioritized. After that, each team member had the liberty to pick one of their best ideas to sketch out and add more details to during the second half of Day 2.

Solution sketches were drawn on sticky notes, showing what customers would see as they interacted with the product or service. The solution sketch moved along with the customer's actions as they experienced the product or service. I asked the team to make their sketches self-explanatory, with only a one-line description for each action, and a catchy title for the entire solution.

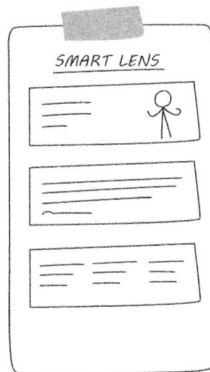

Solution sketch by a team member at the end of day 2

Day 3

Day 3 started with all the solution sketches taped to the wall like an art gallery in a museum. All the sketches were anonymous, to avoid bias. Each team member spent time looking through the details, leaving comments and questions and placing round stickers (dot votes) on ideas that seemed interesting.

Solution sketches at the start of day 3

There were no limits or rules for dot votes. Team members were allowed to put dot votes on their own solution. When they ran out of dot votes, I gave them more. After about fifteen minutes, we ended up with the following:

Solution sketches after silent review

After the silent review, the team gathered around each solution sketch. As the facilitator, I walked the team through each sketch. My goal was to go through each solution sketch and identify clusters of ideas that stood out. I then invited the sketch's creator to add any points I missed. I spent about three minutes per sketch.

After going through all the solution sketches, each team member was given one dot vote —this time a different color—to select their choice. The whole solution sketch or just one idea in the solution sketch could be voted for. The team was asked to consider HMW questions while voting.

Solution sketches with the teams' & decider's votes

Anna had the super vote to select the best idea. Her vote set the foundation for the storyboard. As a team, we took the winning ideas and stitched them together to create a storyboard.

A storyboard has an opening scene and illustrates the flow of events from a customer perspective—all tightly connected into one cohesive story. It was like a movie playing in frames—much like a comic strip but with a lot more details.

Everything seemed to be going great, better than I had expected. It seemed that the whole team was embracing the process. I was particularly pleased with how engaged Stan was being. Then Anna nudged me to take a glance at Tim. I could see resentment on Tim's face.

Storyboard with the most popular ideas

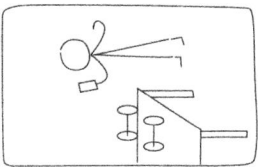

Customer scans the QR code to download the app

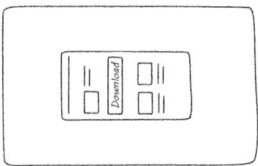

Customer downloads the app

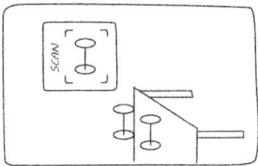

App asks customer to take a picture or scan the QR code of the workout equipment

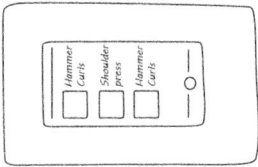

App provides options for workouts

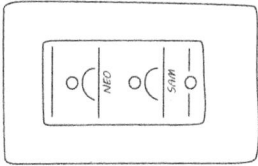

Customers can workout with the AI trainer or can schedule a session with a personal trainer

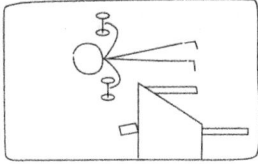

App tells customer to position the phone so the front facing camera can see the customer

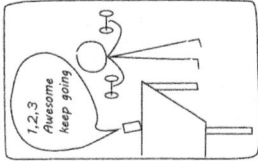

Customer starts to workout. AI trainer or the personal trainer provides feedback

Tim asked me if we could talk. I suggested Anna join us.

"We are eating into our own business," Tim fumed. "Our on-site gym facilities and personal training model has worked really well so far. You're crazy to think we need to do something different."

Anna responded, "I see your point, Tim. But we really don't want to be left behind—our competition and new entrants are already disrupting with digital. If there's one positive thing that can be said about recent events, it's that they've forced us all to think differently."

"Look, Tim," I added, "What worked before simply won't work anymore. We've seen whole categories shift as people have adapted—sometimes rapidly—to new behaviors. Some of them will become permanent."

I could see that Tim didn't like where this was going. I went on. "Business building with digital is important for organic growth. We have great ideas and the market needs what we're inventing."

Tim appeared disinterested. He said, "This new business model will cause a lot of trouble in sales. My people are already under pressure and selling personal training sessions is a big money maker for them. Soon news about these products will come out and I'm just not looking forward to handling the repercussions on my team."

Tim had a point but before we could address his issue sensibly, Anna said, "Look Tim, it's better that we align with our purpose. We need to find what works best for all of us. Sometimes that means leaving the old guard."

Tim misunderstood Anna and responded furiously. "So, you want me to leave? We'll see what happens." He took his bag and left the room.

It was too dramatic.

"What just happened?" Anna asked in disbelief.

I was shocked, speechless. Tim had been a team player on the Towels initiative—his abrupt exit felt like a betrayal.

She continued. "I wanted Tim to find what works best…for all of us. I wanted him to use this as an opportunity to turbocharge sales with new capabilities."

My mind churned, processing. I could see how Tim misinterpreted Anna's point. From Tim's perspective, leaving the old guard meant *find your way out.* I didn't know how far Tim would take things but it would be a blow to lose Tim as an advocate. He was well-respected not just by the SLT but also by the board.

"We'll sort it out," I said. "Let's finish our day."

Day 4

Tim didn't show up. It certainly created a vacuum. I wanted to address Tim's issue before it was too late but building a prototype was our top priority—we'd have customers coming on Day 5 to test it.

I explained to the team that we would adopt a "fake it" approach to turning the storyboard into a realistic prototype—the prototype would appear real, even if it didn't necessarily work like the final product. That was when I discovered that most of the team was uncomfortable with prototyping.

"We don't have enough time to build a functioning prototype."
"Will the customers feel we are just unprepared and too immature?"
"The prototype needs to fully work. How can we go with a half-baked solution?"

These were just a few of the questions I heard. This wasn't unusual. The reality was that the tools we regularly used to create high-quality experiences for our customers were not the right tools for prototyping. The regular tools were too slow. I clarified to the team that we weren't building a real product, it just needed to *appear* real—there was absolutely no need to make a pixel-perfect solution.

For physical prototyping, we used an in-house 3D printer. For digital prototyping (apps and screens), we used slide making software. The prototype only had to *appear* real.

I divided the team as follows:
- *Makers*— Business Designers and Visual Designers to make the components of the prototype as per the storyboard.
- *Stitchers*—Product Managers to stitch the components and ensure we had all the components as per the storyboard.
- *Script writers*—Marketers to create a realistic script that could be leveraged during the interview. Also, they would collaborate with Makers to

collate necessary collateral that would make the entire customer interview as close to real as possible.

- *Interviewers*—Sales and Customer Service managers to interview customers.

After working hard until lunch, we had something close to real. Stan did a walkthrough of the prototype components and Anna narrated the story to see if we needed to fill in any gaps. Around 4 pm, we did one last check to ensure our prototype would help us get the answers to the HMW questions. The prototype was great—I was looking forward to Day 5.

Ever since Mike had a chat with him, Stan had turned out to be a pleasure to work with. But not having Tim present weighed on me. I needed to bring Tim back into the exciting things we were doing.

"Have you heard from Tim?" I asked Anna.

"Nope."

"We should have a chat with him before it's too late," I said. She nodded in agreement.

I called Tim and requested that Anna and I meet him for coffee. While Tim sounded distressed, he agreed.

Anna and I deliberated on new ways to turbocharge sales but we decided to lead with empathy and go with the flow.

"Hey guys, what's up?" Tim asked curtly.

I smiled and shared a few fun moments we had during the day while creating the prototype and told him that we missed him.

No reaction. My attempt to reduce tension didn't seem to work.

Anna dove in. "Look Tim, I wasn't suggesting that you leave Fitness First. You're a great asset to the SLT. But I can see how my statement could be misunderstood. I feel sorry for what happened."

Tim listened quietly but appeared a bit shaky.

Anna continued, "All I wanted was to make the best use of the situation and take sales to a new level with digital, now that we have an opportunity to grow our at-home workout business."

Tim looked curious. "What do you mean by taking sales to a new level?"

"Let me explain. With the new line of business, we can reimagine how we approach sales. We can turbocharge sales with new digital tools and capabilities." Anna paused to let that message sink in.

I chimed in. "An Inside Sales Team." I paused. "How does that sound, Tim?"

Tim's interest grew. "Hmm...inside sales, huh?"

"Yeah. Powered by digital tools, we'll have fitness enthusiasts in the Inside Sales team reach out and connect with the next generation of customers proactively through a community approach."

He thought for a moment. "I guess the goal of the Inside Sales team will be to help—not sell to—our prospective customers on their path to better health?"

"Absolutely!" I replied. "Our products and services will naturally play a role as customers' progress toward better health. We'll no longer sell the way we do now. We'll train the Inside Sales team and define metrics differently."

"Imagine a community of like-minded customers based on their psychographics, behaviors and goals," Anna added. "These communities will be moderated by fitness enthusiasts who will be part of the Inside Sales team. When we pivot our approach to helping instead of selling, customers will trust us."

Tim looked thoughtful and nodded in agreement.

"How about we meet next week to hash things out?" I asked.

"Sounds good. By the way, is tomorrow the last day of the sprint?" Tim wanted to know.

I smiled. "Yes. And I have a role for you. Let's sync at 8 am tomorrow. I'll fill you in."

That night I slept a lot more peacefully. I was excited about sharing the prototype with customers and finding answers to the HMW questions.

Day 5

Tim and I walked into the room where we had set up the prototype. I clarified to the team that we weren't selling our solution to the customers, which was a *push* technique. Rather, we'd follow a *pull* technique. We'd observe. We'd ask questions. We'd learn by watching how customers interacted with the prototype and reacted to its features. We had to have curious minds, asking questions and understanding the "why" behind what customers did as they interacted with the prototype.

We set up an interview room where Tim and I could interview the customers. The interviews were broadcast to the sprint room, where the rest of the team was taking copious notes.

Tim and I interviewed five customers. Why five? Five was a magic number, according to Jakob Nielsen, a usability expert. Extensive research studies confirmed that we would discover 85% of usability problems with just five customers. The ROI of interviewing additional customers was extremely low. We used the following script:

- Friendly welcome—make interviewees comfortable with friendly small talk.
- Context questions—ask questions about the customer's life, interests, etc. to build rapport and understand how the prototype fits into their life.
- Introduce the prototype—set the expectations with the customer that:
  1. It is not a fully functioning product and that there might be a few components that may not be working.
  2. There is no right or wrong answer.
  3. They think out loud.
  4. And most importantly, Tim and I are not the ones who designed the prototype, so it's okay to give direct feedback.
- Tasks & scenarios—introduce a scenario or task and let the customer interact with the prototype. Ask open ended questions that start with the 5 Ws (Who, What, When, Where, Why) and 1 H (How). Never ask close-ended questions that can be answered with a yes or no.
- And finally, the magic wand question—if customers can get 3 of their wishes to come true to improve the product, what would they be?

Anna and Stan were surprised that customers didn't seem to care about the quality of the prototype. In fact, customers were happy to share their ideas to improve the prototype—*co-creation* is the best way to create winning products.

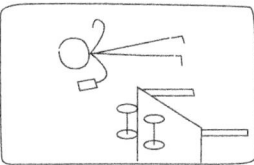

Customer opens the order and finds a CTA to download app

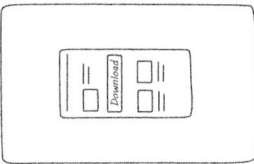

Customer downloads the app

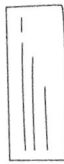

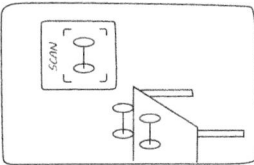

App asks customer to take a picture or scan the QR code of the workout equipment

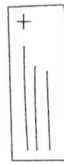

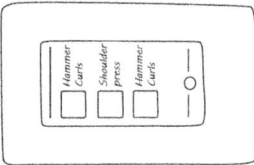

App identifies the equipment and provides options for workout

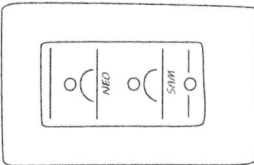

After selecting the workout, App asks the customer to select the instructor

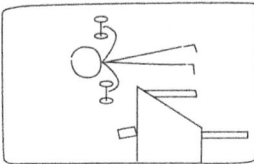

App tells customer to position the phone so the front facing camera can see the customer workout

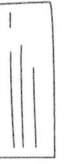

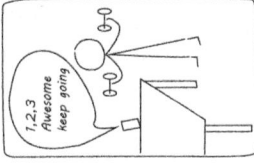

Customer starts to workout. App seamlessly counts the reps, shares inspiring messages and corrects workout form

Storyboard with insights—positive with green plus, negative with red minus and neutral with no sign

The best part of the sprint was that we never lost. It was a chance to learn how the product looked from customers' eyes, revealing problems our team wouldn't have seen otherwise, all under a week.

If the prototype didn't resonate with customers, we saved months of product development and engineering effort, not to mention the heavy cost associated with those processes.

If the prototype did resonate, we were off to a great start.

We completed the fifth interview by 3 pm. We then synthesized our notes; drew insights, themes and patterns, and determined whether we should tweak the idea or abandon it altogether.

We analyzed the patterns and insights, and categorized all the ideas into three buckets:

- Efficient failures
- Flawed successes
- Glorious winners

I reminded the team that a digital-first organization embraced a culture of failing fast and learning smart in order to course-correct rapidly. While we did not have any glorious winners, we had flawed successes for the most part and a couple of efficient failures. We spent the rest of the day refining the storyboard.

The sprint reminded the team why we were working so hard in the first place. Every interview drew the team closer to the customers we were trying to help. It felt magical and unbelievable. "Unbelievable" because it was the first Rapid Innovation Sprint at Fitness First. I felt like our heist team had walked away scot-free after a successful job. It was an amazing feeling.

As I looked around, I couldn't help but notice conflicting expressions on Anna's face. I could tell she was delighted that we had fast-tracked our product design efforts but it seemed like she wondered what was next.

"You happy with our progress?" I asked Anna.

"Yeah…couldn't be any happier."

Wait for it.

"But," she said, "I'm not sure whether we have everything we need to initiate product development. I am not sure where we go from here."

Stacy chimed in. "We envision a cover story. That's the next step in the Digital Innovation approach."

VOICE OF THE CUSTOMER

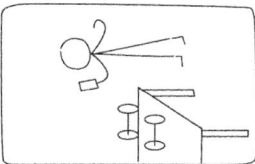

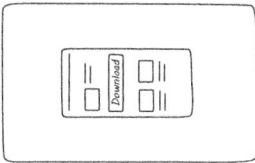

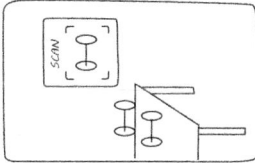

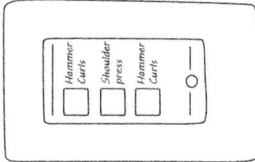

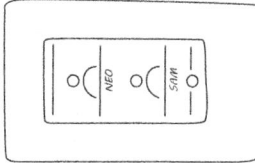

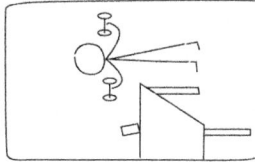

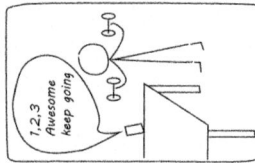

Goal setting is key to set the momentum

How do I know which one to select and when to select?

Inspire me with workouts

The Synthetic voice of the AI was a real put-off

The profiles of the human trainers lacked enough detail to make a good choice

I was caught off guard when the AI would count reps and correct my position

The video call with the human trainer was almost like an in-gym experience

NEW IDEAS

Add option to set goals and intensity of workouts based on equipment purchased

Based on goals, a weekly plan is suggested for targeted muscle groups

"You may like" section to show workouts and the equipment needed, with an option to add to the Wish List

Try life-like speech for the AI

Add training specialties and the ability to rate and review the trainers

Priming the experience with a tutorial at the time of set up

Refined storyboard ready for production

"Yeah, I heard about the cover story," said Anna.

"Great, do you want to share what you've heard?" I asked.

The rest of the team joined in our conversation.

"Okay, let's see." She thought for a moment. "A cover story is written as if it was published in a magazine at a future date where success has been achieved. It talks about the problem and the solution and includes a quote from the customer."

"And how digital solves the problem elegantly," added Stacy.

"Do you know who writes the cover stories?" I asked.

"No, but I guess it must be me. Right?" asked Anna.

"You and Stacy," I clarified.

"What about KPIs?" asked Tim.

"The at-home personal training ecosystem is a new business. We need to add business building metrics to the cover story."

"We'll leverage the mockups from the sprint and add Q&A," Stacy added. "After Neo approves the cover story, we submit it to Susan for her review and approval. Once the cover story is approved, funds are released and the Innovation Pod will work diligently to make the cover story a reality."

Stan cleared his throat and added, "I believe there is a Management Committee as well?"

"That's right. The Management Committee is a cross-functional committee composed of some SLT members as well as relevant business heads and leaders of enabling functions. The goal of the Management Committee is to review the progress of the Innovation Pods and remove any blockers to ensure that the Pods are progressing as per plan."

I looked at Stacy and Anna. "Can you turnaround the cover story in a day or two?" Stacy glanced at Anna to confirm and they both agreed.

I congratulated the team on completing a successful Rapid Innovation Sprint.

I spent the next two days catching up with all the Pod Leads. Each Pod had been progressing as per plan. Even better, I got an email that our second

Title

| Fitness First Launches Virtual At-Home Workouts |

Date of Launch	**Innovation Pod Team**
10th October 2021	Stacy, Anna, Matt, Nina, Michael, Vikas
Focus area	**Business Vertical**
Business Building	Workout Equipment

Summary

Fitness enthusiasts who prefer to workout in the comfort of their home are now able to get guidance from an artificial intelligence training expert or a real fitness trainer from the network of Fitness First trainers worldwide. Customers can plan and schedule their workouts, set fitness goals, and get expert guidance.

Opportunity/Problem Statement

Customers who buy workout equipment for home usage struggle to determine the right workout routine to address their fitness goals. Further, they are unsure of the workout equipment needed to address their fitness goals. They lack guidance and inspiration to workout at home. A survey indicated that guidance of what workout to do and how to do it is a critical factor for going to Health Clubs. The same survey indicated that customers resort to YouTube videos to get guidance, but it is not personalized, creating friction on their path to better health.

Solution/Idea details

Customers who buy Fitness First workout equipment can scan the QR code on the machine to download the Fitness First home workout app. Any customer can also download the app from the app store. After they complete their profile, they are offered suggested workouts that are possible with the equipment they own. They can work out with an AI trainer, which can see and correct the customer's workout movements. It can count the repetitions and inspire the customer to achieve their fitness goals. They can also schedule a personal training session or virtual class through the trainer marketplace. Customers can organize their workout routines, intensity levels and fitness goals. Customer can also purchase new equipment with a quick checkout process.

> **Customer quote**
>
> " As an amateur in fitness, I have been looking for workout equipment and a coach. Fitness First's at-home workout equipment has been a perfect choice. The AI trainer helped me set goals and got me the right equipment. Working out with the AI is great, but I also supplement with virtual workouts with a real personal trainer once per week.

Metrics to track for progress

| Idea to Proof of Concept – 3 months; Sales–~$20 M from year 2; ROI>10X; Time horizon – 5 years |

Optional

| **Potential Annualized benefits** | **Timeline** | **Investments Required** | **Digital technology required** |
| $20 M | 5 Months | $2 M (strategy, planning & first cut of product) | Computer Vision, Mobile app, QR code, AI trainer |

Cover story

Management Committee meeting was cancelled as no Innovation Pod Lead had reported any blockers so far. I was on a roll. It felt good that everything was under control. I decided to head home early.

Seeing me starting to leave, Stacy rushed to me.

"Can we discuss the cover story?" she asked.

"Right now?"

"Yeah. Anna and I worked on the details. We're fine for the most part. But we're stuck at metrics," she said.

For the next thirty minutes or so, we discussed the cover story, mockups and Q&A and refined them further. We specifically focused on the partnerships and collaborations that would be part of the digital ecosystem. We added metrics for business building, keeping in mind the time it took to launch the first cut of the product concept and to commercialize the product.

Since we had gotten feedback from customers already during the sprint, I said, "Why don't you align with Anna on the updates we made and then email the cover story to the Value Realization Office for review and approval?"

"Yeah sure," said Stacy.

"I'll have a chat with Susan about the cover story tomorrow. After her approval, we'll create a service blueprint," I said and stepped out.

The whole way home I was thinking about what the future held for me. I had only four months left, so I didn't have any time to waste. I felt sure our digital initiatives would change Fitness First's future trajectory. Personalization with a 360-degree view would drive marketing and retention. Reducing churn in the supplements business would grow revenue. The supply chain initiative would drive more at-home equipment sales. And the at-home workout ecosystem would create a new revenue stream, globally. All the initiatives had the potential to give a huge boost to Fitness First's profitability, assuming no one dropped the ball.

I needed to make the best use of every single minute.

DRIVING IT WITH AN IRON FIST

With my office guiding the Pods and the Management Committee clearing blockers, we progressed better than expected, at least for a month and a half. Then the bumpy ride started.

The pre-read for the 5th Management Committee meeting contained blockers that, if not resolved, would derail the digital initiatives.

Innovation Pod	Blocker Description	Need help from
At-home workout ecosystem	Risk team is against establishing marketplace agreements with global fitness companies	Vikas, Chief Risk Officer
Supply Chain	Negotiations with regional transportation companies for last-mile delivery stuck in vendor selection process	Tara, Chief Commercial Officer
360-degree view to provide personalization	Supplements business is unwilling to provide access to data	Leena, Supplements Business Head
	Data architecture not conducive for future state	Neel, CTO

Glimpse of the issue log

(The pre-read had details one would expect from a typical issue tracker—priority, dates, resolution needed by, etc.)

As I walked down the hall, I saw Tim and Neel heading to the conference room for the meeting. I went in and took a seat. The Pod Leads, Stacy and Lisa were standing at the far end of the table, ready to share their blockers. A slide projector was in front of them. They started to talk. The clock on the wall indicated it was exactly 8 am. I looked around at the others. We had 100% attendance, with most people looking at the Pod Leads and a few taking a last-minute look at the pre-read.

Stacy went first. She set the context, explained the criticality of the first blocker with the risk team and requested the committee to resolve it. Vikas, our Chief Risk Officer, a clean-shaven man in his fifties, took his time sauntering out from the chair and hoisting up his suspenders as he moved to the whiteboard. He drew a big zero and turned to Stacy.

"That's the number of risk-related issues we've faced since I took over," he said proudly. "I will not let anyone sneak through a risky proposition that puts us in jeopardy."

Stacy seemed anxious and looked at me.

"What's the risk you're seeing, Vikas?" I asked with genuine curiosity.

"We don't share our internal data and intellectual property with anyone." He looked at Stacy. "And your proposition is to share it with other health club companies? Our competitors? That sounds crazy!"

"Correction—just health clubs and personal trainers in non-US countries only. And it is only a small amount of data, just so they can participate in the trainer ecosystem," I said.

"Why does it matter?" he asked.

"It does," I replied patiently.

"Sorry, I don't want to entertain anything that looks like sharing," he said resolutely.

Tim intervened and spoke to Vikas. "I don't disagree with you here. However, I think we should broaden our world view in the digital era." He paused and then added, "Digital has been shaking things up and questioning age-old practices. It did to my sales function. I think you should hear what Neo has to say."

A few heads nodded in a barely perceptible way. The tension was peaking. Finally, Vikas looked at me and gestured to continue.

I decided to share the future state customer experience instead of drowning him in technical details. "Vikas, imagine a customer, anywhere in the world, can connect with a fitness trainer, again anywhere in the world, who could guide that customer on their path to better health. Our marketplace for virtual personal training would make that happen. It'd provide a choice of fitness trainers, track the workouts, guide our customers and inspire them to achieve their fitness goals. Fitness First is currently a US only company—but we can compete globally with a digital business. That's why we need partners in the non-US countries—to cater to our future global customer base," I clarified.

Then I introduced the jargon. "With this strategy, we will create a digital ecosystem and a multi-sided networked platform to turbocharge our future."

Everyone's focus shifted to Vikas. How would he react? I was pretty sure he must be considering the risks of this future business model.

"Sounds interesting and *risky*," he said, then paused. "I'd need to look into the specific risks and how to position us. Perhaps a limitation clause or something similar. I'll work with the legal team and sort this out, say, by our next committee meeting."

"So—you're aligned with the thinking?" I asked.

He thought for a moment and nodded. "Yes. I am principally aligned with the thinking but subject to risk clearance."

Everyone laughed at his legalese response.

Stacy moved on to the next blocker. "Getting additional regional transportation companies onboard has been stuck in the vendor selection process for a while now."

Tara, the Chief Commercial Officer, jumped in. "Look, guys…we requested quotes from different suppliers, keeping in mind your long-term needs. It takes time to get the bids, review them, compare and pick the best ones. You want the best and most trustworthy suppliers, don't you?" she asked, with a tinge of sarcasm.

"What if we break our needs into long-term and short-term?" I suggested.

"What do you mean?" asked Tara.

"We have some specific hot spots where we need to get better at last-mile delivery, fast. Can we focus just on those few areas, to solve the short-term issue?" I asked.

"Sorry but the process is same. Competitive bids are mandatory," added Tara.

"Why don't we try short-term contracts, subject to renegotiation? It might cost us more for last-mile deliveries but we would be meeting customer needs. Can't we make do with that? At least to bridge the gap?" I asked.

Tara kept thinking. After a moment, she said, "Well…I guess that should be *okay* for small volumes. We'll look into it."

"Great! Please run the competitive bids in parallel for our long-term needs."

"Yep, that's the plan," she added.

The Pod Lead for the personalization initiative went next. "As Mike stated during our initial SLT meeting, we have an amazing opportunity to get a 360-degree view of the customer as they interact with our business verticals. We can understand the whole customer experience across our health clubs, personal training and supplements. The personalization initiative aims to combine the data to provide a 360-degree view of the customer and help them on their path to better health. However, the data of each business is siloed."

She summoned her courage and announced, "Our goal of getting a 360-degree view of the customer will fail if we don't get access to the supplements business' customer data. But Leena is not willing to share it. She says it is Personally Identifiable Information (PII)."

The supplements business was acquired a year before Sam took over as CEO. It had been operating as a separate entity ever since. They clocked $150 M sales recently after a year of strong growth.

Leena, the head of the supplements business replied, "I am not willing to approve data sharing. I understand it helps us serve our customers better but privacy is more important. We agree with our customers that we will not use their data for marketing purposes."

The Pod Lead jumped in. "But we are not using it for marketing."

Leena frowned. "If you're not using it for marketing, what else is it for?"

The Pod Lead clarified, "We would use it to create a 360-degree health profile."

"And then?" she asked.

"We will help the customers set a fitness goal and—"

Leena cut her off. "And market our products and services, right? If that's not marketing, then what is?"

"But our goal is to put them on the path to better health," said the Pod Lead anxiously.

Leena's lips compressed. "Look folks…I get the idea of our purpose but I just can't do it. Customers have not consented to it."

Leena had a point. *Customer consent* it is.

I intervened. "What if we ask the customers what they want, subtly?"

"Excuse me?"

"You're right, Leena." I said. "We must get customer consent. Let them opt in explicitly. Customers who opt out won't be bothered and customers who opt in will get the benefits. We'll access their data only after customers give their explicit consent."

Neel spoke up quietly, while typing something on his laptop, "Which is in fact a practice adopted by leading tech companies and many health care companies where privacy is a serious thing."

Everyone looked at Leena, waiting for her response. After a few quiet moments, she agreed. She had to. We didn't leave her an option.

Lisa cheerfully moved to the last blocker. "We're aiming to get near-real-time data from all businesses to get a 360-degree profile. Each business has its own accounting software for consolidating financials and reporting and we discovered that all four businesses have a different architecture. We don't have the expertise internally to move forward," she said, looking at Neel.

"Wait," Anna said, "we will start getting live data from the at-home workout ecosystem very soon."

"Good point—we have to factor that in," clarified Lisa.

Neel didn't seem to be paying attention. It looked like he was messaging with someone on his laptop, perhaps helping put out the latest fire in IT. Then he quietly said, "With our cloud provider's data integration and transmission service live and kicking, we just need to add an *IoT Hub* that connects virtually any IoT device for streaming data. That's a non-issue."

He paused. "What was the other thing you asked?" He thought and then said, "Oh right, accounting software. What about it?" He was still looking at his laptop.

"Well, the technical team is unable to determine how to build data pipelines," said Lisa.

"First, the accounting software has to be integrated with the cloud provider before we talk about pipelines."

"Yeah…that's right. My bad, it was too technical and confusing. I believed the integration approach for one business wouldn't work for other businesses because each business has different accounting software architecture or something," added Lisa.

Neel looked up at her. "Now I get it. Health clubs is using an older version of the accounting software and it's hosted on-premises. The rest of the businesses are on cloud and on a newer version. We may need to explore a combination of an Open Platform Communications protocol and a PI integrator to connect the OSI PI server and push data to the Data Factory and then to the Data Lake so we can crunch data using AI and ML models."

We sat in the awkwardness of the moment, as most of the committee couldn't figure out what the hell Neel was talking about.

Neel noticed the discomfort in the room and tried to play it cool. "Oops…sorry. We need experts from our Independent Software Vendor. I'll get the account manager on priority."

I thought it was important for the committee to understand the basics of data architecture in plain simple English. So, I jumped in. "Just to clear the air on technicalities, we need a place to store data that comes from all businesses—that's called a data lake. Once we store it, we need a way to analyze the data — and the models Neel mentioned help us do exactly that. It's like an engine powering personalization. We analyze the data and that allows us to push the right outputs for personalization."

Neel smiled and said, "Thanks for that, Neo."

Over the next fifteen minutes, we created an action tracker along with dates for resolution and we identified who was on point for resolution. Stacy and Lisa took the lead in aligning the committee on the action tracker.

I was thrilled that we could solve (almost) three issues—assuming Vikas was onboard. That was better than none.

ALL-HANDS-ON-DECK

The Management Committee was working like a charm. We operated as *one team* aligned on our purpose. We questioned our assumptions and current practices. We found a way when we were stuck. We helped each other. We celebrated small wins. Most importantly, each committee member owned the problem and rallied for the success of the Innovation Pods. Aligning the leaders to our purpose and linking their key performance indicators with the Pod outcomes moved the needle in the right direction.

The four Innovation Pods were firing on all cylinders, making tremendous progress. I was particularly amazed by the outcomes of the at-home workout ecosystem initiative. Stacy drove the workstreams in the Innovation Pod with precision, including the partnership with the AI workout start-up, integration with data architecture, mobile app development using low-code/no-code services for the soft launch and last, but not least, content development with our fitness trainers. We were two weeks away from the soft launch. We would be the first ones to market.

Stacy walked into my office for our weekly check-in. She crashed into the chair, leaned back and rested her head. She looked stressed and tired. "Two weeks to go!" she said.

I smiled. "You've been moving mountains the past few weeks. Great job!"

"I don't know." She winced. "Soft launch is round the corner. I want to pick your brain."

"Go on."

"We have ten customers in the US for soft launch." She pulled up a file and flashed it on the screen and said, "Take a look at the rollout plan." Every aspect of the plan was displayed, from customer recruitment, soft launch period and success metrics all the way to dry run, marketplace and app readiness, and waivers. But it was US centric.

"This looks fine." I paused. "Do you have a separate plan for the international soft launch?"

She shook her head. "Sorry...I totally missed that." She considered the status of our contracts. "We have paperwork done with two health club companies—one in Europe and one in India. We're through with risk and legal clearances from Vikas."

"Great. Check whether the folks in Europe and India will be ready to pilot with us."

"Yeah sure. The fitness trainers in India are ready to go—they're from a health club chain in New Delhi," she added.

"Perfect. We should activate our partner network then." I was excited to take Fitness First global with the new business model. It'd be game changing as we redefined how fitness was thought about today. Any customer from anywhere in the world could engage a fitness trainer from anywhere in the world through our platform.

Stacy appeared concerned. "We may have a problem. Recruiting test customers internationally will take time. Legalities and waivers can be managed but recruiting is a long, drawn-out process."

I thought about Mom. It had been more than two months since her surgery. She must be focusing on strength training.

"I can get you one customer," I said. "My mom."

She laughed. "One won't be enough. We need at least a few more."

"Well, let me find a few in India and Europe. Send the criteria."

"Awesome. In the meantime, I'll work with our partner companies in India and Europe to get them ready." She looked at her phone. "Oops...I'm running late for a meeting." And she rushed out.

————

My next two weeks were quite busy overseeing the soft launch and guiding all four Innovation Pods. We did a soft launch with ten customers in the US, four from India and one from the Netherlands. Stacy was on her toes during the three weeks of the soft launch, ironing out kinks and tracking feedback systematically.

We got mixed feedback from customers. Upon further analysis, we found that the feature to automatically identify customers' available workout equipment using the camera on their phone was error prone. It made a terrible onboarding experience for customers. But once we changed the feature to allow customers to add their equipment manually, the next steps—setting fitness goals, selecting a trainer and tracking workouts—went smoothly. Stacy tested the onboarding experience with success and we were ready to commercialize the product.

After the successful soft launch, Stacy and I aligned with the Business leaders on the way forward. We hashed out the details for commercialization and fitness trainer collaboration in the US and within our partner ecosystem. We also agreed that the platform would be run and maintained by the Innovation Pod until a formal business team was set up and that the Pod would support the business teams in the ramp up for the widespread launch during the holidays.

SIXTH DIGITAL-FIRST REALIZATION

Digital Governance Model

Accelerate the digital-first journey through a clear set of Guiding Principles and a multi-faceted Digital Governance model that guides the Innovation Pods and removes blockers.

Digital Governance is the underpinning element that makes a digital-first journey successful. It outlines how leaders hold themselves accountable to achieve the purpose of the organization. It ensures the right people provide the right direction as the organization moves towards becoming digital-first. However, governance models can get complex and chaotic; this is especially true when organizations do not reorient themselves to cater to the nuanced demands of digital transformation.

The multi-faceted Digital Governance Model can be best understood by digging deeper into the expectations of a growth oriented CDO.

The CDO role continues to evolve. A CDO is expected to set the digital-first trajectory and the shortest path to achieve that trajectory. In addition, she must propel growth with the GrowthOps Team. She anchors the Management Committee that removes blockers. She drives the hub that acts as the nerve center to guide Innovation Pods. She also acts as an investment portfolio manager and heads the Digital Governance & Value Realization office. And she ensures growth for the long-term by leading culture transformation across the organization through guiding principles and training. She activates grassroot innovation to increase inclusion and accelerate the digital-first journey. Let's examine each of these in detail.

GrowthOps Team

Digital Giants and forward-thinking startups leverage a methodology called GrowthOps to convert strangers into promoters. It's a discipline that sits at the intersection of product, marketing, and data science with a goal to continuously discover and continuously innovate.

The GrowthOps Team aims to get the largest percentage of the target customer base to experience the core value of a product or service as *quickly* and as *often* as possible. As the target customer experiences the product or service, data is analyzed closely to get insights into customer interactions. The GrowthOps Team identifies friction points and implements rapid innovation and experimentation to systematically unlock strategic opportunities i.e., scale or pivot at speed.

The GrowthOps Team will be headed by the CDO and will include data scientists and growth experts who collaborate with multiple Innovation Pods. The GrowthOps Team enables a culture of experimentation and provides the right instrumentation for each Pod to test, learn and scale or pivot.

Management Committee

The Management Committee includes executives from businesses and enabling functions who must have the power to make executive decisions in their respective areas. Each committee member acts like a director of a venture capital firm, with vested interest in the success of every Innovation Pod. During the committee meeting, Pod Leads present blockers in their respective digital initiative and request help from the committee. Members of the committee deliberate during the meeting and take necessary actions to clear blockers.

The committee must meet weekly to clear blockers in the shortest timeframe possible. Each committee member must have an SLA or acceptable timeframe for resolution. Performance assessments of the committee members should be linked to how effectively they removed the blockers and should be reinforced with rewards and recognition.

Hub & Spoke Model

The hub acts like a delivery oversight powerhouse that guides the Innovation Pods to drive digital initiatives successfully at the spokes, i.e., at businesses or enabling functions. The hub, as the nerve center, churns out frameworks, methodologies, guidelines for the Digital

Innovation approach, playbooks with examples and new digital inspirations. Every Innovation Pod must be activated by the hub.

The hub has two primary goals. One is to ensure consistency in implementation and high execution quality. The other is to guide and support the Innovation Pods on the Digital Innovation approach, agile methodologies and emerging tech and solutions such as low-code/no-code, artificial intelligence, IoT, etc. The hub will be the custodian of the Digital Innovation approach and ensures that Pods live and breathe the guiding principles and follow the Digital Innovation approach diligently.

The hub is headed by the CDO and has Design Strategists—people who balance business strategy and human-centered design—and Specialists—people who have niche skills, like agile delivery or new emerging tech. Design Strategists and Specialists operate at the hub but they collaborate with multiple Pods at respective spokes to co-create digital solutions and unlock possibilities with digital.

Digital Governance & Value Realization Office

The Digital Governance & Value Realization office must function like an investment board that reviews every single cover story, funds the cover stories and monitors the progress of each Innovation Pod. The governance office must: align cover stories with the organization's purpose; drive and ensure value creation; enforce new operating norms and methodologies; and act as a proactive change agent within the organization. The office creates alignment across the organization and ensures that the right digital initiatives are selected to accelerate the journey to achieve the organization's purpose. The office is also directly responsible for portfolio and financial management, value realization and measurement, business and technology sourcing, vendor management, change management and culture. And lastly, but most importantly, they are responsible for building a self-reflective organizational structure that can look at itself, evaluate and refine.

The Digital Governance & Value Realization Office must be chaired by the CDO, in close partnership with the CFO, to drive the value realization agenda. The office must have senior leaders from business and enabling functions and must convene once or twice a month.

Guiding Principles

Every organization requires a set of guiding principles that defines a framework for expected behavior and decision-making. These principles guide the team from the CEO to frontline staff in all circumstances, irrespective of the initiative, strategy or type of work. Guiding principles must become a way of life. Hiring, firing and promotion decisions must be based on how effectively employees live and breathe the guiding principles.

Hire and develop digital talent—Every hire or promotion is crucial to set a precedent and to build the foundation for the type of organization you want to create. You must raise the bar with every hire and promotion. You must spot high-potential leaders and create opportunities for growth. Rewards, recognitions, and promotions must be linked to digital outcomes and metrics.

Start with a why—Lead with empathy to understand the customer's unmet and unarticulated needs. Every new initiative must include a cover story and service blueprint to capture the customer's needs. While solving for the customer, actively question every assumption you think you know about a given problem or scenario. Empower teams to create new knowledge and solutions from scratch to address the unmet and unarticulated needs of the customer, directly or indirectly.

Think big and deliver excellence—People who think big see problems as opportunities. They can visualize what they want and do not feel constrained by the impossible. They explore new ideas. They are risk takers, fearless, creative, and continually raise the bar. They drive teams to deliver high quality products and services. At least 10% of investment should be toward initiatives that create new revenue streams over a multi-year timeframe. Top performing companies set targets on revenue share from new offerings. For example, requiring that 20% of topline revenue come from products or services developed in the previous 5 years.

Ship to learn—Have a sense of urgency and a bias for action to ship the product and course correct with data as you move along. Build the right instrumentation to leverage data and *fail fast to pivot smart.* Speed to market is critical in the digital era to stay relevant and compete better. Create an award and recognize leaders who pushed the limit, failed fast, and pivoted smart.

Humanize tech—Tech must be relevant and useful. It must be purpose-built—it will be so when you humanize tech to solve the problem, and address the customer's unmet and unarticulated needs. Adding tech for the sake of tech will be suicidal. Monitor the solution concepts and question whether the solutions solve meaningful problems from a customer or business perspective.

Frugality—We are in a world with limited resources. Maximize the ratio of value to resources by doing more with less. Embrace constraints and adopt a mindset of simplicity and being resourceful. Aim to offer smart and effective solutions without sacrificing the quality of the user experience. Forward-thinking organizations limit their total investment in IT and Digital initiatives to a fixed percentage of topline revenue, usually in a range of 1% to 2.5%.

Grassroot Innovation

Everyone in the organization must think and act like innovators and problem solvers. This is especially true for the people at the bottom of the pyramid, who usually have greater visibility into unmet and unarticulated needs that emerge due to necessity, hardship, and challenges.

Activate the bottom of the pyramid through a platform to crowdsource ideas. Anyone, irrespective of their role or level, must be empowered to share their ideas by submitting a cover story. If their cover story is selected by the Digital Governance Office, an Innovation Pod must be activated to make the cover story a reality. The one who submits the idea can be part of the Innovation Pod.

The CDO and her team must institutionalize grassroot innovation using technology, gamification, and effective communication.

Ideas to remember

- Digital has created more destruction to incumbents than it has created value. Incumbents often follow a decentralized approach, where digital initiatives are run by business units or departments. Digital means different things to different executives and these efforts will be siloed and will likely not add up to anything significant. Digital initiatives need a holistic direction at the organizational level. Only then will they be worthwhile.

- The level of complexity and the time it takes to become digital-first and to scale big with digital varies from one organization to other. To get a general idea of how complex it will be and how long it will take, look at two elements. One, overall revenue from different channels; and two, how much of that revenue is from digital business models. These two data points can paint a picture of an organization's maturity and how complex the journey will be to become a digital-first organization.

- The structure of the governance model for digital transformation will be equally applicable for any business transformation.

- A truly transformational leader is one who entertains new ideas, adapts quickly, listens, makes difficult decisions, inspires the team, collaborates with partners, shares collective organizational consciousness and leads with a clear vision.

- Traditional organizations should not try to build complex, cutting-edge tech solutions in-house like the Digital Giants. In-house development tends to add people debt, tech debt and data debt. For faster results, traditional organizations should license software products from the Digital Giants or other organizations that have deep expertise in building and maintaining tech solutions. Excessive customization should also be avoided, which adds tech debt. Extract the maximum value from off-the-shelf applications before considering customization. In-house development should be confined to well-understood and practiced technology solutions and should be initiated with a long-term view.

- Successful digital startups usually have a scale-up problem. Building an organizational structure that can help startups scale while retaining a digital-first culture is the key to success.

PART 6
THE FINALE

GO BIG OR GO HOME

We met for our monthly digital staff meeting—the second to last one before my formal evaluation by the board. Everyone was present except Lisa. I sat down and fidgeted. To get the meeting rolling while we were waiting for Lisa, I asked Stacy about her Innovation Pod.

"How's the rollout plan coming along?" I asked.

"Good. We're almost done with marketing plans. We're launching in the US and India simultaneously."

"How is production? And the partner ecosystem?" I asked.

"Everything is under control," she said. "Partners are upbeat about the soft launch results and we are looking forward to add new marketing channels."

"Good." I turned to the Pod Lead of the personalization initiative and asked, "What's the latest on your initiative?"

"Data pipelines are established with all businesses. We have started creating a 360-degree profile of customers and we are defining personalization opportunities," she said.

"So, we now have *one-source of truth* for data?"

"Yeah, we do."

"Excellent."

Just then, Lisa walked in. She sat down and handed me the monthly report that showed how we were performing against our guiding principles and the Digital Innovation approach.

"What does the report say?" I asked, eager for the update.

She smiled. "We are doing much better than the previous month. I can say we're almost there. At least within our team, the guiding principles and Digital Innovation approach have become second nature."

Then she went into a summary of how we performed in the rest of the initiatives. We had come a long way since the beginning of the year. From a disastrous start to running four critical initiatives, full steam.

A bouquet of flowers and something that looked like a greeting card were sitting on my desk when I got back from lunch. Just when I was about to open the card, Mike rushed into my room.

He got straight to the point. "I've heard great things about the Innovation Pods and the progress you guys have made. The Management Committee, Value Realization Office, digital governance...all seems to be working."

"Yeah, that's right." I went over the specifics and how the new structure had been helping drive the digital initiatives. "If all goes well in the next two months, we'll have proved the model. And then we can formalize it organization wide."

Mike shook his head and his demeanor changed in a subtle but distinctive way. He was suddenly confident, even a little aggressive. "No need to wait two months. Let's formalize it right away."

I was stunned. "Wait...you want to formalize it right away?"

"Yep. If the model is working fine, why wait for two months? We're here to accelerate Fitness First's journey to become digital-first. If something works, we have to double down."

"But Sam is on vacation for the next few weeks," I shared nervously.

"That's fine. I'll take care of Sam."

I was apprehensive. Usually I'm a risk taker but with Sam in the mix, I wanted a perfect model to scale. "Should we try with maybe 6 to 8 Innovation Pods before we formalize the model organization wide?"

"No!" Mike shot back. "Let's go big or go home. Think of a roll-out plan and meet me at 8 am tomorrow. Okay?"

I nodded. I was stuck between a rock and a hard place. Mike was a board member, not the CEO. Knowing Sam, she'd be angry or probably furious. I didn't want to be on the receiving end. I was skeptical.

Should I convince Mike to hold off till Sam comes back? But he felt very strongly about formalizing. He made the call; he should have my back if something were to go wrong with Sam.

After thinking about potential ramifications, I decided that Mike was right—formalizing the model was the right thing to do for Fitness First. I'd leave the politics to Mike and would focus on a roll-out strategy. I spent the rest of the day defining what that strategy might be.

The next morning, I reached Mike's office at 7:50 am. Looking around, I figured it must be a temporary setup. There were no pictures or personal belongings whatsoever in the room. Though I wondered why a board member would need an office for himself.

"Good morning, Neo," said Mike as he walked in. He got straight to the point. "I've got thirty minutes to go through your plan."

"Sure. We need a two-pronged strategy. One is to set up the organizational structure Charan recommended—"

"You mean the Management Committee, digital governance and all that stuff?"

"Yeah, even the hub and spoke model."

"I remember all that. And you need to explicitly expand your CDO role to include the *growth* aspect as well, right?"

"Yep, that's the plan."

"What's the other part of your two-pronged strategy?"

"Culture—to bring about a change in mindset and behaviors, among other things. It covers the guiding principles, the digital mindset and grassroot innovation."

I could see Mike becoming slightly uncomfortable when I said culture. Culture transformation is a slow process. It takes time to get real outcomes and sometimes we may not see any.

"What's on your mind?" he asked.

I chose my words carefully, knowing I was broaching a touchy subject. "We must reset the tone at the top."

"You mean the SLT?" asked Mike.

"No not just the SLT. I'm thinking we have to focus on the top 50 leaders to effectively reset the tone at the top."

Mike's interest grew. "Top 50 leaders, huh?"

"Yeah—we want the top leaders to be neophiles and have a high AQ."

He looked confused and said jokingly, "Wait, did you just create a word from your name, Neo?"

I laughed. "I didn't realize that. I guess 'Neo' means *new*?" I tried my best to seem sincere but I didn't care much at that moment. I continued, "Our top leaders must be *neophiles*. Someone who is attracted to novelty and newness. Someone who's ready to explore newness with a growth mindset and who brings new tech interventions to business. We don't want anyone to have neophobia."

I was pretty sure Mike wanted every single employee of Fitness First to be a neophile.

"Interesting. What is AQ?" Mike asked.

"Adversity Quotient. Leaders must have grit and perseverance to succeed in the digital world. If there is one thing that's certain in digital, it's *obsolescence*. The rate of change in digital is incredible."

"Couldn't agree more. Our leaders must be resilient to face obstacles, thrive despite uncertainty and pursue uncharted paths to unlock possibilities with digital. And they need to do it before the competition does."

"Yeah—they must have a high AQ. Their thinking must go beyond our industry."

"How do you think we can get them there?"

"We'll do two things. First, we'll launch a series of experiential learning sessions for the top 50 leaders."

"Experiential sessions? On what topics?" Mike asked.

"First, digital leadership. Second, product management. And third, the Digital Innovation Approach and growth—we want to build a culture of innovation, working backwards and experimentation. We'll make the cycle of 'experiment, learn and iterate' second nature."

"Experiential sessions alone won't make the cut, Neo. You'll have to think of something more."

He was right. A classroom session on these topics would only get the leaders ready to a certain extent. We had to give them hands-on experience with live digital initiatives. "What if we have each leader be part of an Innovation Pod and contribute to a digital initiative?" I suggested.

He thought for a moment and said, "I wonder if we can take it one step forward. Why don't we tag a leader with a Pod Lead to drive a digital initiative?"

"Like reverse mentoring?"

"Yeah. I've seen reverse mentoring work wonders. The wisdom of the leader and the digital mindset of the Pod Lead will help each other up their game," he suggested.

"That's a brilliant idea."

"What else for the top 50 leaders?" he asked.

"One more thing. A monthly learn and share session to create a culture of continuous learning." I paused to let it sink in. "We must address the fear of failure that is deep rooted here."

"Agreed. But what happens during these sessions?"

"During each session, we'll have five leaders share one of their high-impact digital initiatives that they are particularly proud of. Impact is defined by value created or by lessons they can share from their failures."

"I doubt whether this alone would encourage leaders to push the limits," he said.

That made me think *Leaders may not be motivated to try new things just for the sake of sharing during a session.*

"What if we recognize them with an award?" I suggested. "Like a Digital Resilience award for leaders, who pushed the limit, failed fast and pivoted smart."

"Cool. And the ones who created the highest value could be awarded a Digital Path Maker award. We'll link it to their performance reviews, so they have the drive to push the limits. Why don't you define the criterion for both?"

I nodded. "Finally, we need to make changes to our policies to keep them in line with the guiding principles. I'll work with HR on that but we can't expect radical change overnight," I added.

"I can see that. I feel that if we do a good job in aligning the team with our purpose and have hiring, performance reviews and firing based on adherence to guiding principles, everything should fall into place."

I nodded in agreement. "Well, with experiential sessions, reverse mentoring and monthly learning and share sessions, I think that in a year, each leader will have imbibed a digital mindset, experienced the guiding principles in action and delivered business outcomes on digital initiatives. And most importantly, become a neophile."

"Yeah, I'm hoping so too." He paused. "Didn't you say something about grassroot innovation?"

"Yeah, we'll have a platform to crowdsource ideas. Anyone, irrespective of role or level, can share their idea by submitting a cover story. If their cover story is selected by the Digital Governance Office, an Innovation Pod will be activated to make the cover story a reality. The one who submits the idea can be part of the Innovation Pod."

"Nice. Let's gamify idea submission across the four businesses and make it exciting for everyone. It'll create a multiplier effect," he added.

"Sure." I was hesitant to introduce startup collaboration but I thought I should plant the seed. "Startup collaboration is the other area we could explore to accelerate digital adoption. In fact, we are partnering with a startup from India that developed an AI fitness trainer. They agreed to license their AI to us. It's part of our at-home workout ecosystem."

"Yeah, I've seen a number of digital startups disrupting the health and wellness space. What are you thinking of doing next?" he asked.

"Well, we'll identify focus areas first. These areas can be defined based on mega trends in the health and wellness space or based on a specific business problem. Then we can invite startups to collaborate with us through a hackathon."

"What's the model for collaboration with startups after the hackathon?"

"It gets a little tricky there. We should cross that bridge when we get there but I can share a couple of models now." I paused. "First, we could do a simple commercial engagement where startups solve the problem like a vendor or we could form a hybrid team with a few people from Fitness First working in collaboration with the startup like *one team*."

"I prefer a hybrid approach. Infuse a startup culture into these initiatives and it will slowly trickle into our organization."

"Yeah. We're doing the hybrid approach with the AI trainer start-up. Another model of startup collaboration is to be a strategic investor and define a new business model that combines our value proposition with that of the startup's to create something new and game changing."

Mike went into deep thought. "I guess startup collaboration is demanding and needs to be carefully thought through. Why don't we try to expand our work with startups next year?"

I nodded. "Agreed—we already have our plates full."

As I was about to talk about organizational structure, I heard someone knock on the door. I could see that it was Sam's Chief of Staff. Mike asked him to wait. We jumped back into our discussion. Over the next fifteen minutes, we hashed out the organizational structure, specifically the team composition for the Management Committee and the new team structure for the digital organization. He suggested I work on the details and formalize the new model with the help of HR and the Communications team.

As they say, *when it rains, it pours.*

REKINDLE

While walking back to my office, my mind was clouded with the tasks needed to formalize the new model. I texted Lisa to meet me in ten minutes. I walked into my office and started making a list. Suddenly, I smelled the aroma of flowers. My EA didn't have a routine of putting flowers in my office. Then I remembered the card and bouquet. My EA had taken the flowers and put them in a vase with water. Some of the flowers were already in bloom. And the card—it was nestled in the flowers. How nice of her, I thought.

I opened the envelope and unfolded a greeting card that looked hand-made. It was from Riya, *Congratulations Dad…You are a rock star!* and below was a handwritten message from Tina saying congratulations on the achievement. What was that about?

I video called Tina. She answered with a bright smile.

"Congrats!" she said.

"Hey, thanks…I got the flowers and the card. But what's the congrats for?"

"Didn't you know? You were in the news."

"News? Me?"

"Yeah—it's about your at-home workouts." She tried to show me the newspaper but aside from my picture the details were barely visible.

"What was it about?"

"It's about a startup founder who was *fired* from his own startup, then created an innovative new business within just twelve months. They spoke about your grit and how you connected customers with fitness trainers all over the world. They interviewed Mom, too, about her fast recovery with personalized training. She was overjoyed."

"Nice! Although I wish they didn't mention that I was fired."

"That's okay. You can use some of the news for your upcoming evaluation anyways," she added.

"Yeah…I guess so." I thought about Sam and how she'd react to the new organizational structure.

Tina took a long breath. "You know…I've been thinking about some of the things we talked about in the park when you were here." She paused. "I have to say, for a long time, we've been drifting apart. I've watched you get more and more wrapped up in your startup and then at Fitness First. I got wrapped up myself in taking care of Riya and Mom. I lost sight of what was important."

I wasn't sure where she was going with this conversation. She continued.

"When we were living in the same house, I felt as though you took me for granted. Since we've been living apart, I have had a lot of time to think about our relationship. And one thing has become more and more clear to me—I definitely want more of you, not less."

It felt good to hear.

"Look, Neo," she continued. "I want us to give each other what we need. I want Riya to grow up and be a good person. I know you care about us—I just don't want you to take us for granted."

"I won't. I wish I could be around you all the time but my work is so demanding. I can't ignore my job," I said.

"I never asked you to. Just don't ignore us. I can live with your work."

I smiled and said, "I can't wait for us to be together again."

"Only two more months to go," she said.

I saw Lisa at the door. "Hey, I gotta go. Love you," I said and hung up.

As Lisa walked in, I jumped up. "You need to deprioritize everything you have for today and tomorrow. We're going big and I need your help."

She had no clue what the heck I was talking about. I brought her up to speed about my discussion with Mike and his goal to formalize the new model. She was wary but we pulled together a detailed roll-out plan to bring the new model to life. The week after that was filled with announcements, rejigs and gossip across the organization. Not to mention my team's euphoria with the new structure, new team and expectations. I marveled that we were going to accelerate the journey of Fitness First toward becoming a digital-first organization.

It looked like a fairy tale until Sam came back from the vacation.

BEGINNING OF THE END

It was 4 pm on a rainy November day. Rain was beating at the windows of my office. Outside, the world was gray and blurred. In two months, I would have witnessed all the seasons in Seattle…and completed my one-year contract at Fitness First.

An hour later, my phone rang. It was Sam—she was back from her vacation. I decided to let it go to voicemail. After a few moments, I called Mike. I wanted to confirm if he spoke to Sam and aligned her. But the call went straight to voicemail. Darn!

Sam called back. I ignored her again.

I went to the window and stared into the storm. Half an hour later, it was as dark in my mind as it was outside the window. I turned away and sat at my desk, waiting for Mike's call.

Then I saw something unexpected. Sam was storming toward my office. I felt my stomach twisting.

"What the hell did you do?" she exploded as soon as she opened the door.

I felt threatened. I stammered. "Sam, please relax. I can explain what—"

"Explain what? Why you're burning money?"

"No, that's not true. I've been frugal all along."

"Then what the hell is this request to add *thirty* new resources to your team?"

"We are expanding, Sam. Let me explain all that. I thought Mike would—"

"What about Mike? You're building your own empire in the name of digital."

She wasn't allowing me to speak.

"Sam…we have this new organizational structure to—"

"To make me insignificant?"

I thought she might jump across the table and strangle me. "No! You're an important part of the new structure," I said.

It didn't make any difference. She was outraged. "The new organizational structure is a gross waste of time and resources. You're playing a game. Your plan is to hide your inefficiencies behind this so-called new structure."

"No, that's wrong. First, take a look at this presentation." I handed her the printouts of the new model and its benefits.

She took the presentation and threw it back at me. The papers scattered over the floor. "I can see what's happening here clearly, Neo. I'm calling for a board meeting. See you there!" She left with vengeance.

The door slammed shut. I tried to process what had just happened. I was in utter disbelief. Her accusations were terrible and painful. I did everything the right way, in the best interest of Fitness First.

I sat in the dark of my office, turning the conversation over in my mind. Enough was enough. I sent a text to Mike with the details of what had happened. I decided to talk to him and end things here and now. I just couldn't take it anymore.

I left the office in distress. The elevator doors opened—I stepped in and my EA entered the elevator behind me. She gave me a timid look. The doors closed.

It crossed my mind that I would soon be fired…again. Twice in a year. Sam would blame me for everything going wrong at Fitness First. It occurred to me that I was doomed from the beginning. Not once did Sam appreciate my efforts. Getting fired now would only accelerate the inevitable. I was never going to become the permanent CDO.

I walked through the garage to my car. I didn't go home right away. I drove around for a while until I was tired of it. An hour passed; I didn't care where I was. As I was driving, I tried to clear my mind of what happened. I drove in silence, watching brake lights mock me as I splashed through puddles. I was hungry. I exited the freeway and found a pizzeria.

I parked the car, unbuttoned the collar of my shirt, and took off my coat. I got a table at a corner and indulged myself, ordering two Long Island teas and a half and half medium pizza with double cheese, peri peri chicken, chicken tikka, black olives, and onion. Pain increased my appetite.

After an hour, Mike called. I calmed myself down and gave him a minute-by-minute chronicle of what had happened with Sam. He needed to know.

He listened patiently and said, "First, I'm sorry that I couldn't talk to her. I had an appointment with her on the first day she was supposed to be back—I didn't know she would cut her vacation short. Looks like someone tipped her off."

"That's okay, Mike. I've been calling you for hours."

"Yeah…I was in an all-day offsite with no network."

"Listen Mike, I want to end this now. It's better for me to make an orderly exit on my own terms than to get fired again."

"Are you crazy? You're part of the growth story here."

"I don't know," I paused. "It just doesn't feel right with how things are going."

"Let me get this straight. Do you have a problem with Fitness First or with Sam?" he asked.

"Well…I like the team, the challenge and the opportunity. But it's not going well with Sam."

"I can see that." He paused for a moment. "Let's see how the board meeting goes. And then we can discuss this?"

I took a deep breath and said, "Mike…win or lose, I know I did my best."

"I know, man! I think you should take it easy and let the wisdom of the board prevail," he said and hung up.

A week later I got the invite to the board meeting. The rumor around the office was that Sam had been working late nights on her presentation, running her staff ragged. At that point I had no interest in impressing anyone. I decided that I would share what I did, honestly. And then it would be up to the board. Either way, I knew I was going to be with my family in a few weeks.

SHOWDOWN

I got dressed and had breakfast, feeling like a prisoner waiting for the gallows. I would have never guessed a granola bar and French toast would be my choice of a last meal before the inevitable. As I drove to work, I remembered the first day at Fitness First and thought about the dramatic way my life had unfolded since then. I walked to the board room a few minutes before 9 am. We were in the most formal room in the building, the one with a mahogany table and expensive black leather chairs. The room provided a captivating view of Mount Rainier. I went to the window and tried to distract myself.

Sam walked in along with the Chairman, talking cheerfully about her vacation and the fun things she did. As the board members settled in, my mind reeled back to the day I was fired from Digi Gate. The boardroom, the backdrop of what happened, the purpose of the meeting—it all reminded me of what I went through a year back. But this time, I was prepared. I pulled myself together and got ready to defend myself from the imminent ambush from Sam and the board.

Sam adjusted the mike at her desk and announced, "Good morning, everyone. I want to talk about our failed digital transformation efforts for the past three years. You all know how the previous two CDOs failed us miserably. I thought that the third would be a charm. But I was wrong."

The Chairman went first. "You need to break that down for us, Sam."

She cleared her throat and spoke confidently. "Neo formalized a new organizational structure that led to a massive waste of leadership time and resources. It adds layers of bureaucracy and slows us down significantly."

What? The very purpose of the new structure was to kill bureaucracy and put us on a fast track. I wanted to stop her. I looked at Mike but he motioned that I should remain quiet.

"Do you have any evidence to prove that, Sam?" asked one of the board members.

"Yes, before the new structure, we had twelve digital initiatives in flight. Once Neo created the new structure, the scope was narrowed to only four initiatives. Productivity was cut to a third," she explained, calmly. "Meanwhile, we are burning cash and not seeing a clear ROI. Our company has poured almost $100 million into digital initiatives, cash that could have otherwise been used to drive our quarterly revenue targets."

I seethed at the gross misrepresentation of the facts.

The Chairman stepped in. "Do you have an understanding of why it all went wrong?"

"Yes. I've spent a long time on the root cause. The heart of the problem is a leadership capability issue. And I take blame for that," she said.

For a moment, I was relieved that she was taking some accountability for her inability to drive a digital transformation but it was short lived. The spotlight stayed on me.

Sam sighed, looking contrite. "Neo should never have been hired. I believed Neo's startup experience would help him drive digital initiatives at the group level. And he came highly recommended by Mike. But he couldn't manage the digital efforts of multiple businesses. He failed to prioritize initiatives and he was too narrowly focused on the health club business."

She then presented a few documents that provided a skewed picture—the outcomes of the first two Innovation Pods. Some board members flipped through the details.

"Your recommendation, Sam?" the Chairman asked.

And here it came.

Sam looked at me sadly. "I am sorry to make this recommendation but I feel it is in the best interest of Fitness First. We must terminate Neo's employment immediately, before he does any more damage. And then we must reprioritize our resources to drive sales through our established channels. If we do this, we can turn around our numbers within the next three quarters."

I looked at Mike. His unflinching look made me wonder what he was up to.

The Chairman nodded. "Okay, thank you, Sam. We'll review a few more details before we conclude."

I was glad that the board wanted a holistic view. I had ten-odd minutes to salvage my career. I could honestly say I wasn't all that nervous. As I handed the presentations to the board members, Mike stood up to address the board. I wondered why he was stepping forward. Maybe we would both present to the board.

He looked at me and said, "Chime in as needed, Neo."

I had no idea what was going on. I thought it was me vs. Sam and the board. I wondered why Mike was driving the show.

Mike started with the purpose. "At the beginning of the year, I shared Fitness First's transformative customer-centric purpose with you, Chairman, and with the board members. I am delighted to say that we are well on our way to becoming a purpose-driven organization. It helped us prioritize the right initiatives, be more ambitious, align our efforts, inspire richer innovation, and make faster decisions. Thanks to Neo, for steering us to become a purpose-driven organization."

He then continued with the new digital business model and ecosystem. "A traditional organization like ours should not just focus on digitizing the core business. We must add new business models that are powered by digital. Neo has made a big impact on our core business, improving premium subscriber retention, and creating a hyper personalized experience through our app that integrates the product offerings of all our businesses. He has also created an entirely new business by building an ecosystem of fitness experts from across the world to serve our customers working out at home. Because of Neo, we have the beginning of a global digital fitness platform."

He then referred to the media coverage we got in India. "We got great feedback from our international partners already. And we are about to scale up our marketing during Thanksgiving, keeping in mind the gift-giving season and New Year's resolutions to stay fit."

Sam tried to intervene but the Chairman asked her to let Mike finish.

Mike continued, "What I am particularly intrigued by is the small, autonomous team called an Innovation Pod that implements a unique five-step approach for digital innovation." He then addressed the report Sam shared. "While the early efforts of the Pods failed, which is what you saw in Sam's reports, they've now been corrected with the new organization structure. We have multiple Innovation Pods working in parallel to add new revenue streams, solve supply chain issues and much more."

He looked at Susan and said, "Not to mention, the budget expenses have been completely aligned with Susan, who is known to control the purse strings very carefully."

Susan smiled. "I agree with all that Mike said. To specifically address the ROI issue, Neo helped me redefine the measures to evaluate the success of digital initiatives. I'm satisfied that we are on a path to unlock new revenue streams and cost savings through our digital initiatives. In fact, I'm confident that we'll see a strong return on invested cash next year, using traditional measures as well as the new ones."

Mike continued. "Last, but most importantly, Neo is working to change the culture and tone at the top of the organization. He has a solid plan to activate the bottom of the pyramid with a platform to crowdsource ideas, while resetting the tone at the top by focusing on the top 50 leaders with reverse mentoring, experiential sessions on digital leadership, experimentation, and digital innovation. All of these will deliver incredible impact."

As he shared the details, board members meticulously reviewed every single detail in the presentation. And then the call for final words came.

"And your recommendation, Mike?" asked the Chairman.

SUCKER PUNCH

Mike gathered all his energy to give his unqualified recommendation. "Chairman and board members...we've made tremendous progress this year in our digital efforts. If we stay the course, I am confident that we will become a digital-first organization in a couple of years." He looked at me and said, "Thanks to Neo. This wouldn't have been possible without his relentless efforts." What Mike said after that was a shocker. "He did all of this with little to no support from Sam."

Sam was clearly boiling with anger at Mike's assessment but she restrained herself, not wanting the situation to get any uglier.

"Mike, thanks for the details," the Chairman said. And then another shocker, "On behalf of the board, I want to thank you for accepting the special assignment to assess Sam's performance as CEO and to closely monitor the progress made in our efforts to become a digital-first organization."

My eyes went wide. I was stunned. I stared at Sam, whose face was rigid. Had she known that Mike was evaluating her? She must have. As I thought about the time I'd spent with Mike in the past eleven months, his active involvement in the day-to-day affairs of Fitness First started to make sense.

"Neo," the Chairman said gravely, "please step outside. We have a decision to make about you."

I nodded and stepped out of the room, feeling apprehensive. Sam remained in the room and the Chairman had not asked her to leave. I wondered if she would find a way to turn the board against me, against Mike. A rush of adrenaline shot through my body as I processed the shocking events of the meeting. At that moment, I had more questions than answers.

I called Charan and was surprised to get hold of him right away. I filled him in on the developments. He didn't seem surprised.

"Neo, what you have done is quite impressive. If you did not realize it already, you drove the business transformation of Fitness First with digital," said Charan.

As I thought about it, I realized that digital was a microcosm in the broader realm of business transformation and that digital transformation is actually *business transformation* driven with digital.

He continued, "I don't think you have anything to worry about. You will have a long run at Fitness First. So, congratulations in advance for becoming the permanent CDO."

"Wait, the verdict is not in just yet."

"I know…but I believe you will make it," he said. "Good luck and keep up the great work."

I felt a surge of desperation. Before he hung up, I said, "If I really get the permanent role, I'm afraid that luck won't be enough. I'd need your help again."

"Look…even if I had the time, I don't think it's a good idea." His answer disappointed me.

"Why not? It seemed to work fine so far."

"Neo," he said in a stern voice, "as your responsibilities grow and you embrace new challenges, you must learn to rely more and more on yourself. Asking me to come over will increase your dependency. And that doesn't do you any good."

I refused to see his point. "But what if I'm stuck and want to learn?"

"What is that you specifically want to learn? Spell it out for me."

I didn't have an answer.

"You call me when you have clarity – congrats again. You will soon hear good news." And he hung up.

The next moment, I saw Sam exit the conference room. She shot a hostile look at me. Then she turned toward the elevator. After about fifteen minutes, I was called inside the room.

As I settled in, the Chairman said, "Neo, we've been carefully reviewing all the details. And I want you to know that we are pleased with your grand vision for Fitness First and the way you've been rallying the whole organization to achieve that vision."

My heart jumped. *Here comes the "But."*

The Chairman continued, "But we cannot offer you a permanent role as CDO."

I kept my face still as I felt disappointment crashing over me. Looks like Charan was wrong, probably for the first time.

The Chairman's voice was even, somber. "Your experience and your drive make us feel strongly that you will be a great CEO to take Fitness First to all new heights."

What? Become the CEO? I couldn't believe what I was hearing. I looked around, trying to find Mike. Then I thought of Sam.

"But what about Sam?"

I heard Mike speak from across the table. "She's been fired."

A chill went down my back as I remembered everything that had happened that year. My interactions with Sam and her erratic outbursts. The highs and lows. At one point, I was in deep trouble and I almost gave up. My career had been one inch away from crashing; and the unbelievable hours I was putting in at work had pushed my family life to the brink.

But I didn't give up. Against all odds I continued to fight. And I wasn't alone. Charan introduced me to new, sensible approaches. My team enthusiastically backed me up. Mike inspired me, believed in me, and cleared the way all along like a true transformational leader. Tina had supported me, taking care of Mom and Riya and had believed in me from the beginning. I made it. And now I was being asked to lead Fitness First?

I heard my name. I snapped to attention. The board was expecting a response from me.

"It's okay if you want to take some time and let us know your thoughts," said the Chairman.

Without giving much thought, I blurted out, "No...I don't think I can be the CEO." I took a deep breath and thought for a moment. "If there is anyone who deserves it," I paused for dramatic effect, "it's Mike."

I looked at Mike and said, "If not for his transformative leadership and timely interventions, I wouldn't have delivered what you saw today." I turned back to the Chairman and said, "I am happy to work as the CDO for the group under Mike's leadership and the board's guidance."

The room was quiet.

Realizing the gravity of what I said, I added politely, "I respectfully decline the offer, Chairman." I paused. "But I am fine with whatever the board decides is in the best interest of Fitness First." And I stepped out of the conference room.

My adrenaline soared, my heart was racing. I decided to take a stroll in Bellevue's downtown park to calm down. As I walked to the park, my mind didn't stop swirling. I walked past the water wall and the fountain, trying to distract myself. Everything around me looked riveting. I stopped to watch the pure joy of kids playing. I spent a good amount of time walking in the park till I felt relaxed. As I walked back, I thought again about the offer to lead Fitness First. I felt I was right in respectfully declining it and suggesting the right man. I wasn't ready yet.

After an hour, I got a text from Mike that read: *Mr. CDO, let's go make a dent, together. Will call you after the board meeting.*

I felt elated and video called Tina. After sharing the turn of events since I last spoke with her, she said, "I'm really proud of you. Congrats on officially becoming the CDO."

I was overjoyed.

She continued. "Although I think you deserved to be the CEO."

"Thanks, but I'm not there yet."

"Hmm," she said.

"And the family paid too big a price for this achievement. It would take my time away and make it worse if I was the CEO," I finally said.

"Neo, you're being too hard on yourself." Tina continued, "It was me who suggested that we spend this year apart, to make this opportunity work. Let's face it, if you hadn't taken this opportunity, it might have spoiled every good part of our marriage. Besides, this is the time for you to feel proud.

You didn't have to step on anybody to get this achievement; you won it fair and square."

Tina was right.

"So…when am I coming back to my homeland?" She asked with a radiant smile.

"How about we celebrate Thanksgiving in our new home in Bellevue?"

"Yay!" She couldn't contain her excitement.

I was thrilled that everything was finally falling into place. My work was sorted. Tina was happy. Mom was recovering fast. I was ready to start a new chapter in my life.

LIVING THE DREAM

It had been five years since the family moved into our new home in Bellevue. Tina got back to work at Microsoft and Riya was now in fourth grade. Mom found the US easy to adjust to; she quickly made Indian friends in the neighborhood.

That day, I woke up before the usual time. As I entered the bathroom, the sensors in the Magic Mirror recognized me and started reading news headlines. I was beta testing the Magic Mirror for Fitness First. We were experimenting with how a mirror, which is so essential to our daily life, can double as a health and wellness companion. Not every feature of the cover story of the Magic Mirror was live yet but some features like gamifying teeth brushing, skin vitality analysis and vision testing were live.

The mirror started playing a video that looked like a blast from the past. It struck me that I had just completed six years at Fitness First. It was great to see the mirror curating the pictures intelligently from the past six years and making me feel elated—a true wellness companion. I thought back on the many innovations we launched. The failures we celebrated. The transformation of Fitness First into a digital-first organization, my promotion as CEO last year and Mike becoming Chairman of the Board. I felt euphoric and emotional, with tears welling up in my eyes.

What we had achieved as a team was incredible. A well-deserved day off was on my mind. That is, until I asked the mirror to show me my schedule for the day: a quick meeting with Mike at 10 am followed by the 12th Innovation Summit.

I never missed an Innovation Summit. We launched the summit a year back when Mike and I took on our new roles, with Lisa as the new CDO.

We felt that Mike and I should have a special focus on cover stories in the business building category. I was continuing to mentor Lisa and we were still evolving the role of the CDO. We looked forward to the point in a couple of years when the CDO role would no longer be required because digital would be fully ingrained into the DNA of Fitness First. Lisa and Stan had formed a great working relationship and Stan was helping me groom her to be the next COO when he retired.

I headed to work for the Innovation Summit, promising Tina I'd meet her for lunch. As I got into the glistening glass-topped driverless car that I was using to carpool, a digital avatar beamed from my smart watch, suggesting I get an immune booster smoothie and showing a list of nutrition partners on my smart watch screen—my smart watch had sensed that I was a bit tired and didn't sleep well last night. I placed an order and selected the option for drone delivery, which would take 16 minutes and 23 seconds to arrive at the drop off point next to Trinity Towers.

As I entered my office, Hana, a computationally created virtual being that looked and behaved like a human, flashed on the glass panel of my office. We had installed the personal assistants in most offices, thanks to our partnership with one of the Digital Giants. AI assistants had evolved significantly in the past 5 years and they could do most of the job of traditional EAs, plus much more. Productivity had increased significantly and the assistants reinforced our digital mindset. After congratulating me on my work anniversary, Hana briefed me on key product updates.

Mike flashed on the glass panel, asking if I could swing by a few minutes early. As I walked to Mike's office, I saw a team from an Innovation Pod moving virtual post-its around on one of the glass screens, building a service blueprint. It was fulfilling to see that every Innovation Pod was living and breathing the guiding principles. We had forty-seven active Innovation Pods and counting. These pods were now woven into the fabric of how each business unit and enabling function operated.

As I entered Mike's office, he was asking his virtual assistant, Sue, about growth projections that were displayed on the glass panel. For the next thirty minutes, we discussed sales growth, year-over-year targets and how we could activate more Innovation Pods. The digital ecosystem that had taken Fitness First global had boosted the top line substantially and it was powered by the India growth story. Stacy had taken an active role in the growth story and had decided to relocate to Bengaluru to expand the Asia Pacific market.

Flashing again, Sue suggested that we join the 12th Innovation Summit. After a quick briefing, we spent time quietly reading and noting questions on cover stories. All the cover stories perfectly aligned with the purpose of Fitness First: *To be the best in the world at helping individuals and families on their path to better health.*

Virtual health club in the metaverse and VR compatible fitness equipment

The first two cover stories were no surprise: they addressed the fitness needs of customers who were now spending most of their time in the metaverse, an always-on network of connected virtual universes that is experienced in virtual reality or augmented reality. One cover story proposed launching the world's first full-fledged virtual health club in the metaverse with personalized virtual body weight exercises and virtual fitness communities that will help customers stay fit in a social, fun, and interactive way. The second cover story pitched a new circle-shaped treadmill design that would allow customers to walk around the metaverse while exercising in real life. Mike and I agreed that both cover stories warranted further exploration, since they had the potential to future-proof our traditional health club business.

Smart Toilet meets Supplements Business

The third cover story was an interesting one—it was from a janitor who had a conversation with an employee with an upset stomach. The janitor proposed that Fitness First partner with a Japanese plumbing manufacturer that had recently launched the world's first smart toilet. The new toilet could tell what's wrong with a customer's health and provide wellness recommendations. This was achieved by an array of sensors to perform skin and waste analysis. If Fitness First offered the toilet for sale, we would be able to leverage the data to connect customers with our ecosystem of nutritionists and medical professionals and to create personalized nutrition plans. Customers could also purchase personalized, premium quality supplements that would be created in real time with 3-D printers and shipped via drones powered by our logistics partner, a tech startup that was selected during last year's hackathon to address last mile delivery challenges.

"We have come a long way," said Mike. "Smart toilets…who would have thought?"

I laughed. "I'm really pleased that grassroot innovation has taken hold. I didn't even know this toilet was in the market." We decided to ask the janitor to spend some time with one of our Innovation Pod Leads, to work on the details more.

It was inspiring that everyone in the company was championing new digital business ideas in ways that we, at the top, would have never envisioned. We had successfully democratized innovation across the breadth and depth of Fitness First. Moreover, everyone was incredibly aligned with our purpose, guiding principles and the digital governance model. We were operating in a decisive and courageous way, taking big, bold bets and moving rapidly.

Fast had become the new normal—a dream come true for me. A dream every organization must aspire to achieve. It's the digital-first future that helps you stay relevant. Relevant for customers, relevant for stakeholders and relevant for the world.

When you change the way you see the world, you change the world you see!

Ideas to remember

- Leaders must have grit and perseverance to succeed in the digital world, since the rate of change in digital is incredible. Transform the leaders. Make them neophiles. Ensure that they have a high Adversity Quotient.

- Invest in upskilling the entire organization on key topics such as digital leadership, product management and the Digital Innovation Approach. This creates a culture of innovation, working backwards and experimentation. It makes the cycle of "experiment, learn and iterate" second nature. Although culture transformation is a slow process, it is critical to invest time and effort to upskill the entire organization.

- Implement reverse mentoring by having a leader co-pilot a digital initiative with a Pod Lead. The wisdom of the leader and the digital mindset of the Pod Lead will help each other up their game.

- Create a culture of continuous learning through "learn and share" sessions. They are a great way to showcase success, as well as communicating lessons learned organization wide. During these sessions, recognize successes and celebrate failures.

- Align company policies to ensure adherence to guiding principles. Hiring, firing and promotions must be based on how effectively employees live and breathe the guiding principles.

- Collaborate with startups to reinvent the core or for business building. First, identify focus areas based on mega trends in your industry or based on specific business opportunities or customer problems. Conduct a hackathon and invite startups to submit their ideas in line with the focus areas. Collaborate with the winning startups and ensure a win-win proposition to both incumbents and startups.

  Let's take a look at Vedanta Limited, a mining and metals major—a sector usually known for slow innovation. Under the visionary leadership of Chairman Anil Agarwal, Vedanta launched a startup accelerator program called Vedanta Spark to build technological capabilities by partnering with startups. Through the Spark program, it attracted more than 1,350 startup registrations from across 19 countries. After a process of evaluation involving business executives and industry experts, 23 startups were shortlisted which held the potential to deliver a business impact of around $45-50 M in one year.

Akarsh K. Hebbar, executive sponsor and advisor of the program said, "Vedanta Spark is a refreshing boost to Vedanta's cultural DNA. As we speak, we are already thinking about the next cohort of start-ups and finding new ways to collaborate with startups."

Startup collaboration is a step in the right direction toward accelerating digital adoption.

- To become a digital-first organization, change is inevitable—change in thought, change in approach, and change in how you work as a team. It's the new way of doing business. When everyone in the organization is aligned with the purpose, guiding principles and the digital governance model, fast will be the new normal.

ACKNOWLEDGMENTS

First, I want to thank the many clients I've worked with in Europe, US, and India who have allowed me to advise and drive their complex transformation journeys. The insights I shared in this book are the outcomes of my interactions with many extraordinary digital leaders. Special thanks to Tatwamasi Dixit and Vikas Kamran for mentoring me as I navigated some of the transformation journeys.

I'm forever thankful to my Dad, Mom, and my brother, for being my greatest teachers. Your trust, support, and positivity shine through my work.

I especially want to thank our beta readers and feedback providers for the countless discussions during my journey authoring this book. Your insights gave me well-rounded perspectives and made the book a lot more interesting. This includes terrific people like Kalyan Guntha (my brother), Varun Manian, Praveen Vukkallam, Raj Neraveti, Jayaprakash Bhaskarbatla, Sandeep Maram, Samik Raychaudhuri, Chetan Anand, Satish Kalala, Ranjan Jain, Tim Bowman, Suresh Namala, Sumedhas Dixit, Vignesh Soundararajan, Rohit Tuteja, and Manoj Jacob.

I'm grateful for my friends Pavan, Vinay, Sandeep, Naveen, and a long list of others, and the communities that are part of my life and my formation.

And of course, I reserve so much thanks for my always supportive wife, Gayathri, and my wonderful boys, Yuvraj and Sahan, for asking me 'why' and grounding me to the purpose. The dinner table conversations we had discussing Neo's journey are something I fondly remember. I love you all more than I can say.

Last, but most important, thanks to Shahrul, who has been an amazing soundboard during the long and complex journey of authoring this book. I'm eternally grateful for our countless discussions on The Hero's Journey and balancing the heart and mind of the fable, which made the book highly readable.

– Vamshi Guntha

First and foremost, I would like to praise and thank God, who has granted me countless blessings and opportunities. Second, this book would never have existed without Vamshi, who graciously invited me to collaborate on this project, and whose wealth of knowledge and drive to succeed inspire me every day.

The ideas that I contributed to this book are the product of my observations of and interactions with extraordinary business leaders, including Jeff Bezos, Mike Sievert, Callie Field, Marcus East, Nate Brooling, Crystale Lapham, Jeff Wilke and Todd Genovese. I am especially grateful to my long-time partner on T-Mobile's digital transformation, Kate Boatman. I owe a debt to my many colleagues at T-Mobile and Amazon, particularly Lisa Hillmann, Nate Snodgrass, Melisa Barbera, Kaveesh Chawla, Sejin Siegel, Jason Hein, Bill Grdanski, Kamran Emad, Rohit Makkad, Jennifer Rolfes, Puneet Garg, Annie McGettigan, and Kirk McGettigan.

I'd also like to thank my family and friends for their constant support and how they have shaped me over the years. My mother who taught me to read, and my father who taught me entrepreneurship. My brother Shaari, who shares my love of great stories. The incredibly accomplished Osman family motivates me to strive higher. And of course, I must thank Jedediah, Cullen, Matthias, and Nana for being pillars of strength over the years.

– Shahrul Ladue

ABOUT THE AUTHORS

Vamshi Guntha is the Founder of Propl Inventions, a firm dedicated to making organizations digital-first. He is also a VP of Digital Innovation at Revel. Vamshi's passion for transforming businesses with digital and hi-tech startups is reflected in his writing, speaking, and consulting. He has advised CEOs and their executive teams on their digital-first journeys through Propl, PwC Digital, Deloitte, and Revel. The widespread appeal of Vamshi's thought leadership has yielded him a diverse client base, including a mix of Fortune 500 companies, mid-size organizations, and startups. He is also on the board of a hi-tech startup and a fast growing Corporate Venture Capital entity.

Vamshi lives in Bengaluru with his wife, Gayathri, and their two sons, Yuvraj and Sahan. You can reach Vamshi at vguntha@propl.in.

Shahrul Ladue specializes in guiding executives in launching new high-growth initiatives and creating economies of scale with digital. Shahrul was most recently the head of Digital Strategy for T-Mobile, USA, where he reported to the Chief Digital Officer. Prior to T-Mobile, Shahrul spent many years at Amazon, where he was a founding member of Amazon Business and Amazon Clothing.

Shahrul lives in Seattle. You can reach Shahrul at sladue@propl.in.

To learn more about Propl Inventions, please visit www.propl.in.

Printed in Great Britain
by Amazon